Now I know in part;

then I shall know fully,

even as I am fully known.

Awakening the Soldier
Published by Robert Ming
24681 La Plaza, Suite 250
Dana Point, CA 92629
© 2012 Robert Ming

ISBN-13: 978-1481226967
ISBN-10: 1481226967

Awakening the Soldier

Robert Ming

Contents

The Western Kingdom

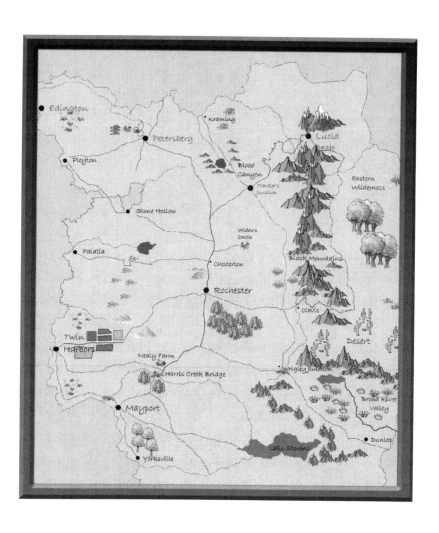

Dedication

To Jonathan and Katie,
for continuously asking
when the next chapter would be done,
to Susie for her patient editing,
and to Wesley and Grant
for the motivation to finish.

Acknowledgements

Special thanks to Eric Browning
for the outstanding cover art and affinity for the edgy,
Nancy Williams for her editing expertise and eye for prose,
to Jaclyn Russell and Jessica Powers
for their perspective and suggestions.

.

1. Contact

The steel-blue flash was almost blinding. Again. Again. Again. The swings came with such force they almost knocked the sword from his hand. As fast as he could block one strike, the next one came. Reeling back from the sheer power of the attack, Vic struggled to regain his composure.

"Who are you?" Vic yelled over the clash of metal. Jab, jab, parry, miss. He defended against his attacker with skill, but knew the strength of his foe was formidable. "What do you want?" No answer, and the fight continued. His attacker advanced with blows of tremendous force. Vic took two steps back and tried again. Block, block, attack, block; again he was forced to take two steps back. Vic couldn't make any progress at all. What about poor Steven? His apprentice couldn't be doing well. A glance back confirmed his suspicion: Steven was stumbling backward as he struggled against the second attacker.

"Roll! Fall back!" His instructor's voice helped Steve snap out of his punishing retreat. He dove and rolled, but it was only a few seconds before vengeance was on him again. Vic couldn't look anymore, and a kick in the chest reminded him why.

Vic went flying backwards, far enough to get a clear view of his attacker for the first time. He was huge. At least seven feet tall, a hooded black cloak concealed most of his body, but not his arms or hands. Was that scales he saw? Pointed scales like small mountains flowed down the arm to the hand like chain mail. Its face was concealed by the hood, but a demonic pair of red cat eyes shown from the dark hood. A chill went down Vic's spine. What was this thing?

Vic blocked the next few blows but the swings rained down so heavily that he knew he couldn't last. A pleading cry from Steven rang in his ears.

"VIC!"

He glanced in Steve's direction just in time to see him impaled on a nearby tree by the second cloaked warrior -- a sight he thought would surely be his last. A burning sensation brought him back as the tip of his attacker's sword ripped across his chest. A final blow he blocked, but it sent him to his knees. A kick in the head from his attacker and Vic lost all sense of direction and began to black out. His head hit the hard dirt and he squeezed his eyes shut as he waited for the death blow to arrive, but it didn't. Instead, he felt a blast of wind, a scream, and then silence.

Deep in a dungeon, two chained prisoners fell limp in their chains. Their keeper watched them drop, then turned to his master, "Kravon has failed."

"What? The fool. His target wasn't even trained yet. How could he fail?"

"Someone must have intervened."

Rage filled Dramon and he raised his hand to strike the grotesquely malformed jail keeper, but relented when he saw him cowering before him. "Obviously. Well at least that settles it. I was right. I knew they were watching him. Now we are too. He must be an important recruit."

"But we lost him."

"He'll be back, and when he returns, we will be ready. Send word to all my outposts. If anyone spots him I want to know."

"Yes, my liege. What will become of Kravon?"

"He has failed. Let him rot. He will be lucky if I ever call him back again."

"By your command."

It had been almost a year since Victor Bremerton faced those demonic attackers on the road outside of Yorksville. The otherwise pleasant midsummer afternoon was seared into his memory. Not only was it the day he lost his first and only apprentice, but it was the first time he had ever been utterly defeated in open combat. As a soldier for hire, he didn't have much room for error. There were usually no second chances. You are either the best, or you're dead. It troubled Vic to know there were creatures out there who were so much better and stronger than he was. What were his attackers and why was he still alive? Did someone or something actually defeat his attackers and save his life? He may never know, but now he was forced to spend his 21st birthday under a stranger's roof recovering from injuries he still didn't understand. It was a good thing he was in good shape or his recovery would have taken much longer. Now his physical wounds had healed and his strength returned, but there were still many questions left unanswered. Victor often found himself revisiting those mysterious few minutes.

"...excuse me, Sir, that'll be four pieces of silver."

"Right, sorry." He snapped out of his daze and doled out the small coins from his side bag. "Do you know how far it is to Lucid Peak?"

"About three days journey, but what business would you have there? There's nothing at the Peak but old ruins and swindlers."

Vic had heard the folklore before, but was hoping it wasn't true.

"You watch yourselves up there," the vendor continued.

"Don't worry about us," Derek replied with a slap on the vendor's shoulder, "We can take care of ourselves." They smiled at each other and turned to go.

Derek was quickly becoming a good friend. Ever since he and Vic met on the road outside of Mayport about a week ago, Derek had not left his side. Vic was always cautious about who he befriended, especially lately. Even those he had known for years were suddenly changing, or disappearing, but Derek inspired a sense of trust. He seemed honest and at peace with himself, rare qualities these days.

Anyone who saw them together would have thought they were brothers. Derek was a few years his senior and about two inches taller than Vic's six feet. He had striking green eyes next to Vic's blue but otherwise they looked quite similar. Both had sandy brown hair they kept back, sharp facial features and an athletic build. Those days growing up when Vic had wished for a big brother, Derek would have been the perfect choice.

It also might have been the way they met, which Vic thought was a strange twist of fate. Shortly after leaving Mayport, Vic spotted old Mrs. Nealy on the road up ahead. She was unmistakable, driving the same rickety cart and wearing the same broad brimmed hat she always wore, and it looked like she was getting into trouble just like she always used to! Two bandits had jumped out in front of her cart. Vic couldn't believe it. This was like old times!

It was Mrs. Nealy who gave Vic his first soldier-for-hire job six years ago, when Vic was only fifteen. Vic's mother had sent him over to Mrs. Nealy's farm to help her bring in the harvest. Back then, she was still trying to farm some of the crops her husband used to grow before he died, and every season, she needed help. When the crops were ready, Vic agreed to accompany her to market. On this very road as they were returning from market, he was sitting in the back of her wagon when two bandits, much like these, jumped out from behind some bushes. Without a moment's hesitation, Vic jumped out of the wagon and attacked the first bandit. Even at 15, Vic was an excellent swordsman and in just a few strokes he had them both on the run. Needless to say, Mrs. Nealy was thrilled with Vic, and from then on, she happily paid him to ride with her to market every week for the next few years.

Others heard of how successful he was, and pretty soon Vic was doing similar odd jobs around town. He developed a reputation as a skillful swordsman with a pleasant demeanor and quick wits. His new profession arrived none too soon because the very next year, the rest of his family was killed when the family farm burned to the ground in a tragic fire. It was these odd security jobs that kept food on the table. After the fire, he had little interest in rebuilding the farm, so he sold the land and bought a small place in town. Especially through those hard times, Mrs. Nealy had always been like a grandmother to him.

Now instead of carrying vegetables, she carried homemade wicker baskets to support herself. She wove them with care and hand painted each one. They didn't bring home much, but it sustained her and gave her purpose. She didn't go to market as often and Vic was busy doing other things so he didn't ride with her anymore, but they were still very close.

The road to Mayport ran through one particularly dark and dangerous thicket of trees as it approached Harris Creek Bridge. That's where she was when Vic spotted her this time. Unfortunately, he wasn't in the back of the wagon; he was a considerable distance down the road.

"Oh, no you don't!" He said to himself, and kicked his horse into a gallop.

The bandits had jumped out in front of her as she was bringing her cart up to the narrow bridge. There wasn't enough room to turn the wagon around, so there was little she could do to escape. Vic wanted to yell, but she was still too far away. He *had* to save her. Only the thunder of his horse's hooves was loud enough to drown out the beating of his heart.

It didn't take long before the bandits noticed him barreling down on them and the taller of the two grabbed Mrs. Nealy's money bag and dove into the thicket. He emerged on horseback and turned across the bridge to leave. His partner was close behind but as Vic approached, he saw that the partner was heavier and an inexperienced rider. The road forked ahead and the leader went to the right, and his partner to the left. Vic stayed with the leader.

As the road straightened out, Vic could tell that this chase would be over quickly. He had a better horse and was a better rider, so he gained on the thief rapidly. When the rider sensed that that Vic was about to attack, he pulled his horse up short and jumped off.

Vic followed with ease, and the minute he hit the ground, his sword was out and he was in a full charge toward the bandit. In the first few strokes, Vic could tell this was a two-bit thief with minimal skills. Before he even knew what was happening, Vic had wrenched the sword from his hand and kicked him down to the ground. The bandit ended up face down, with Vic's foot on his back. He was out of breath and begging for his life.

"Just shut up!" Vic said as he let him feel the cold tip of his sword on the back of his neck. "That was a pretty stupid stunt you pulled back there. You have to steal from a poor, defenseless old woman?" Vic didn't have the stomach to kill the man, but didn't want to just let him go either. "You're so pathetic you don't deserve to live, but I don't have the heart to kill you either. Go take this message to your friends: that woman is *off limits*. The next person who tries to touch her will end up dead. Understand??"

Vic punctuated the point with a shove into his back with his heel. The man winced. Still panting and shaking, he sheepishly agreed.

"Here's a little present to remind you never to do something so stupid again." Vic swung the tip of his sword through the soft fleshy part of the man's right buttock, just enough to make him bleed. The man yelled in pain. "You better have a doctor stitch that up, my friend, and use the time in bed to figure out what you're going to do with your life, because this isn't it!"

Vic left him on the ground holding the wound on his butt and twisting around to try and see what Vic had done. He walked over to the man's horse and took Mrs. Nealy's money bag from where it was hanging. He gave the horse a good slap and sent it running, then mounted his horse to head back to Mrs. Nealy.

"You can't leave me here!" the man yelled.

"Your friend should be along shortly, IF he is a real friend," Vic shot back.

As Vic returned to Mrs. Nealy and her wagon, he was surprised to see two men with her. One was the second bandit, but the second he didn't recognize. Vic approached cautiously, ready for another fight, but the stranger quickly spoke up.

"You should have seen her fight!" the stranger pointed his thumb at Mrs. Nealy. "Feisty one, isn't she?" He winked at her.

Mrs. Nealy smiled at the stranger and turned back to Vic. "Still feisty, but didn't do much fighting this time. That's always been Vic's job."

"Aah, you must be Vic," he smiled. As Vic approached, he saw that the stranger was holding the second bandit at knife point. "Mrs. Nealy has been telling me all about your adventures together over the years. I guess this was just the latest installment." Derek poked the man with the knife just hard enough to make him complain a little. "I was about 100 yards behind you when you spotted them. You broke into a gallop, so I did the same. When you took the right fork, I took the left to catch the one you left behind, and here he is! Unfortunately, he seems to be a little light on cash. Did you catch yours?"

Vic pulled out Mrs. Nealy's money bag and smiled, "Sure did! Here you are, Mrs. Nealy." Vic carefully handed her the prized bag of proceeds, and then followed with a big hug. "I guess I should visit more often?"

"That would be nice!" Mrs. Nealy kissed him on the forehead. "Whatever would I do without you?"

"You know, you really shouldn't be on these roads alone, Mrs. Nealy. We've gone over this before."

"You know me better than anyone, Vic. I can't stop doing this, and you wouldn't want me to. I'd rather die on this road than wait at home for someone to find me dead. This is much more fun!"

She seemed completely content with the day's adventure. Vic smiled, "I didn't think you would listen to me!" He turned to the second bandit and the smile vanished from his face, "But you'd better! Your friend is down that road less than a mile, and he is injured. If you're any kind of a friend at all, you'll head down there and help him out. Most importantly, make sure you spread the word that this woman is off-limits. Go find someone else to pick on." Vic pointed down the path and Derek gave him a push in the right direction. As soon as he was free, the man tripped over himself to get out of there as fast as he could.

"Think he's smart enough to know better next time?" Derek asked Vic.

"Nope. I'm not sure he could even repeat what we just said! Maybe his friend will remember better."

The three of them rode together reminiscing as far as Mrs. Nealy's farm. "You boys want to come in for a snack? Maybe a little peach cobbler? Roasted venison feast and a wild party?" She winked as she said it.

"Mrs. Nealy, it's not even lunch time!" Derek was really starting to like this lady.

"Well, I had a good morning and sold out fast, so we should celebrate!"

"You know I would love to," Vic helped open the gate to the farm, "but we have a schedule to keep today."

"You could even play in the mud in the back like you and Catherine used to do!"

"Catherine? Mud wrestling?" Derek gave Vic a good poke with his elbow.

Vic blushed, "Seriously, we need to go, but I promise to drop by on the way home. Okay?"

"Such a sensible young man these days. You've grown up so nicely, Vic." She smiled and put her hand on his cheek. "See you soon."

She waved them on their way and Derek and Vic continued down the road together.

The more they talked, the more Vic realized how much he and Derek had in common. Amazingly, Derek was on his way to Lucid Peak too, and both were in a hurry. Neither had a traveling companion, and especially with the countryside growing more dangerous by the day, both knew it was a good idea to have someone to watch your back. Vic hadn't seen Derek fight, but he hadn't had much trouble with the bandit so Vic surmised he could hold his own just fine.

Before they knew it, six days had passed since they left Mrs. Nealy. The two were glad to finally be nearing their destination, because both were tired of traveling and quietly anxious about what lay ahead. They would spend the night in Traveler's Junction.

Vic had never been this far from Mayport and was enjoying the quaint little town they found. As the road crested and the city came into view, the setting sun opened up a panorama before them. Rolling green and brown hillsides disappeared into the rocky mountainside. The air was cool and thin, but refreshing for the tired travelers. Snow patches were scattered on the mountains up the road and each little farmhouse had a wispy stream of smoke rising from its chimney. The shadows were long and the orange sun bathed the countryside in autumn colors.

Traveler's Junction, as the name suggests, was where two main roads in the region met. The road they had been following ran from the Southern Sea, along the mountain range, northwest to Blood Canyon, a treacherous canyon about two miles to the northwest, and then up to the coast near Kraming. The other road began inland, ran up to Traveler's Junction, and then became the trail to Lucid Peak. Traveler's Junction was the last resting stop before Lucid Peak and the pair needed to buy supplies for the next few days.

Unlike most other mountainous areas, Lucid Peak was a common meeting point for traders. Due to the rough mountain range that ran all the way down to the desert, it was very hard to get products from the Western Kingdom where Vic and Derek lived, to the Eastern Kingdom where neither had ever been. The only real choices were by sea, by the long desert route all the way around the mountain range, or through the mountains. With its large plateau at the crest of the mountain, Lucid Peak was an ideal place to meet with other traders, as long as you only

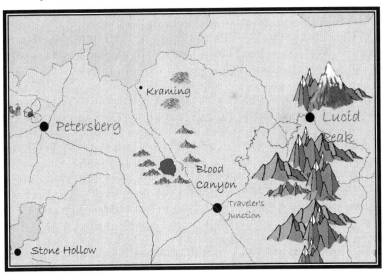

planned to buy what you could carry home. It was much easier to make the trades in the middle, with each trader returning the way he came. Lucid Peak's location on the crest of the mountains also made for some spectacular views; it was one of the only places where one could see the entire kingdom.

Though there were several routes to Lucid Peak, Vic had heard of a strange old man named Percival who came highly recommended as the best guide in the area. Percival was known to frequent the Traveler's Junction tavern and Vic thought it was probably a good idea to charter his services for tomorrow's travels. The road to Lucid Peak was well known for the number of travelers who never arrived at their destination. Even if most of the incidents were due to buyers returning with too large a load, or sellers with too large a purse, Vic knew it couldn't hurt to have an experienced guide. Unfortunately no one was able to tell him exactly how to find this Percival character.

As they approached the edge of town, they spotted some merchants in an open air market who were packing up for the night. Vic approached a gruff looking mountain dweller with a cart of dried fruit and nuts. He tried to ignore them, but with a little persistence and a few extra silver pieces, the man agreed to make one last sale. While they were finishing up, Vic asked the merchant if he knew where to find Percival.

The old man looked up for a minute and then chuckled, "You'll find him, or he'll find you. Either way, you won't miss him!"

It wasn't a very satisfying answer, but at least it was consistent. Every time he had asked someone how to get to Lucid peak, they all said to go with Percival, if you can find him. As they walked away, Derek said what Vic was thinking.

"What's with the vendors around here? Doesn't anyone want to work?"

"That's just what I was thinking! A vendor that doesn't want to sell and a guide nobody can find?"

"Put up a sign, pick a starting point, even a donkey with a logo would be helpful. We get nothing."

"Must be nice."

"Think the tavern will be open?"

"Hopefully the bartender will be at least a little interested in selling us a few drinks."

"Look alive everyone, real live customers!"

The Tavern was right on the city square, and not hard to find. Even though it wasn't quite dark yet, the tavern's lights provided a warm welcome. In a town of mostly travelers, it was the only place that still looked welcoming after the sun went down. The locals were on their way home, leaving only strangers in the streets, most of whom were drawn to the warmth and laughter of the tavern.

Vic thought the tavern was a better deal than the inn, so he chimed in first, "I'll check the tavern for that guide of ours. Wish me luck." he said to Derek as they entered the city square.

"Great, I'll check out the inn," Derek nodded toward the only other prominent building on the square, "maybe we can actually sleep in a bed tonight."

A warm soft bed sounded great to Vic, but he quickly remembered the last inn they had visited.

"Try to find a room without rats this time, OK?"

Ouch. Derek remembered that night too. "Will do," was all he replied. It was hard to sleep with rats sniffing at your toes all night.

They headed in opposite directions across the cobblestone city square. When Vic was about to enter the tavern, he looked back over his shoulder at the inn. A young boy had been pacing anxiously in front of the inn since they arrived in the courtyard. He was probably 10 or 11 years old so it wasn't anything to be alarmed about, but Vic took note of him. These days, everything was worth noticing.

It didn't used to be that way, but in the past few years, even before his near-death experience outside Yorksville, Vic had noticed strange things happening. People would disappear without a trace. For a while, rumors circulated around Mayport that a dark horse and rider would ride at night outside of town. The Mayport jail was once broken into and ransacked when it was supposedly empty. Most common folk never took any of this seriously, blaming the stories on kids playing pranks, robbers or freak accidents, but Vic knew better. A few times he had even been hired to help find someone's missing relative, but to no avail. He couldn't explain it, but he knew something was wrong. Just under the surface, a tempest was brewing. That cloaked warrior on the road outside of Yorksville was the first time he had ever seen a manifestation of this tempest with his own eyes.

The first few times he had tried to explain this feeling to others, they laughed at him, or called him superstitious, so he learned to keep his feelings to himself. For a while, he thought these occurrences were confined to Mayport, Yorksville and the other coastal towns where he grew up, but lately he had been traveling enough to know better. It wasn't his imagination, and it wasn't only in Mayport. Something was wrong and it was affecting everyone.

When Vic was a boy, things were different. People lived their lives in small towns, minding their own business and trusting their friends. They would usually deputize one of their friends to act as local sheriff and that was all they needed to keep them safe. Occasional bad apples would wander through, but they were quickly given the message that they weren't welcome and they would leave as fast as they came. There didn't used to be an undercurrent of fear.

These days, people were always looking over their shoulders. What were they looking for? It was hard to tell, but strange stories circulated in abundance. Last month, Vic heard that Mrs. Witherspoon, one of Mrs. Nealy's best friends, simply disappeared. She was out picking berries one day and never returned. There had been a traveling salesman in town that day, but no one knew him or saw where he went. Mr. Witherspoon was distraught. The whole town canvassed the countryside looking for her, or her body, but they found nothing. There wasn't even a sign of a struggle.

Vic had even heard stories of monstrous shadowy figures like the ones that attacked him. Last month, he overheard the Mayport sheriff talking in low tones to the mayor at the local tavern. The sheriff said he had found a local mercenary, Jefferson Kroger, just outside of town almost dead. He had clearly been in a swordfight and was gravely injured. He kept mumbling something about red eyes and black coats. "Too strong, too strong," he would say. Jefferson lasted about a week before he died and no one was ever able to figure out what he was talking about. Now that Vic had met one of these creatures up close, he knew exactly what had killed Jefferson.

So Vic had to keep his eyes open. He was looking as much for threats as he was for answers. That was one of the reasons he agreed to travel to Lucid Peak; maybe along the way he would be able to fill in some pieces to the puzzle. He hoped that each new piece would lead him closer to the truth. Maybe he could even find some weakness of those monsters that attacked him.

As Derek approached the inn, the boy stopped pacing and headed straight for him. Was the boy friend or foe?

2. Scrolls

Vic's first instinct was to run to join Derek and his hand reflexively went to his sword, but something made him pause. Derek seemed perfectly at ease with the situation. Did he know the boy? Neither smiled as they approached. It wasn't the greeting of old friends, but there was no fear either. The boy walked straight up to Derek without hesitation and then stopped. It was almost as if the boy had been expecting Derek; even waiting for him. This was strange and Vic wanted to know more. He slipped around the corner of the tavern and pressed himself against the side of the building. The dusk left just enough light for him watch the scene from the shadows.

How could they be expecting each other? The thought was preposterous since there was no way the boy could have known they were coming. Not even Vic knew where they would be stopping that night. He and Derek had never discussed it. In fact, Vic was considering not stopping here at all. Having a guide would be nice, but not at the expense of losing daylight. If they had arrived earlier in the day, they probably would have kept right on walking to cover more ground before nightfall. Nevertheless, this certainly looked like a prearranged meeting.

Derek and the boy spoke in hushed voices. Vic strained his ears to hear, but was too far away to make out any words. They drew even closer to each other and continued talking. A meeting of some kind was taking place, but why? Was Derek some kind of spy?

Just then, Vic heard a noise in the bushes nearby. He shot a glance in the direction of the noise. Nothing. He scanned the nearby forest. Still nothing. Something was there, but he couldn't see what it was. In any case, he didn't want to be caught by an animal while hiding behind the tavern. A cold breeze blew across his face and he knew – time to get inside.

Vic looked back in the direction of the inn just in time to catch the boy handing Derek what looked like a tiny scroll tied with a red ribbon. Is that really what he saw? It was getting darker by the minute and Vic had to strain to see. Yes, there it was again as Derek placed it into his bag. It was a little scroll. With that, the boy ran off down the road and Derek went into the inn.

"Get a hold of yourself, Vic. Don't jump to conclusions," he thought, "Let's see what Derek has to say for himself." With one more look around to make sure no one was watching, Vic slid out of his shadowy hiding place and resumed a casual walk into the tavern.

A young farm girl was on her way to the barn to give her horse one last rub down before bed. As she opened the back door to her house she saw a small scroll tied with a red ribbon lying on the ground, and next to it, a beautiful pearl handled dagger. Her heart leapt inside her chest. Her time had finally come! She carefully picked up the scroll and the dagger and went back into the house.

"Ma! Pa! Come see!"

It was a simple home; nothing fancy, but warm and safe. All three met at the wooden kitchen table where the girl carefully laid the dagger and the note. They all stared at them for a minute.

"Well, aren't you going to open it?" her father asked.

"I suppose so." The girl was so excited her hands trembled as she slid the ribbon off the scroll and unrolled it. It said, "Rebecca, On the path to Lucid Peak, past the ridge but before the clearing grows the great oak. At midnight the moonlight strikes its trunk in only one place. Plant the blade of this dagger in the tree at that spot. Go with my favor." It was signed "Renatus."

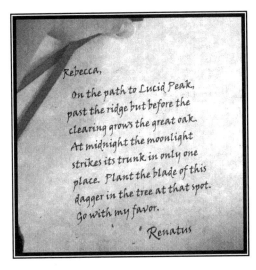

"Ma, he signed it himself! I can't believe it! I know exactly where that is. Molly and I used to play around that oak tree all day long during the summer. I've never been there at night, but it shouldn't be too hard to find."

"He always prepares you for the tasks and sends just the right person for the job." Her mother smiled.

A look of concern came over the girl's face, "Do I have to go alone?"

"No," her father said, "I can come with you, but it is your assignment. I will only be there to protect and help."

"Right!" Her face brightened up again. "Let's saddle up the horses!"

He was the youngest of seven brothers and even though he was only 10 years old, he grew up watching his mother, father and brothers receiving scrolls and following their instructions. He had already done several himself and they always gave him great satisfaction. They were mostly small tasks he didn't understand, but that didn't matter. He didn't need to be a hero, and really didn't want to be seen. In fact, he liked it best when they required sneaking around at night. That part was fun.

His scroll said simply, "Put one bow and one arrow into the small shed in front of the Western Tower at Widow's Castle. Use the method of your choosing." Yes. This was going to be fun.

After dinner that evening, he grabbed a bow and arrow and snuck his way across the two fields that separated their farm from Widow's Castle. He knew the way well. He had been there many times with his father and had heard the awful stories of what went on inside. When the patrol guard had walked around the corner out of sight, he crept up to the shed to plant his bow and arrow. Hmm. Locked. Time for some quick thinking.

The boy ran out into the open space in front of the shed where the guard frequently passed, and placed his bow and arrow carefully on the ground. Then he ran back to the bushes and watched silently. The guard came back around the corner at his usual interval and when he came upon the bow and arrow, he stopped. He scanned the area for any sign of movement. Seeing none, he finally shrugged his shoulders, picked up the bow and arrow and headed for the shed. The clanking of his keys told the story and in a minute, the shed door swung open and he placed the bow and arrow inside. He closed and locked the door, then resumed his patrol. Mission accomplished. The young agent was headed home.

3. The Tavern

The room was noisy and smoky, about how a tavern should be. On one side, an old wooden bar was tended by an even older man. On the other side, small hand cut wooden tables made from tree stumps, with matching chairs, cluttered the room. Neither looked very welcoming, but the patrons didn't seem to mind and they left very few open seats. Three burly men sat at a table in the corner and were singing badly. An occasional laugh broke through the drone of conversation. Along the back wall, a large stone fireplace warmed visitors and provided the main source of light for the room.

After pausing for a moment in the doorway to take in the scene, Vic headed for the bar. As he took a stool, the bartender walked over and plunked a drink down in front of Vic.

"Lookin' for Percival, ain't ya?" he asked, a wry little smile on his face. "Not hard to spot ya, at least not for me." His voice was gruff and his skin like old leather, but his eyes were smiling and young. "I've been watchin' you folks come in here for years. Always lookin' for somethin'. So what'll it be?"

"Looks like you already got me a beer."

"That's an ale, young man, and the question is what're YOU lookin' for?" he asked as he poked Vic in the chest with his wiry finger.

"I'm not looking for anything, I'm meeting someone."

His eyebrows raised and his eyes brightened. "Maybe, but I think you're lookin'. OK, let's hear about the meetin' first," he replied, "I'm always interested in a good get together. So let's hear it, lad, what brings ya here?"

Although he seemed harmless enough, Vic wasn't about to tell a bartender he'd known for exactly 30 seconds his entire life's story. Even so, he seemed like a pretty insightful judge of character. Vic really *was* looking for something. He desperately wanted answers, but not from this guy. Vic had things to do. "Thanks for your interest, but I think I'll save my stories for another day. So how about it? Where can I find Percival?"

"Oh, he's around," then he smiled, "but if you intend to go anywhere with Percival you better start tellin' that story. I bet you don't have the slightest idea what he looks like, now do ya? Well I do, and I like good stories, so start talkin'."

Vic smiled. This bartender was not only a good judge of character, but a pretty decent chess player too.

"You drive a hard bargain."

"That's the deal."

"How about a nice tip?"

"Nope."

Vic looked around the room at all the people who could be Percival, then sighed. "Alright, here it is. I hope you think it's worth it. Some people say I'm a soldier-for-hire, but I say I get paid to help people. Ever since my parents were killed and our farm burned to the ground almost five years ago, I go from place to place helping people solve their problems. Sometimes I'm catching poachers stealing pigs, sometimes I join a posse tracking down a jail breaker. Sometimes it's tenants that don't pay their rent. Whenever someone's got a job they can't handle, they get word to me and I come around and help them. I never know where I'll be the next day, and although I head back to Mayport between jobs to catch up with friends because that's where I grew up, there really isn't much for me there. Just give me a job and I'll get it done."

The bartender was wiping down the bar in front of Vic as he told the story, occasionally looking up and smiling.

"Today, I'm helping a farmer friend of mine, Tom Claybrooke, who farms about 20 acres of land in the lower plains south of Mayport. About 10 of those acres haven't been fertile for the past 4 or 5 years. For some reason nothing seems to grow there. It was really starting to put a strain on Tom's family and there wasn't much hope of bringing the land back until Tom got wind of a new type of wheat seed that can grow almost anywhere. He was excited until he heard that the only place to get it is from a traveling salesman who comes to Lucid Peak every year about this time. Tom took a nasty fall off his horse last year and even though he was in no condition to go, he was determined to make the trip. I knew he shouldn't go, so I volunteered to come for him, and I wouldn't take no for an answer."

"This salesman is supposed to be there until the day after the full moon, and I need to meet him there to make the trade. By my read, we've got about three days until the full moon, and Lucid Peak is about three days journey. That's why I wanted to meet Percival, to make sure I get to the meeting point on time. I've never been to Lucid Peak and I've heard the road can be treacherous, so I figure, it never hurts to have a guide."

"More than that, it could kill ya' not to," the bartender soberly cut in.

"So that's my story. Now it's your turn. Where can I find Percival?" Vic was glad for some conversation, but he was growing weary of this bartender and had doubts about whether he would deliver on his side of the bargain.

"So you're just here 'cause you're gettin' paid to be, eh?" The bartender obviously didn't think the story was done yet.

"This one's free. Tom's like family to me, and he needed help. As I said, I help people. So no, I'm not getting' paid for this one. Now can we get on with the introduction?"

The bartender smiled, looked over at the fireplace for a few moments, and then looked back. His smile vanished and he looked Vic straight in the eye. "No introduction tonight. You find yourself in front of this tavern tomorrow morning at dawn with your bags packed and your boots on. Don't be late." Then he smiled and stepped back. "Drink's on the house." He slapped the bar in front of Vic and let out a hearty laugh, and then turned away to help another customer.

Vic tried to call him back, but he was gone. The conversation was over. There was no way to know if the bartender could deliver or not, but it didn't really matter. Vic and Derek would be ready to travel tomorrow morning at dawn whether Percival showed up or not. They had to leave then anyway if they wanted to meet the trader in three days, guide or no guide.

Vic sat for a few minutes taking in the sounds and smells of the tavern. The warmth of the fire was relaxing after what had already been a long journey. He finished off his ale and headed for the door. It was time to talk to Derek about that boy.

4. The Inn

It was fully dark now, and the moon had not yet crested the rim of the valley. The night was clear and cold, and was getting colder. As Vic stepped outside, the brightness of the tavern lingered for a few moments before his eyes adjusted to the darkness of the night. There was no one around. Other than the stars that filled the night sky, the only light was coming from the door behind him and a dim lantern in the window of the inn where he was headed.

Vic made his way across the square and found the inn door unlocked. As he walked in, he was greeted by a warm fire in the fireplace with a big black cauldron hanging above it, and the smell of beef stew in the air. At first it looked like no one was around. The counter was wiped clean and the lamp in the window was turned down low. Vic was about to ring the bell on the counter when he heard a voice from near the fireplace. "So let's see, you must be our traveling hero." The voice was of a young woman, soft and playful. "I was beginning to wonder if you were really coming." Vic turned to the big stuffed chair by the fireplace to see a young woman uncurl her feet from the chair and close the old book she was reading.

"My name is Angela. My father owns this inn and he told me you would be coming. Your friend has already rented a room upstairs." She put the book on a nearby table and brushed off her apron as she stood up.

"Sounds good. I'm glad to hear you had a room available."

Angela smiled, "I can take you there if you like, or if you're hungry, you are welcome to some stew. I thought you might not have eaten so I kept some warm for you."

Smelling the stew was the first time Vic realized that he hadn't eaten since that morning. "I'd love some, I'm famished!"

In the light of the fire, Vic got a better look at his considerate host. She had long dark hair, light skin and striking features. Vic guessed she was around 20 years old. "So what brings you to Traveler's Junction?" she asked while ladling the hearty stew out of the cauldron over the fireplace.

"I'm going to meet a salesman at Lucid Peak. He's only here once a year and I have a friend who really needs the seeds he sells."

She handed him the warm bowl and continued, "Well if you don't mind me saying, you don't look much like the farming type. I see a lot of farmers, and a lot of soldiers, and the farmers don't usually carry those." She motioned to the sword he had pulled onto his lap when he sat down in the second stuffed chair. "Do you make this trip often? I've never seen you here before."

"No, this is my first time," he said between bites. The stew tasted as good as it smelled and warmed his insides through and through.

"Of many?" Angela looked up from the stew she had been stirring.

"Probably not. We're hoping that with these seeds, they can make it through the next few seasons." Vic paused, then continued, "and I'm not sure I would want to make this trip again."

"Don't you like it up here?" Angela smiled as she asked.

"I like it well enough, but there are some people at home that I would like to get back and see."

"Ooooh," she nodded, "I see. So, what's her name?"

Vic felt himself blush. His feelings about Catherine were so confusing, even to him, that he was surprised Angela had discovered her so easily. "What makes you think there's a woman?"

"There isn't?"

"Well, I didn't say that."

"Right. Like I said, what's her name?" Angela was clearly having fun with this whole line of questioning and was thoroughly enjoying Vic's discomfort.

"Her name is Catherine, and it's her dad who needs the seeds. Her birthday is three days after mine and we grew up together. We've been very good friends since we were kids."

"Friends?" Angela asked.

Vic smiled, "Yes, friends."

OK, it was definitely time to end this conversation. Catherine was the real reason he had come all this distance in the first place and it took Angela less than 5 minutes to figure it out. What was it with everyone in this town? He had just spilled his guts to a bartender and now he was about to tell this beautiful stranger about his love life? Vic tried to think of a way to get the topic back onto safer ground.

"Her dad injured himself last season and was not well enough to make the journey, but he was determined to go anyway. The only way I could talk him out of going was to offer to go myself."

"I see," she said, a little quieter. "So it really wasn't just for her? That would have been so much more romantic."

The funny thing was, like the bartender, she was right. Tom's injury was part of the reason Vic volunteered to come, but the real reason was Catherine. When the road was particularly long, or the sun beat on his face with no shade in sight, he wondered why he would make such a crazy journey. On those days, his thoughts would drift to Catherine. Angela was right, he was not a farmer, and this kind of thing was one of the reasons why he could never see himself becoming one. He was, however, smitten by Catherine.

One look into her deep blue eyes and the journey to Lucid Peak would seem like a few seconds. She captivated him. The way she moved; the playful look in her eyes when she teased him. They grew up in the same town together, and they were very close friends. Every summer when the days got long they used to set out to find adventures together. Catherine was the daring one. She loved to explore, play practical jokes on people and generally find the fun in life. Vic was never the one to suggest their adventures, but he always looked forward to them. He was at his best when he was helping her get into, and out of trouble. Catherine would find the cave to explore and Vic would draw the map to get them out. Catherine would "borrow" two horses from a neighboring ranch for a ride in the forest and Vic would get them back before the rancher noticed. When they were younger, she would dream up practical jokes to play on her older brother and Vic would help her figure out how to make them work. Vic had less time for fun when his family died, but he ended up spending more time with Catherine and her family. She was never afraid to speak her mind, and even though Vic thought it was smarter not to jump to conclusions, he loved watching her debate her father and brother on the silliest things.

It wasn't until last summer that Vic began to think of Catherine as something more than a best friend. The night before the attack at Yorksville they sat under the stars and watched the moon trace across the sky. It wasn't the first time they had spent much of the night talking, but it was the first time they had both felt such a strong attraction. As he was about to leave, both knew he would be gone on his next job for several weeks. The last embrace seemed to last longer, and her sweet smell lingered with him long after he walked her home. He had fallen for her, and he knew it. Unfortunately, they never had the chance to figure out what they were going to do about it.

Instead of returning home after a few weeks, it was nine months before he returned. The attack had left him near dead, and if it wasn't for the kindness of that Yorksville farmer and his wife who found him and nursed him back to health, he wouldn't have made it home at all. It was a full seven months before his strength had returned. Just as he was strong enough to leave, harvest time had arrived, and his kind rescuers needed all the help they could find. Staying to help was the least he could do, after they had done so much for him. For a month and a half he worked long hard hours in the sun, until the harvest was finished. The work helped his strength return faster, but all he could think about was getting home. As they celebrated the end of the harvest, he bid them farewell and headed for home, with just enough time to make it back before the first frost of winter.

When he finally returned home, Vic found everything different. Months of wondering about him had taken their toll on Catherine, and her parents finally sent her away to her aunt's house in Rochester. The change of pace had helped her forget about Vic, and she wrote home with stories of new friends and adventures.

When Vic finally returned, she was still away. She finally returned to visit from Rochester, but their first meeting was awkward. They had both changed and neither knew how to act around the other. She was only home for about a week and then went back to Rochester. Vic wanted the old times back, and even more he longed to tell her how he felt, but it all seemed wrong now. It was a few days later that her father mentioned the new seeds, and Vic was quick to volunteer for the trip. He and Catherine would have plenty of time to work things out when he got back. Maybe he could stop by Rochester on the way home and see what she was up to.

With these new seeds, Tom was hoping to be able to plant the barren land and maybe after a good season, he would have enough seed to sustain future crops and make some money, but someone had to get the first seeds. The trip was both necessary, and a good distraction. Vic didn't have any other work lined up, so it was easy to see why he should go instead of Tom. By now, Vic had been on the road about a week and in just a few days, he should have the seeds in hand and could head for home. At times like these, he couldn't wait to get there.

Vic finished his bowl of stew, handed it back to Angela and stood up from his chair. "Not that I wouldn't love to stay and tell you all about her, but I've got a big day ahead and I need some rest. It has truly been a pleasure chatting with you, and your stew was simply perfect."

Angela stood up with him and gave a slight curtsy. "I'm glad you enjoyed yourself," she smiled, "I'll show you to your room." The pair went up the stairs to a room at the end of the hallway. Angela opened the door and then handed him the key. As he walked in, he noticed Derek's traveling bag on a table, and no other sign of Derek. Vic turned back to Angela, "Do you know where my friend is?" he asked.

"No," she said politely, "he left shortly after he checked in. He said he had some business to attend to and would be back later." Angela lit the lamp on the wall and then turned for the door. "My father and I live in the first room at the top of the stairs. Just knock if you need anything. Good night." She closed the door as she left.

The conversation with Angela had kept him distracted from the mystery he had observed earlier, but now he faced it squarely again. Who was that boy, and more importantly, *where was Derek?* His actions earlier had been peculiar enough, but now he was out alone at night in an unfamiliar town. There was nowhere else for him to go, was there?

Vic walked to the window to take a look around. The moon had been climbing and was now high enough in the sky to peek over the valley walls. The night was clear, but it was also cold, and at this altitude, cold could kill.

If Derek hadn't left his traveling bag, Vic might have thought he had left for good and wouldn't be coming back. Neither one had asked for a commitment of any kind, but Vic expected Derek to at least say goodbye. Vic looked at Derek's traveling bag still sitting on the table. Derek obviously didn't intend to be gone all night, and it was already getting late. If Vic didn't go after him, there was a good chance Derek would never make it back.

Vic didn't have to ponder for long. He checked his sword and dagger, wrapped himself up in his cloak as tightly as possible and headed back downstairs and then out into the night.

Vic gazed through the silent town square and up the road they arrived on. During the day, it would have been teeming with people who might have seen Derek, but at night, there was no one out to ask. The tavern was still full of activity, but Vic had been there earlier and knew they wouldn't be much help. That's not where Derek went.

Maybe he went to see someone in town? Did that boy live nearby? Angela might know. Turning back inside, Vic went to ask her.

Vic was relieved to get back inside out of the cold as he pulled the door shut behind him and headed upstairs to Angela's door. He rapped gently.

She was dressed for bed, but not asleep yet when she answered the door.

"Is something the matter, Vic?" Angela asked, a look of concern on her face.

"I'm not sure. Derek hasn't come back yet and I was wondering if you saw him talking with anyone else who might know where he is."

"Hmmm. The only person I remember him seeing was a young boy he spoke with briefly before he walked in the first time."

"Do you know where I could find the boy?"

"No, I'm sorry. He wasn't from around these parts. We know pretty much everyone who lives here, and I've never seen him before. He arrived in the early afternoon and stood right in front of the inn for several hours pacing back and forth. He looked so tired I offered him a little something to eat and drink while he was waiting, which he gratefully accepted. He seemed very hungry, and was waiting for someone. Derek must have been who he was waiting for because after they talked, he never came back."

"Did you see which way the boy went after they finished talking?"

"I can't be sure, but I thought he headed in the direction of Blood Canyon. I don't think I saw him head down the main road, and we certainly did not rent him a room."

"OK. I don't know what it means yet, but it helps. Thanks, Angela."

Vic was genuinely glad for the help, but he didn't like what it meant. Derek didn't go to meet someone in town, he got wrapped up in some kind of business with that boy and he headed down the road to Blood Canyon. Vic had no proof, but he was sure of it. He walked back out the door into the cold.

Was he really going to do this? He could see his breath making smoke in the clear night sky. He didn't know the road and didn't even know where to look, but somehow he thought he could come to Derek's rescue? Leaving the safety of the inn to help Derek was crazy, but the situation seemed strangely familiar to him. He finally realized why. This was the same way he felt back home when he would run off to get Catherine out of some mess she had gotten herself into. He didn't know what was up ahead, but his friend was in danger and he knew he could help. He wanted to kick himself for wasting so much time. Derek hadn't abandoned him or betrayed him, he was in trouble.

It was now or never, so off he went. The excitement of the adventure was thrilling, but it was fear that pushed him into a run. Not fear of what lay ahead, but fear he was too late to fight by Derek's side. Fear that Derek was already dead, and that he had died alone.

It had been a long day, and Harold was tired. He was the foreman at the cannery in Kraming, a small town on the northern coast. He lived alone and it was just past sundown when he arrived home. Like every night, he walked into his small cottage, hung his coat on the peg, lit the lamp on the wall, and then plopped down into his one big chair. He was starting to take off his boots when he noticed something out of place on the kitchen table. It was a small scroll wrapped in a red ribbon.

His neck stiffened and the hairs on his arms stood up. Now? Really? No news for weeks and word comes now? Harold sunk his foot back into his boot and walked to the table. He unwrapped the scroll and read its characteristically brief message. "Blood Canyon. 2 hours past sundown. Stay hidden." He was glad to be back in service again, but wished it could have been a day when he wasn't so exhausted. It only took an hour to get to Blood Canyon from here, so he still had time. He left his boots on, but went back to his chair for a quick nap.

In the forward command center, the Timekeeper opened his eyes and turned to Renatus. "He will not arrive in time."

Renatus lowered his head. "Harold needed this. He longs to be used again. He needed to complete this assignment as much as I needed it completed." Renatus looked back to the Timekeeper, "Percival is the only other capable soldier nearby, isn't he?"

"Yes, sir."

Renatus sighed. "Wake him up." He turned to face the nearby fireplace. "How I long for the day when so much of the load will not have to be carried by so few."

"Our numbers are growing, sir, isn't that cause for rejoicing?"

"Yes, but what good are numbers when they are unwilling to answer the call?"

"Your plan is in motion, things will change."

"Yes, but I will not make them serve me. They must choose that for themselves."

5. Blood Canyon

The road to Blood Canyon was aptly named. The wandering path suddenly turned and clung to the side of a cliff on its way to the bottom of the canyon. The downward segment was not well marked and travelers were unprotected from the wind that swept up the canyon face. At places it was no wider than a single horse and rider, and the gravel was often loose and unpredictable. It was even worse at night.

Fortunately, Vic spotted the first turn and drop off, and stood there to examine the road ahead. The danger of the descent stood in stark contrast to the beautiful meadow at the bottom. The bottom of the canyon was quiet and inviting, even whimsical. Not far from the base of the cliff, a glassy lake slipped into a lazy river that wandered down the valley. It drifted all the way down the valley's length as far as he could see. Even though the water looked like ink in the moonlight, he thought that many people would visit its banks to enjoy an afternoon if the trek up the canyon face wasn't so perilous. Why didn't someone fix this road? From the lake heading north, the trail was wide and easy, meandering along the side of the river all the way to the small fishing town of Kraming on the northern coastline.

Vic could see almost the whole trail that snaked down the canyon face. Could Derek be somewhere on the road ahead? Vic's eyes scanned back and forth down the trail. On one switchback before the bottom he spotted something. It was hard to tell at that distance in the moonlight, but it could be the outline of a man.

The figure was near the bottom of the road, crouched behind a large boulder. Wounded? Resting? Hiding? Waiting? Vic couldn't tell, but he was determined to find out.

The moon was now higher in the sky and lit everything with its eerie gray light. He wanted to keep an eye on the figure below, but had to keep his eyes on the trail. This trail was not to be taken lightly. He tried to hurry, but it was a slow process.

After what felt like an hour of tedious descent he was finally close enough to see the figure in some detail. It was Derek, and he certainly wasn't hurt. He was hiding - crouched behind a small rock. Vic immediately scanned the area at the base of the canyon to find Derek's target. At first he saw no one, so he quietly pushed downward as fast as he could until he was about two switchbacks away from Derek. He was finally able to see what Derek was looking at, and it made him freeze.

Coming up the trail in the distance were three riders. They rode three abreast, and the one in the center had his hands bound behind his back, and a rope around his waist which was tied to one of the other horses. His clothes were tattered and worn and his head hung low in defeat. The two with him were something entirely different. Clothed in black from head to toe, they rode massive black horses and wore long black cloaks. Neither figure moved in the saddle or spoke a word. They methodically proceeded up the valley floor, and one had his arm extended to grip their captive. Scales on his arm glinted in the moonlight.

Could these be Derek's prey? Was he insane? Did he know what he was getting into? These two were no ordinary prisoner guards. These were the monsters that had assaulted Vic on the road outside of Yorksville. The sight of them sent chills down his spine. He couldn't make out the faces under the hoods, but he saw the red glow of their cat eyes reaching out from the darkness under their cloaks. Many nights he had seen figures just like these in his dreams, and many days he had spent wondering what he would do if he saw one again. Was he now going to face them voluntarily?

He also noticed another feeling he remembered. It was something oppressive. Every muscle in his body was tense. His palms were sweaty as he gripped his sword and his heart pounded. He wanted to help Derek, but not against them. He had been in this fight before and knew where it would lead: it was going to be a slaughter. Maybe Derek was good, but this wasn't going to be a fair fight.

Vic's eyes turned back to his traveling companion. Derek was keenly aware of the oncoming party, and had not yet seen Vic. His eyes were glued on his targets. He moved back and forth behind the rock to get a better view of them as they rode up the valley floor along the river. As they got closer, Vic realized what Derek had planned.

Derek's hiding spot was on the first switchback, putting him about seven feet higher than the group that would be coming from below. The travelers were now a mere thirty feet from his position and though they were on horseback and he was not, he should be able to take out one of the guards with a surprise attack, leaving only one. If Vic could get down there, at least it would be two on one. Even then this would be no cakewalk, but at least they might have a chance.

The party reached the end of the canyon, but instead of turning to their left as the path began the switchbacks up the long face of the canyon, they stayed in the clearing and turned their backs to Derek to face the path that they had just arrived on.

They were waiting for someone! If Derek was going to attack, now was the time, but they were stopped twenty feet away. The plan wasn't going to work, or so Vic thought, until he saw Derek attack.

From the moment Derek attacked, everything was a blur. Derek leaped from behind his rock on the ledge of the first switchback. Not to the ground as Vic had expected, but twenty feet straight through the air! His jump threw him silently into the air, first with his hands outstretched, and then in a mid air flip, then descending with his sword in striking position. Derek dropped just alongside the closer horseman and with one well placed slice, beheaded the guard, and tumbled to the ground in front of him.

The jump alone was impressive, but the precision of the cut was amazing. A bloodcurdling scream ripped through the quiet night sky and echoed through the canyon.

How does a man without a head scream?

All at once the memories flooded back into his head. That was the same scream he heard just before he blacked out on the road outside of Yorksville! Vic wanted to jump in and help, but instead he was petrified with fear.

The cloak from the dead guard tumbled to the ground in a heap and then disappeared. The head? It too was gone. Both vanished into thin air, but the other horseman didn't, and now the fight was on. The other horseman was already off his horse and heading toward Derek.

The duel that ensued was like nothing Vic had ever seen. Combat usually has a predicable pace, each combatant sizing up the other and moving to exploit weaknesses. Vic knew all too well that it took different tactics to beat different foes. A slow and weak opponent could be taken by brute force. A fast opponent could be beaten, but only after wearing him down for a while. A taller and stronger opponent would often leave an opening with too wide a swing or too slow a block. As much a teacher as a student Vic loved watching a battle to learn, but this battle fit no mold.

The guard was a towering menace and swung a huge sword, but with speed no normal man could muster. In sheer strength, it was awesome. A blue flash of light emanated from the swords with every contact, as if the very essence of the metal was challenged. Derek was done for. Surely there was no way he could fight back. Vic knew what to expect, but again, Derek amazed him.

Three times in a row the warrior struck, and all three were blocked by Derek. Then the strikes stopped. Where was Derek? Did he fall? No, he had moved behind the warrior. How could he have moved so fast? Vic had no idea, but there he was, on the other side of his target and on the attack. One, two, three strikes by Derek. All blocked by the guard. As strong as the guard was, Derek was keeping him off balance thanks to his speed. The guard was pushed back into his horse, then leapt to the side and planted himself for the next attack wave from Derek.

But where was Derek? The guard looked side to side. Where did Derek go? The guard spun around just in time to find Derek behind him and on the attack again. One, two, three, four, five. The guard didn't even have time to change his sword position. Derek was winning! The guard stumbled back and Derek was coming from on top of him and pounding him into the ground.

The guard swung at his feet; Derek jumped. As he came down he swung and caught the guard's arm. First blood. The guard roared in pain like an angry mountain lion, then rolled and came up ready for more. Derek was there within a blink and

41

again, the engagement was a blur of flashing blue light and steel. The duo quickly moved to a nearby patch of trees and then much to Vic's dismay, the battle was shielded from his view. A few moments later, they emerged, the guard with his back to Vic and retreating as they fought. Derek clearly had the upper hand now. Two seconds later, Vic saw the end of Derek's sword protrude from the middle of the guard's back. Again, a bloodcurdling scream pierced the night sky.

Derek quickly sheathed his sword, and ran for the prisoner, who was still sitting motionless in the saddle through all the commotion. Vic thought this was odd since Derek hadn't cleaned his sword and a good swordsman knows never to put a bloody sword back in its sheath. Another odd thing was that both black horses didn't seem so large anymore. They stood in the same places, still saddled and harnessed in the same way, but now appeared about the same size as the third horse carrying the prisoner. Had they really changed or was it only his perception? The moonlight could play tricks on a person, but Vic knew what he saw.

Derek began untying the prisoner from the horses, but then stopped and turned toward the river. Vic strained his eyes and ears to see what he was looking at. Off in the distance Vic saw a small cloud of dust. Other than the flow of the stream, the night was deathly silent at first, but a few seconds later Vic heard the distant sound of horses at a gallop. Not less than three. Maybe more. These must be the reinforcements. OK, Derek, you did well, but now was the time to run!

Derek did not disappoint. In a flash, he finished untying the prisoner and was leading his horse back up the first switchback. He would never make it. With the speed of the gallop and the pounding of their hooves getting louder every second, the reinforcements would get there before Derek had crossed the third switchback. More relevant for Vic, they would spot him any second and he had nowhere to hide. Now was the time to let his presence be known.

"Derek!"

Immediately Derek looked up at Vic, now only one switchback above him. With something between amazement, incredulity and exasperation, Derek yelled back exactly what Vic expected to hear, "What are **YOU** doing here?"

"I…"

"Never mind," Derek replied. He was clearly in control of this situation and Vic was perfectly content to follow his lead. "Grab the horse. Take the prisoner to the inn as fast as you can. I'll stay down here to hold them off so they don't follow."

"You'll never be able to take on that whole group alone," Vic shot back, "you need my help."

"You wouldn't have a chance," was all he replied.

Ouch. That hurt, but it was true. Vic had watched the last battle and knew he was no match for what they were doing down there. "Help is on its way… I hope," were Derek's last words as he spun around and ran back down to meet the oncoming posse.

This was not going to be pretty, and both Vic and Derek knew it. Without help, there was little chance Derek could take them on and win, and without the time Derek would buy them, Vic would never make it to the top with the prisoner. By now, Vic was running as fast as he could along the uneven path and the steep slope, pulling the horse and prisoner behind him. Three switchbacks later, he was still going, and now his legs and chest were starting to burn, but there was no stopping. A scream filled the night air. One down, good job Derek. Vic didn't stop. His life, and that of this prisoner, depended on it. Shortly after, he heard another scream and he couldn't help but look. He glanced for a second to the bottom of the canyon to see how Derek was doing.

Things were actually better than he expected. From the empty horses, there had been five riders. Derek had obviously hidden again and taken down the first horsemen with his initial jump, and then one more, but it looked like three remained. His clear advantage was his speed. As before, Derek moved faster than they could keep track of, and he kept moving to the outside of their group as they tried to surround him. Vic forced his way up the hill with all his might, and the fight below seemed to go on forever. Finally, as he was nearing the top Vic stopped to rest, and glanced down to see the fight below. He could see that Derek was clearly tired, but still standing. The group moved out of sight and into the trees, then a second later – good move, Derek! He swung around from behind a tree and brought the full side of his blade into the stomach of one of his rivals. Another bloodcurdling scream and another pile of black cloth on the ground, but this time Derek didn't get away unharmed. One of the other guards took advantage of Derek's exposed arm and gave him a good upward blow to the shoulder. Derek was down, stunned, and another guard was coming down right on top of him.

As he saw Derek go down, Vic's stomach leaped to his chest. He wanted to yell. He wanted to help, but he couldn't. He was too far away now, and couldn't help anyway. All he could do was watch.

Derek rolled just in time to avoid a blow to the head, but he wasn't even back on his feet when a strike came from behind that tore through the back of his leg. He crumpled to the ground again. He was done for. Another second and one of the two remaining guards would finish the job. And then Vic heard the last thing he expected, another scream.

One of the guards had been approaching Derek with his sword over his head. This was the death blow that surely would have finished him, until a dagger went flying through the air and into the guard's back with such force that it kept going and took his empty black cloak with it. The cloak flew through the air straight over Derek's head and pinned it to a nearby tree. Help had arrived, but was it too late?

The surprise shocked the last guard who reeled around just in time to find another dagger cutting through the night air, producing a fifth scream. Vic tried to see who had come to help, but the trees blocked his view and he had to keep moving. If Derek was still alive, he would be fine, now that he was in friendly hands. Vic had reached the top of the trail and now turned away from Blood Canyon on the path back toward Traveler's Junction.

The questions swam through Vic's head. Everything had happened so fast it was hard to believe this wasn't a dream.

"Who is this guy on the horse behind me and what am I going to do with him?" Vic wondered. The prisoner would never make it to Lucid Peak. Derek was obviously willing to give his life to free this man so he must be important, but he sure didn't look like it. He was almost unconscious and could barely stay on the horse he was riding. What if Derek never made it back?

Just then an idea came to him. Vic would ask Angela to take care of the man until he returned from Lucid Peak. Maybe by then he would be well enough so that Vic could figure out what to do with him. Maybe he would even get word from Derek about how he was doing, and what to do with this newly freed prisoner.

It was no easy task getting the prisoner off the horse and up to his bedroom, but after considerable trouble and much more noise than he thought Angela and her father could ever sleep through, he finally got his new ward into Derek's bed. It had been a long day of physical and mental stress and Vic collapsed onto his own bed in complete exhaustion. Hopefully everything would make sense in the morning.

Harold woke up with a start. He was still in his chair with his boots on. The room was dark except for the gem mounted on his pocketwatch sitting on the table. It was glowing so brightly it lit the room. He had missed the rendezvous and he was gripped with panic. He grabbed his coat and sword, stuffed the scroll in his pocket, raced out of the cottage and headed for Blood Canyon. Was he too late?

6. A New Day

Vic awoke to the sun's rays on his face from the nearby window. What a nice new day, he thought. Last night must have been a bad dream. No, it was a nightmare. He turned to the bed across the room, half expecting to see Derek sound asleep, half expecting to see the prisoner he now vaguely remembered rescuing last night. Instead, he saw nothing but an empty bed.

Empty? The man from last night was in no condition to go anywhere. He couldn't have gotten up on his own, could he? A bolt of adrenaline shot through him and suddenly he was wide-awake. Had more guards come for him in the night? He reached under his bed for his sword. There it was, cold and in its sheath just where he left it. He scanned the room again, this time taking stock of everything and looking for anything out of place.

A closer look at the bed showed that its covers had been pulled all the way down, not like you would when getting out of bed yourself, but like someone else might do when trying to lift you out. Nothing else was out of place. *Even the door was locked, just as he left it.* Whoever did this had a key, leaving three people he was aware of: Derek, Angela and her father.

Vic opened the door and intended to head straight for the caretaker's room, when he heard the bell on the front door jingle. Was it Derek? Another guard? The late arriving rescuer?

Vic took up a spot at the top of the stairs where he could just barely see the front counter through the reflection in the parlor mirror. "Nice move, Vic," he thought to himself, "hide in the middle of a hallway where no one could possibly miss you!" Nevertheless, on short notice, this would have to do.

The front door squeaked as it shut. "Morning," said a gruff voice.

"Good morning," replied Angela, in the same welcoming voice that had greeted Vic the night before. She sounded in good spirits and not the least bit concerned. Working at an inn probably let her see all types, but Vic got the impression she made them all feel as warm and welcome as she had made him the night before. It was unusual to have people arriving in the morning, but her voice certainly didn't show it. "How can I help you this morning?" she asked.

"I was told to...well..." the burly voice stammered. "I got this...um...oh, I see, this is for you, isn't it?" From his vantage point, Vic could see the front counter but didn't have a clear line of sight to the visitor. "Suppose so. Well, here it is." The sound of his heavy boots signaled his approach to the counter. Vic caught a glimpse of his shoulder as he set something down, and though he couldn't quite see it, the jingle of coins made it all clear. The man had just laid a pouch full of money on the counter in front of Angela. This time, the gruff voice sounded softer, almost distant, as if reminiscing about an old friend.

"I always wondered when I would get the call to pass this along. I knew it wasn't mine, but it's been sitting on my mantle for nearly four years. I was starting to think I might get to keep it, but then the word came. Good enough for me. It's nice to finally do my part."

"That's all we can do, we each have our part." Angela replied. "Thanks for doing yours." There was an awkward pause.

"Well, I best be gettin' along," he finally said.

"King's favor on your journeys," she said as the door swung closed behind him.

King's favor? That was a strange thing for Angela to say. There hadn't been a King ruling the land for over a hundred years. Vic remembered the many tales about a king and his kingdom that his grandfather used to tell by the fire when Vic was young. They were stories about an age of peace and prosperity that seemed to have gone on forever. No one could tell for sure what was real and what was folklore, but the stories were always replete with magic and powerful creatures, and they always ended with a great war waged against the King and his armies.

As the stories go, one of the King's top generals had turned against him and, in a massive mutiny, a third of his army turned against the King. Rather than fight among the innocent people, the King drove the rebels out of the land and into the Eastern Wilderness. After many years of fighting on the Eastern borders, the King decided to take his soldiers on the offensive and leave the territory to take on the enemy. As he left, the King appointed governors in charge of the twelve districts of his kingdom and instructed them to carry on in his absence until he returned. As time went on and still the King did not return, people began to believe the King had died in battle or would never return. The longer he remained absent, the more the governors began to fight among themselves. Eventually, there was open conflict between several neighboring governors. One was even assassinated and their two regions joined. Finally, the three northernmost governors declared their independence from the kingdom.

For the next few years, civil war ripped through the land as various factions vied for control of the kingdom. With the sides evenly balanced and coalitions too self interested to stay together for long, no clear winner emerged. The civil war raged on and kept the land unsettled for many years, depleting the resources of all sides and leaving chaos in its wake. Eventually, the people tired of the constant conflict and revolted against several of the governors. This finally brought an end to the war because without the laborers, crops weren't harvested and the soldiers had no food. The resulting peace was really just the absence of open fighting, never real peace and stability. In time, the regional barons who were really just the largest landowners, began trying to enforce some kind of justice for their regions and maintain order.

It wasn't until many years later that a single baron named Lord Dramon began to gain power and a following. Many say he wasn't the heir of a governor at all, but had stolen the family seal and claimed power. He was much more shrewd than the other governors and realized that to keep the people loyal to him, he would need to bring them economic stability. He established a more organized trading system and built up a militia not to directly attack his enemies, but keep the peace for the traders. People mostly had to fend for themselves, but he encouraged commerce and allowed the ambitious to amass great sums of wealth and did not interfere with the use of their riches as long as they continued to pay his taxes and did what they were told. By the time Vic was born, the fighting had generally subsided, but there was no centralized government of any kind.

So why would Angela wish the man "King's favor" for his journey? It seemed childish, but Vic didn't really care. He wanted to find out about the prisoner, about Derek, and now about the money bag. He started walking down the stairs, a little more noisily than he normally would. Maybe with a few well placed questions, he could find out what had just transpired.

"Good morning, Vic," Angela greeted him warmly with a smile, then her face became more serious. "Did you ever find Derek last night?"

Hmm. He should have known she was going to ask, but he hadn't thought ahead about how to answer. The truth would probably end up something like "Well, my friend vanquished a squad of hooded black creatures at superhuman speeds while I stood there and watched, then he gave me a prisoner to care for that I didn't know and now Derek might be dead, but I left before I could find out. Oh, and I lost the prisoner, have you seen him?" No. The whole truth wasn't going to work this time. Maybe a little less than complete would be better.

"Actually, yes, I did find him. Did you happen to see another man leave my room this morning? Derek sent him back here with me last night, but this morning he was gone."

"I did," Angela replied as she straightened the counter and picked up the pouch her previous guest had left. "I got a message that he needed to eat early and be on his way, so I prepared him a meal and woke him up this morning so he could be off. I'm sorry I didn't wake you to tell you, but you were sound asleep and the message was clear that he would be dining alone."

A message? Did Derek send her the message? Well that was good news. At least maybe that meant Derek made it out alive.

"Do you happen to still have the message handy so I could take a look?"

She smiled, "No, sorry."

"Was it from Derek, by any chance?"

She paused, "No, not really, but don't worry, the man from your room last night will be fine."

He will be fine? How would she know? There was no way a message could have gotten to her so fast either, it was the middle of the night when Vic and the prisoner had returned and Angela must have woken the stranger before dawn. Vic was getting suspicious. She was holding back information and it was starting to bother him.

"Oh, and one more thing," she continued, "this is for you." Angela put the coin pouch on the counter in front of him and pushed it over to Vic.

"For me?" Even if he didn't take it, he wanted to see what was inside so he picked it up. From its weight, it was indeed full of coins. Vic opened the mouth of the pouch just enough to see the glimmer of gold inside. It was quite a sum.

"Why for me?" He wasn't exactly accustomed to people randomly giving him bags of gold. Even more strange was that she had only received it from the visitor barely a minute before. She didn't even stop to count it. Now Vic was more than suspicious. Was she trying to pay him off?

"It's from a friend," she replied, "and speaking of friends, what time were you going to meet that guide to Lucid Peak?"

The guide! In all the excitement of the evening, he had completely forgotten about meeting Percival. Without Percival, the chances he would actually make it there on time and in one piece dropped precipitously.

"I can't believe I forgot," Vic answered, "we were supposed to meet at the Tavern at dawn." He leaned over to look out the nearest window and saw the sun well in view and starting to climb in the sky. "I hope he hasn't left yet." Vic looked at the pouch and then back at Angela. She still hadn't answered his question and from her face, she wasn't going to. The frustration was too much for Vic to contain.

"Why are you giving this to me? What am I supposed to do with it? You tell me that the man in my room last night is fine, but you don't tell me how you know, and now you're giving me more money than I would make in a year for no reason at all. This just doesn't make any sense! What's going on around here?"

Instead of being angry with him, it looked like she felt sorry for him. She smiled and put her hand on his shoulder. Her voice was soft and understanding, almost like she would speak to a child, "I'm sure you will understand everything soon enough. For now, just hold on to it until its purpose becomes clear. When it is time to use the money, you will know."

Vic couldn't be mad at her when she was so sweet in return. He sighed in frustration. There was no time to figure things out. He had to find Percival. He turned and practically flew back up the stairs and packed up his things. He returned as fast as he could to the front desk and Angela.

"Angela, would you mind holding on to Derek's things until he returns? For some reason I can't explain, I believe you. I think you're right, and I think Derek will return. Right now, I've got to run."

Angela smiled, "Of course. Oh, and I made a little something for you to eat on the trip. Safe journey!" She handed him a small package wrapped in brown paper and tied with a string.

He was so confused he stood there dumbfounded for a moment. It was all too overwhelming. He took the package, but didn't really know what to say.

"It seems like saying 'thank you' just isn't enough, but I'll say it anyway. Thanks." Vic was so amazed by the recent turn of events he could barely understand what was going on. The one thing he knew was that he absolutely *had* to get to Lucid Peak on time. Tom Claybrooke was depending on him and he could not bear to return to Mayport empty-handed after such a long journey.

"You're welcome," she said emphatically.

As Vic pushed open the door, he paused and looked back to Angela, "King's blessings?"

She nodded. "Yes. King's blessings. Now go!" and she pointed at the door. Vic knew she was right, and he went.

The butcher slammed his cleaver down on the cutting board again, lopping off another chicken wing. His cart sat in its usual spot along the side of the town square.

"Chicken. Every day, more chicken," he said to himself.

He watched Vic run out of the inn, across the square and into the tavern. A few minutes later, Vic left the tavern and headed up the road to Lucid Peak alone. He wiped his bloody hands on his already bloody apron.

"And sometimes something more interesting."

He reached into the bottom of his cart and rummaged around until he found what he was looking for. It was a note he had received two days before.

"WANTED: Information leading to the capture of Victor Bremerton. Armed and dangerous. Use extreme caution. Lord Dramon." A crude drawing of Vic completed the message.

He stared at the image for a minute, then tore off a corner of the sign. With the pencil behind his ear he scrawled his own reply, then rolled the note and placed it in a small cartridge. He carefully placed the cartridge on a ledge on top of his cart, raised a small yellow flag and then walked away. He walked through the square, chatting with the other vendors. While he talked with a nearby fruit vendor about the weather, a large hawk-like bird swooped down to his cart, grabbed the cartridge and flew off. The vendor acted as if he didn't even see the bird, but when he had finished talking, he walked back to his cart and quietly removed the yellow flag.

7. Catherine

"You can't expect him to go through something like that and not be a different person." Catherine's cousin Bethany was just finishing up the hem on a beautiful satin evening gown. It was nearing the end of their work day and the two ladies were trying to wrap things up and head home.

"I know, but what about me? He could have told me, or sent a message or something. Even a homing pigeon would have been nice."

"Catherine! He almost died! Don't you think he would have sent word if he could have?" Their days were long, but their conversations about everything and anything were always engaging.

"I know, but it wasn't nice. He went on an adventure without me!" Catherine kept working as she spoke, her fingers quickly making their way around a sleeve that needed to be re-stitched. "We always did fun things together."

"I don't think this adventure was any fun at all," Bethany said a little more soberly. "Think about poor Steven."

Neither of the girls knew Steven very well, but he had been nice enough and it was hard to believe he was gone.

"You're right. I guess I shouldn't be so hard on Vic. You remember when I got Dad's note saying Vic had returned? I was really mad. Where did he go for all that time? The more I heard about what happened the harder it was to be mad, but even so it was all so strange and uncomfortable. I thought he was dead, and then to find out he wasn't..."

"You were confused. We all saw it."

"It was shocking. I didn't know how to respond."

"Do you still have feelings for him?"

"That's just it, I don't know, and I sure didn't have time to think about it. I felt the attraction in the room when I was with him, but there was something different about him. He looked great," she smiled at Bethany, "but he was somehow more sober, reflective. I didn't even really know what to say. I wanted to joke around like usual, but it didn't seem right, so we ended up with this awkward silence. If it wasn't for Dad talking about his crops, I don't know what would have happened."

"Do you think he still has feelings for you?"

"I think so, but it was hard to tell. I don't think *he* really knows either."

"Maybe he just needed some time to figure it out."

"Yeah, I guess that's right. Then he left on Dad's trip. Now I probably won't be there when he gets back."

Bethany finished her piece and rose to hang it up. "Sounds like you *both* needed some time to figure things out. I bet it will be different when you get back."

"If he's there!" Catherine continued working on her piece as Bethany finished up. "Sometimes I want to forget about him and get on with my life, and sometimes I think I can't live another day without him next to me! I'm so confused. Maybe I just need to get my mind off the whole thing."

"Well, tonight should help with that." Bethany was packing up her things to go. "I know Samantha can't wait. She's been looking forward to this for weeks."

Catherine finished her piece and held it up to examine her work. "Samantha just wants to find a man who can afford her. For Samantha, a poor man would never do. She would chew him up and spit him out. That's why she wants to go to the theater, that's where all the men with fat purses go."

"You could find a man there too, Catherine," Bethany poked fun at her cousin. "Something new might be fun."

"Maybe so, but I wouldn't get your hopes up. That show has been cancelled more often than it has played lately. I hear they are having problems with the cast, but who knows." Catherine hung up her piece and grabbed her coat. "Come on."

The cousins kept chatting as they locked up the dress shop and started walking down the cobblestone street. They passed other shops and street vendors, also wrapping things up for the evening. Everyone seemed as eager as they were to put the day behind them.

Several blocks later, they arrived at the Rochester city square where remnants of the daily marketplace could still be seen. Most of the carts were gone, but the littered street showed their prior locations. The ladies cut straight across the middle, something they never could have done at midday when the square was congested. Half a block down a narrow street on the far side of the square, a small two level flat waited for them quietly.

As they were about to open the door, Samantha came running down the street toward them with a distraught look on her face. "It can't be!" She ran all the way up to them and grabbed Bethany by the shoulders. Both ladies were terribly concerned.

"What is it Sam? Is everyone alright? Was there a problem at the store?"

Samantha tried to catch her breath and when she finally did, she looked straight at Bethany and her eyes welled up with tears. It looked like she was about to burst.

"They cancelled the show tonight!"

"What?"

"They cancelled the show!   We can't go to the theater tonight!"

Bethany and Catherine stood there dumbfounded. Not because the show was cancelled, they had been warning Samantha that it might happen for weeks. They were in awe at Samantha's ability to overreact.   The cousins looked at each other, then burst out laughing.

"THAT is what you came running down the street to tell us?" Bethany shook her head at Samantha. "Come here, Sam" and Bethany opened up her arms and gave her a big hug. Samantha fell into her arms and sobbed.   She cried like every living person in the world was gone. One day Samantha would be a star herself with drama like this!

When her sobs had softened to a whimper, Catherine grabbed her hand. "Do you want to come in for a while and have some dinner? I'm sure Aunt Mabel wouldn't mind."

"Looking like this?   How could I?   What a terrible impression I would make." Samantha began straightening her hair and dress. She did look awfully disheveled after her run and cry. Depression obviously didn't cure her vanity.

"I'm going home to bed.   What else is there to do on a terrible night like this?"

Bethany used her most motherly voice, "Now you go straight home and be careful, OK?"

Samantha nodded, and then ran off down the street.

The cousins watched until she turned the corner, then looked at each other and burst into laughter.

"Wow, she's in particularly bad shape tonight. Do you think she'll make it?"

"Oh, I'm sure she will. She won't even remember what she was crying about by the time she gets home," Bethany turned and stepped up onto the threshold of her house. "Let's see what Mother's making for dinner!"

When they opened the door, they were greeted with a warm fire in the fireplace and the smell of the evening meal already cooking.

"Hello ladies, welcome home."

Catherine's Aunt Mabel was a pleasant, round woman with red cheeks and a ball of bright red hair. Her apron seemed to be permanently attached to her front side and her smile was as infectious as her food was delicious. She made her living by cooking for any who came to her table. She asked her guests only to pay what they could afford, and they always gave her more than enough. Sometimes she would have only the three of them for dinner, and sometimes she would have as many as twelve. Tonight, there were four guests waiting in the parlor before the meal; three travelers and Mr. Miller, an elderly widower who frequented their table, as much for the conversation as for the food.

The ladies removed their coats and then proceeded to the kitchen to help with the preparations. "Do you need any help, Mother?" Bethany asked as she peeked her nose over the large cauldron hanging over the fire, "Smells good."

"No tasting young lady, you can wait like the rest of us!" Mabel chided. Bethany only smiled back at her and began setting the table.

"So who are we having for supper tonight?" Catherine asked.

"Silly girl, we're not eatin' em, we're servin' em! They look like a nice lot and should make for some interesting conversation, and hopefully pay the rent too."

Since their home was a stopping point for random travelers, dinner was often fascinating. They had eaten with princes, salesmen, young and old, rich and poor. They could never be sure whether one would try to rob or hurt them, but they were usually safe enough as long as there were several visitors. There were a few inns in town, but the tavern's cooks were not much to speak of, so there was little choice for those who wanted a more hearty meal.

"Well let's see, there's Mr. Saunders from Palatia. I think he's a livestock trader, but I'm not exactly sure. Then we have Bartholomew Chilton, he's the personal assistant to the Baron of Edington. He said he is here to buy some new horses for the Baron's stables. Then we have a strange little man by the name of Eunice. He looks like a gypsy if you ask me, but it's hard to say. He doesn't talk much and gave me a gold coin as a deposit, and said he would give me another if the meal was to his liking. Not the silver pieces you see most of the time mind you, but polished gold. He's sort of shifty, always lookin' over his shoulder for something, who knows what. Then of course, there's old Mr. Miller. It's always nice to have him around, and he always pays well."

By the time the women had finished talking, bread and meat were on the table and the soup in the pot had been ladled into hand carved wooden bowls. Aunt Mabel poked her head through the door to the sitting room and announced that dinner was ready. Bethany and Catherine waited beside the door until the four gentlemen had found their seats, then they sat down for dinner as well.

The dinner conversation was pleasant, but not nearly as satisfying as the food. Aunt Mabel lived up to her reputation. Every dish had that special little something, sometimes a spice, or a twist, or a glaze. Catherine never could quite tell how she did it, but Aunt Mabel always made things that were so good you wanted to try and make them yourself, but when you did, they were never quite as good as when she made it. Mabel had a gift, and she joyfully used it to benefit many hungry travelers.

As the gentlemen finished their meals they departed one by one, eventually leaving only Eunice. Mabel went upstairs to finish up the day's chores, and Bethany started cleaning up. It made a nice opportunity for Catherine to talk with the gypsy. He probably had lots of good stories to tell, but he had been silent most of the night, and her curiosity got the best of her.

"So, Eunice, what brings you to these parts?" Catherine asked in her nicest unassuming tone.

"I sell stones," was his reply. "Very special stones. Would you like to see one?" He looked at Catherine with a smug smile.

Eunice was a shifty character. He could be playing a trick or be loaded with diamonds, it was impossible to tell. Catherine would never have wanted to be caught alone with him, but she loved a good adventure. Here in her aunt's kitchen with Bethany nearby, she felt safe. "Sure, I'll take a look."

Eunice swung open his coat and reached for a well worn leather satchel tied around his waist. He pushed the remaining dishes away to make some room, and then proceeded to dump the bag's contents onto the table.

Right there before her eyes rolled six of the most beautiful gems Catherine had ever seen. They were different shapes and sizes, each artfully cut and polished. Not quite translucent, they seemed to have a slight blue glow to them that made them enchanting to look at. Bethany was walking back to the table and was about to pick up another plate when she saw the gems.

"Oooooh," both girls involuntarily exclaimed at the same time. "Those are beautiful," said Catherine, "I've never seen anything like them!"

"And you won't either," the old man quipped. "These are very special gems. Special indeed. Some say even *magical*. You won't find these at your corner marketplace."

"They must be worth a fortune," Bethany marveled, with a slightly sad tone in her voice. She was obviously thinking there was no way she could afford one of those stones for herself.

To Catherine, it was like Bethany wasn't even there. She only heard one word he had said.

"Magical?" Catherine asked. Now that was an adventure she had never been on.

The gypsy's grin broadened. "These are coursite gems. Some say that you see strange things when you hold them. Some say you can see the future. I've seen them play tricks on a man's mind. Makes you see things that aren't. Lots of people think it's fun. Either of you ladies care to try?"

Catherine would usually jump all over a chance like this. She loved doing fun new things, but this time something was different. There was power emanating from those gems. She could feel it. The hair on the back of her neck was standing up. This was not a game. Bethany had no such concern.

"Sure, I want to try!" Bethany jumped in.

Before Bethany had a chance to grab one, Catherine grabbed her arm. "Are you sure?" Catherine looked cautiously into her eyes. This was a switch that surprised Bethany, she was puzzled to see Catherine shying away from a new chance at fun. She could see Catherine's concern, but quickly shook it off.

"How could something so beautiful be dangerous? Look how they sparkle!" Bethany wasn't going to be dissuaded. She turned back to Eunice, "So how do I do it?"

"Just pick one up and close your eyes, then tell us what you see."

Bethany reached for one of the larger broach sized gems and picked it up. Somehow it looked larger in her hand once she picked it up.

"Wow," she said in a subdued, almost reverent whisper, "it tingles." She closed her eyes and began to roll the gem around in her fingers. Finally, she put it at the center of her hand and made a fist.

When she gripped the stone more tightly, Bethany winced and started to sway in her chair, as if she were getting a little dizzy. "Bethany, are you OK?" Catherine asked as she grabbed her arm. "Do you need to put it down?"

"No, no... not yet... I'm OK," she answered back, in a somewhat distant voice, but clearly not wanting the experience to stop. Catherine was not convinced, so she kept watching closely; ready to wrench the gem from her hands if anything looked like it was going wrong.

Bethany continued to sway a little, and made some strange noises until suddenly she gasped and dropped the stone on the table. She was obviously shaken up. Their strange guest had been watching with an impish grin.

He laughed at her. "You saw something, didn't you?"

"Yes, I think so."

"Someone you know?"

"Yes. I felt like I was falling and I was going to hit the ground. I think I saw my brother too. It looked like he was in pain but it was really hard to tell. Is he OK?" Bethany looked fine physically, but the images she saw had stayed with her.

"It's hard to say," Eunice smiled, "the stone does strange things to those who touch it. Some say everything it shows is real, but we don't know *when* it was. It could be the past, the present or the future. Some say it plays tricks on the mind and creates images from your deepest darkest secrets or reveals your worst fears. No one knows for sure, but people pay me for the chance just to touch it. Some even come back and find me over and over to try it again. I'm the only one who knows how to get them, so you won't find them anywhere else." He turned to Catherine, "Your turn now?"

Catherine had been watching the scene with some skepticism, but the energy from the gem was calling to her. To Catherine, Eunice looked like a strange little man trying to play a trick on two unsuspecting girls, but she absolutely couldn't walk away without her turn with a gem.

Catherine turned to Bethany, "You keep an eye on me ... and HIM. Don't let him get away with anything, OK?"

"Don't worry, Catherine, its harmless fun." It was good to see that Bethany had recovered her usual carefree spirit, but Catherine was worried.

"OK, I guess I'm ready." Catherine didn't look ready, but she stretched out her hand and picked up the gem Bethany had just dropped. As she held it in her fingers she felt the same thing Bethany had described. It was that tingling sense that started at her hand and crept up her arm. There really *was* something special about this gem. It made her shudder all over.

"I really feel it," she said. The tingling was growing more intense. "Now what?"

"Wrap your hand around it and close your eyes."

Catherine did so and rather than seeing the darkness she was accustomed to seeing when she closed her eyes, she immediately started to see much more. First there were colors, brightly swirling in and out of her view. Then gradually the swirl of color gave way to shapes. Everything was still too blurred to make out what she was seeing, but it was becoming clearer and clearer by the second. Through her mind's eye, Catherine kept looking into the blurred images to try to make sense of them when all of a sudden everything came into focus.

"OH! I see something," Catherine exclaimed. Eunice smiled. He was glad to see his sale was going well. He sat back in his chair to watch the pretty girl experience her first "high" with the gem.

"It looks like us, but we're so small. Oh, that's better, we're bigger now. Looks like we're going to have someone over for dinner."

Bethany was glad to see her cousin seemed to be enjoying the experience, but didn't want her to get confused, "No, Catherine, we already had dinner."

"I know, silly, I mean someone else. He looks nice. Look, here he is now."

At that very moment, there was a knock at the door. Catherine opened her eyes and gently put down the gem. Bethany and Eunice sat there in stunned amazement looking at Catherine.

Aunt Mabel yelled down the stairs, "Is one of you going to get that?"

"Coming!" Bethany yelled back. She almost knocked over her chair as she snapped out of her amazement to answer the door.

Eunice continued to stare at Catherine. They could hear Bethany greet a man at the door. He came in and started inquiring about dinner. A few moments later, Bethany came back through the parlor door and headed for the pot that was still resting on the side table.

"Looks like you were right, Cath, he does look nice and he wants to have some dinner."

Catherine and Eunice both peeked through the open parlor door as it was swinging closed and there in the parlor stood a man in his sixties with a pleasant smile and a long flowing cloak. He was well groomed and of a pleasant disposition.

Bethany left the room with a bowl of stew for the new guest, who she served in the parlor. Eunice finally broke the silence. "Is that the man you saw?"

"Yes." Catherine was absolutely sure of it.

"How did you know he was going to knock on the door?"

"I saw him."

"You saw him knocking on the door?"

"No, I saw him walking up the steps to our house and he was going to knock on the door. As he did, I opened my eyes."

"You mean what you saw actually happened?"

"I guess so. You sound surprised. Isn't that how it is supposed to work? You said people see things and that's just what happened to me."

Eunice paused, "Most people don't see much, and when they do, they don't see what's actually happening like you did. Would you like to try it again?"

"I'm suddenly very tired, but yes, I would like to. May I?"

"Go right ahead." Eunice motioned to the gem that was still sitting right in front of Catherine on the table. The experience was strange, but not painful. It was probably a fluke seeing things so clearly like she did, but only another try would tell her for sure.

Eunice was not sitting back in his chair this time, he was intently watching Catherine. Though he would never admit it to a potential customer, he had never run into anyone who could accurately interpret what they saw. For everyone else it was just a game, a cheap thrill to pass the time. For Catherine, the gem was different.

Catherine picked up the stone like before, and felt the same tingle. This time it ran right down her spine. It was the same intensity, but somehow the feeling was already familiar. She wrapped her fingers around it and closed her eyes.

This time the colors came and went more quickly and images started coming into focus right away. There was a small boy leading a horse. She didn't know where they were, but the boy seemed sad for some reason. The horse had a beautiful multi-colored blanket on its back but with no rider. It walked slowly with its head down, like a horse that had worked many years.

Eunice could tell she was seeing something and wanted to know what, "Do you see something?"

"Oh yes, I'm sorry, I forgot to tell you. It is a boy leading a horse with a beautiful colored blanket on its back. They both seem sad. They are walking slowly on a lonely road, as if they don't really want to get wherever they are going. It looks like they are coming into town. They're walking past a sign but I can't seem to read it. Oh there it is, Wrigley Junction, yes, that's it. They are meeting someone there, but now the picture is fading away."

Eunice sat up in his chair. He was visibly shaken but didn't say a word. Catherine kept talking.

"Now it's changing. This one is scary." Catherine flinched. "A man…" she flinched again, "he's being hurt very badly. I can't see who's doing it, but there are several people surrounding him and one is beating him. He isn't doing well. They're saying something to him but I can't hear them. Oh no … no… one man pulled out his sword, I can't bear to watch."

Catherine put down the gem and opened her eyes. She had no idea who the man was that was being beaten, but she felt for him and didn't like seeing him hurt when there was nothing she could do about it.

"If that's what your stone is going to show me, I'm not sure I want to try anymore." When she looked over at Eunice, she noticed how white he was and that his face had none of the grin it had earlier. He had a distant look in his eyes.

"That horse you saw, did it have a long brown mane with a red rope weaved through it?"

"Why yes, it did."

There was a long pause before Eunice spoke again. "I was that boy." He could barely continue. "It was over forty years ago. I loved that horse, and it was the last thing of any value we had. My father was ill and couldn't work. When we had sold everything else I finally had to take our horse to town to sell it so we could eat. I used to ride that horse while it pulled our traveling store from place to place. Without that horse, I knew we could never make our living the way we had before and that my Dad was probably going to die. That was the hardest thing I ever did, not just because I loved the horse, but because it was the end of hope. I vowed I would never be that poor again, and I haven't been."

"I'm so sorry." Catherine didn't know this man, but felt like she had just been with him through his deepest, most difficult experience. "Thank you for letting me use your gem," Catherine said as she pushed it back across the table toward Eunice.

The gem sat there in the middle of the table for a moment while both stared at it.

Eunice reached out and pushed it back to Catherine, "No, I think you should have it. What you have, young lady, is a gift. I know you can't afford what I would charge for it, so I'm not going to charge you anything. The one thing I ask is that you allow me to tell a few others about your gift. To everyone else, these gems are just a toy; something to make them feel different and see strange things they can't understand. To you, this gem is the key to the whole world. You should keep it." Eunice collected the rest of the gems, returned them to his bag and started gathering his things.

"I'll be back tomorrow night with someone I would like you to meet. Will you be here?"

"Yes, I will."

"Excellent." He bowed slightly, "Then I must be off."

Eunice left the kitchen and found Aunt Mabel. He gave her another three gold coins and then disappeared into the night. It was long after most had retired when their last guest finished his meal. As he left, Bethany barred the door and turned to Catherine who had been resting in a nearby chair.

"I'm so tired. Using that stone is more draining than it looks."

"What happened in there?" Bethany was curious since their experiences with the gem seemed to be quite different.

"I don't really know, but he let me keep the gem."

"What? He let you keep it? I'm so jealous! Why did *you* get to keep it? Did he leave one for me too?"

Catherine smiled, "He said I had a gift, and that it would be better used with me than with anyone else he would sell it to. He's coming back tomorrow night to bring someone to meet me. Apparently, what I saw was a big deal."

"It sure was, Cath. You know what I saw - nothing but a few strange images and sensations. Mostly, it scared me to death. You saw a whole scene and told us all about it. That was pretty incredible if you ask me."

"In a way, it felt so right," Catherine paused, "but it terrified me too, especially when I couldn't control what I saw. Maybe when he comes back tomorrow I'll learn more. Who do you think he will be bringing over?"

8. The Journey

The chances of finding Percival this late in the morning were not good, but Vic would never stop wondering if he didn't stop by and look for him anyway. He stepped inside the tavern to take a look around.

What had been a bustling room of people the night before was now cold and quiet. One weather beaten old man sat in the corner eating a late breakfast and a teenage boy cleaned up behind the counter. There was no sign of the bartender who seemed to know where to find Percival, and no one else was around. He was too late. Now without Derek, he would have to travel alone.

These were dangerous times, and with all Vic had seen the night before, the thought of being on that road alone at night left a sinking feeling in the pit of his stomach. On a well known road or through a busy town, traveling alone was a risk, but an acceptable one. On an unknown path over rugged terrain on a multi-day journey, it was foolish even to try. Until recently, he would have thought he could defend himself pretty well but now he wasn't so sure. *Who were those warriors and how did Derek move so fast?* He could still remember the blue flashes of light and steel as the swords collided. He would be no match for one of those creatures, so he would have to stay on his guard and steer clear if he spotted one. His best chance was to cover as much ground as possible during daylight and maybe catch up with Percival and his group. Unfortunately, they were probably several hours ahead, if there was a group at all.

On the way out of town, the path was as clear as the day. The sun was still rising overhead and a cool mountain wind was at his back. There was a sign on the outskirts of town that said "Lucid Peak – 20 miles". He was on the right path, and needed to hurry.

At first the path was relatively straight and level and his pace was almost a jog, but soon enough the altitude gain made him slow down. The beautiful mountain panorama was both refreshing and annoying. If only he could take the edge off the pace to enjoy the view; but not today. The old growth trees that covered the valley floor had probably been there for hundreds of years, maybe they would still be there when he came back.

Every bird or rodent made him jump. A young squirrel jumped into his path and stared right at him with its little tail all fluffed up. "I'd rather be running through a nest of alligators while late for dinner," Vic said out loud, talking as much to himself as to the squirrel. The squirrel cocked his head, confused by the strange man, and then scurried off behind a large rock. "Have fun in your hiding place." Hiding places were plentiful with large rocks and trees all along the path. If someone planned to ambush him they would have no problem doing it. Images from the night before kept flashing through his head, as did the words of his mother many years before telling him never to travel alone.

The hours passed and he stopped only to eat some of the lunch Angela had packed for him. As day wore on into afternoon, he started liking the little creatures that would jump onto his path. They broke the monotony of leaves crunching beneath his feet. He was tired of maintaining high alert and was now more focused on catching up with his guide. Soon, the shadows would be getting longer and then he would only have a few more hours of daylight left. As he rounded a bend, the trail seemed to take a slight decline, and plunged into a dense area of bushes that were cut into a crude archway and tunnel. From his vantage point, Vic could see where the trail emerged again after about twenty yards, but this covered stretch concerned him. It looked like a great place for an ambush. He stopped to listen. He stood as still as the slab of stone next to him, listening intently to the gentle breeze, until he recognized the faint sound of running water.

The water explained this phenomenon ahead of him. It was the junction where a river, now probably no more than a stream, crossed the path. The thick growth on the riverbank along with the formation of the mountainside here left no other way around, and the cool mountain spring water would be a refreshing break. He drew his sword with one hand, held his walking stick in the other and plunged in. If someone or something was hiding in there, he would know soon enough.

As he entered the dense bushes, the first thing he noticed was the low clearance and lack of light. His eyes adjusted to the semi-darkness but he still had to crouch to avoid brushing his head against the twisted branches that formed the natural ceiling. He could tell by the cut marks on the bushes that it was only the frequent travelers who had kept the vegetation from closing the path altogether. Even better, these cuts were fresh with the sap still running from the leaves. That was excellent news – the group was not far ahead.

As he moved farther into the bush-tunnel, the sound of running water grew louder and the ground softer. Unfortunately, the leaves overhead also grew thicker, allowing less light to filter through. All at once, the dirt became mud, and Vic felt splashes from the running brook in front of him. It was difficult to see exactly where it was in the darkness, but Vic could see enough to make out the water about five feet in front of him. Now he needed some light. Vic plunged both his walking stick and sword into the bushes overhead and pulled them apart, looking for just a glimpse of sunlight from the sky above. After a considerable amount of trouble, he finally found a spot that brought some indirect light into the darkness below.

On the ground in front of the stream, he could see footprints in the mud, at least three sets, maybe four. Luckily, the soft mud left clear impressions when each person crossed the stream's path. It was hard to tell how many had crossed, but a few of the prints were distinctive. There was at least one heavy adult, and one younger child, and a few others that all blended together. It appeared that all had been able to cross the stream without difficulty, as the tracks on the other side did not appear any different than those on this side and there was no evidence of falling near the water's edge.

That was great news. With one younger and one heavy set traveler they couldn't go very fast. If he kept pushing ahead, he may still be able to catch them before nightfall. Before resuming, he took a few minutes to refill his water flask and wash his face in the cool mountain spring water.

Vic had no trouble crossing the stream, which was swift but not deep. As he emerged from the thicket of bushes he checked the sky. Not good. There was no sign of the sun, which had dropped behind the mountainside. Dusk was fast approaching. Unless he found the group soon he would have to spend the night alone. The cool breeze was turning into a biting wind, which meant he would have to build a fire — a roadmap for anyone planning to do him harm at night.

Vic again picked up the pace and fortunately, as the path wound around the next corner, it straightened out for a while and lost some of its steep incline. He carefully climbed the face of the rock wall to his right just enough to get a view of the path ahead. In the distance was a small clearing with a rock enclave surrounded by trees. From the middle of the trees, a twisting ribbon of smoke was rising into the sky. At last, he had found them!

Vic made his way back down to the trail, grabbed his pack and started half walking-half running as fast as the terrain would permit. Now that hope was in sight, he forgot all about the soreness of his legs and feet and about the growling in his stomach.

The next half-hour passed in what seemed like no time at all. Vic was heading across the clearing straight toward the strand of smoke. It wasn't until he was just about upon the encampment that he started feeling apprehension about who he would meet there, and whether they would welcome his presence. As he approached, he was greeted by a gruff voice yelling "Halt, who goes there?"

"Victor Bremerton, I've come to meet Percival, my guide to Lucid Peak. I was delayed this morning and missed the rendezvous, but would like to join you, if he is in your group."

An older man whose back was to him facing the fire rose from the ground. "So you would like to join me, would you?" It was the bartender! Percival waved to the makeshift watchman to let Vic through.

"You're Percival? I thought you said I could *meet* Percival in the morning! You didn't mention that I would be meeting *you*!"

"All in good time, my friend. It must have been quite a chore to catch up with us, you must be tired." With that, Percival motioned for Vic to take a seat by the fire and scooped some of the stew from the pot he had been tending.

"It may not be your mother's stew, but it'll give you what you need," Percival said as he ladled it into a bowl he set out for Vic.

As Vic sat down, his whole body began to remind him of what he had forgotten. He really *was* tired. His legs ached, his feet throbbed, and he was famished. By the time Vic arrived, darkness was just taking hold of the mountainside, and night would be here before he finished his stew.

As Vic ate, he took stock of his surroundings and his new traveling companions. Standing watch near the edge of the grove of trees was a large man with a plain brown cloak and a scar across his neck. He was heavy set, unshaven and his hair unkempt. It was hard to tell whether he always looked like that or if it was only from the hard journey. Either way, his expression made Vic think that he had been complaining all day and had made the rest of the travelers as miserable as possible, and it earned him the first watch. He was the one who made the deep impressions by the stream.

On his right, Vic saw a boy of about 13, huddled close to a man who could only be his father. The boy had fear in his eyes, but looked healthy and strong. His father sat next to him but was his opposite in appearance. Most of the time, his eyes were closed and when he opened them, they had a distant, glassy look. His complexion said he wasn't well, and it looked as though the day's travels had taken their toll. He looked weak and his breathing was shallow and congested. The boy was leaning against his side, but unlike his father, his eyes were wide open as he stared into the fire with a concerned look on his face. The father needed the rest more than his son.

None of these gave Vic any concern, but the last traveler, who sat directly across the fire from Vic, was another story. From the moment Vic arrived, this stranger had not taken his eyes off him. His steely gaze was unnerving and seemed to accentuate the scar on his left cheek. His forearms were muscular and his sword was the weapon of a trained warrior. The way he scanned the area made it clear he was not at ease, but he didn't speak a word.

What were all these people doing here, and why were they going to Lucid Peak? Vic marveled at the cross section of humanity. Tomorrow, he would have to find out more.

Vic's observations were distracted by Percival, who announced that it was time for everyone to get some rest. He proceeded to set his bedding down by the fire, and the boy and father did the same. The portly guard stayed on watch, but the strange warrior did not move a muscle.

Vic got his bedding out and spread it by the fire, but he was not in any hurry to use it while this stranger stared him down from across the fire. After what seemed like an eternity, the stranger stood to his feet and walked over to sit down next to Vic. Finally, he broke the silence.

"If it wasn't for me, you would be dead. Has it been so long since Yorktown that you've already forgotten? Maybe you're not so smart after all."

His mind raced. How did this stranger know about Yorktown? Could he have been there that day? Someone obviously stopped those two cloaked warriors from killing him, but he didn't really see what happened. Vic was skeptical, but he took the bait. If this man knew something about what happened to him outside of Yorktown he absolutely *had* to know.

With his straightest poker face and flattest possible tone of voice, Vic asked, "How do you know about Yorktown?" He hoped to get another clue about where this stranger got his information without giving away any more than he had to. The stranger looked at him again, this time puzzled. He leaned a little closer to Vic, and looked into his eyes. Suddenly, Vic felt a heat run up his spine and into his head. It was like this stranger could look right through him, right into his soul. After a few seconds that felt like hours, he started shaking his head.

"Impossible. I just don't believe…you mean to tell me…" His words trailed off. He grabbed Vic's cloak, threw it open and patted down his waistline, as if looking for something. Shocked by his actions, Vic let him do it. All he found was the pouch of coins Angela had given him, which he seemed unconcerned with. The expression on his face had now turned to anger.

"Show me your hands." He commanded. Vic slowly produced his hands, now even more curious about the reason.

"I can't believe it, I just can't believe it!" He shouted now, throwing Vic's cloak closed again. "He sent me all the way out here for a guy that doesn't have a clue? I'm not doing this." At that, the stranger started to walk off.

"Wait, where are you going?" Vic shouted after him. The stranger never turned back as he walked into the black of night alone. Part of Vic wanted to go after him. He was so desperate for answers about what happened in Yorktown he would have followed him for that reason alone, but for some reason he wanted to try and talk him out of leaving as well. It felt like something horrible had just happened before his eyes, but he didn't understand what. This man held the secrets Vic needed to understand, and was heading into the black of night alone.

Vic started to get up to go after him when he was overwhelmed with an irresistible urge to sleep. It wasn't just exhaustion, he had been drugged. He looked at the fire, and it began to blur and swirl. He was barely able to pull himself over to his bedding, and not a moment too soon. Vic collapsed and was instantly fast asleep.

From across the fire, Percival looked sadly after the stranger who had left, and then smiled slightly at Vic. He looked at Vic like a father sees his infant who finally falls asleep after fighting what he needed most. His guests would sleep well tonight. He had made sure of that.

9. Decisions

When the travelers awoke, they were greeted by a crisp, clear morning, and the smell of bacon on the griddle.

"Nice to see you all slept so well," Percival greeted them as he held the griddle over the campfire. He never looked up, but Vic thought he saw a slight smirk on his face. "Thought you might want some breakfast."

As Vic sat up, his head swam for a moment and he felt a dull pain in the back of his head. When the wave of dizziness passed, he remembered the feeling from the night before.

"I might eat some of that," Vic finally said, "if you promise me it's nothing like your stew." As he spoke, he looked around at the other travelers and noticed that they had the same expressions on their faces as he did. All were awaking from Percival's drugged stupor. "Your stew was a little more than I could handle."

"Don't worry straggler," he replied to Vic, "now it's time for walkin', not sleepin'. I told you it would give you what you needed. Lots of city folk have a hard time sleepin' when you get way up here in the wild. To keep up with me, you need your rest."

Well that was about as close to a confession of guilt as Vic needed. At least he seemed harmless enough in his motives. Vic looked around again. No sign of the strange warrior who had stomped off into the night.

"So what happened to the other guy?" Vic asked as he took a plate from Percival. He motioned to the spot where the strange warrior had been sitting the night before, "Did he ever come back?"

"Nope."

"You know where he went?"

"Nope." Percival kept right on cooking.

Vic kept prodding. The stranger knew information about Yorktown and Vic had a burning desire to know what it was. Vic suspected that Percival also knew more than he was letting on.

"Did he say anything when he left?"

"Nope."

"Did he say where he was going?"

"Nope."

Vic was getting frustrated.

"Don't you care at all about those who put their trust in you?"

That one hit home. Finally, Percival paused and looked up from his frying pan. "I care deeply," he said solemnly, "he has left the path and may never return. It was sad to see him go, but it was not a surprise. He has been dissatisfied with the path he was on for quite a while." Percival looked off into space for a moment and then went back to his cooking. "I've shown many the path. It's what I do; but I've never actually been around when someone decides to leave the path. Maybe his heart was never really in it, and maybe he'll be back. We may never know."

Vic was confused, but struck by the emotion of the answer. Percival was talking about the stranger as if he had known him for a long time, but didn't they meet two days before? No, they were close, and whatever happened last night was much more profound than Vic understood.

"People come up to Lucid Peak for a variety of reasons. Most come to find something, or someone; and some don't even know why they come. The important thing is that you go where you're supposed to be." Percival lifted some of the bacon out of his frying pan and gave it to the boy and his father who were sitting nearby. "I'm not sure why he came on the trip at all. He must have been instructed to come. He has been this way before, but this time I had a sense that he wasn't going to make it to the peak. I've done this so long now, my gut tells me about people, and it's usually right.

"So what does your gut think about me?" Vic asked as Percival handed him a few more strips of bacon. He stopped and looked him straight in the eye, much the same way the stranger had done the night before. He looked right through him into the very reaches of his soul.

"It tells me you've come a very long way and are determined to make it. You are strong and have good instincts, but have no idea where you're going. You'll make it to the top, but then the challenge will be to find what you're really looking for. How's that sound to you?"

Vic whistled. "Not bad at all." Vic lowered his voice a little and motioned over to the boy and his dad, "What does your gut say about them?"

"They have some difficult choices to make and the road ahead will be hard. If they have the will, they can both make it, but they will need help. When the time comes, will you help them?"

Help them? Vic was puzzled. What could he do about two people he had never met before and knew nothing about? It was hard to understand how he could have a role in their future.

"I guess I would help, if I could."

Percival stopped his cooking again and looked back up at Vic. "You will." He said it with a certitude that was chilling. After a moment, he turned back to his pan and took the last piece for himself. He stood up straight and looked around at the group. "It's time. Pack up your things. We leave in five minutes."

The announcement caused the intended stir in the campground as everyone began to collect their things and prepare for the journey ahead. Things seemed to be proceeding as planned until Vic heard a loud thump. The boy's father had been trying to get up with the help of a walking stick, but didn't have the strength to make it up. He had crumpled into a ball at the base of a nearby tree. The boy helped pull him into a sitting position, but the man's face told his story. He was not well enough to stand let alone climb a mountain. The boy grabbed his hand and tried to pull him up. At half his father's weight, it was like a mouse trying to move an elephant. The group had already begun to gather around.

"C'mon Dad, you've got to get up, we're almost there."

"Son, I can't. I just can't." His words were broken, and full of as much sorrow as they were exhaustion. I've come as far as I can, and you've been such a man through all this. I could never have made it near this far without you ..." his words trailed off.

The boy turned to Percival. Panic and desperation were in his eyes as he pleaded for help. "Can we carry him? Is it much farther? I know we can make it. We HAVE to make it."

The boy was not giving up, but the expression on Percival's face said it all.

"Son, the road is not long, but it is steep. It will be challenging enough for you to make it on your own. If we tried to carry your father, none of us would make it. You will have to find another way." Percival was solemn, but not without hope in his voice.

"Can I go and bring it back?"

Percival paused for a moment and looked to the sky. "Yes, I think you could, but how would your father fare alone? It is a day's journey there, and a day's journey back. Two days is a long time for an ill man alone in the woods."

There was silence for a few moments, broken only by the whistling of the wind in the trees and a distant bird.

"Aw, blast it all," the large man in the brown cloak was the first to speak up. "I'm in no hurry, I can stay with him for a few days." He turned to Percival, "You'll take me back up again after the boy returns?"

"Certainly, I wouldn't want you to miss your journey."

"Well that settles it then. You folks hurry along and come back quick. We'll be waiting right here."

The man threw his pack down by the tree and lumbered over to sit down. Vic had a good feeling about them. They would be good for each other, if the father lived.

Percival pulled a small package from his bag and set it on the man's pack. "Here are some rations. I'll buy more at Lucid Peak for the return trip. This should be a good place for you to stay while we make the journey."

The boy knelt down next to his father and grabbed him by the shoulders. "Father, did you hear that? I can go to the peak for you. I can make it, I just know it. Then I'll return with your medicine and everything will be back to normal. You stay here and lie still and the friar will take care of you. Promise me,

Father." His voice cracked. "Promise me that you will hold on until I return. Promise me you won't give up, Dad. Please."

Tears welled up in the father's eyes and he nodded, as he made the promise he hoped he could keep. "I promise. Now go quickly, son." He smiled at his boy, and then closed his eyes and rested his head back against the tree. Immediately the boy stood up and turned to Percival.

"Let's go!" There was an urgency in the boy's voice and everyone felt it. Percival smiled and then grabbed his pack. "We go," he stated with finality, and they did.

Now that the group was trimmed down to Percival, Vic and the boy, Percival had no reason to hold back. The boy was young and strong, and he knew Vic could keep up, so the pace they set was about as fast as one could safely traverse the rough terrain. Percival took the lead, followed by the boy, and Vic brought up the rear.

At points along the way, the terrain would become so rocky they literally had to jump from boulder to boulder. Hardly a path at all, there were many places where they easily could have turned the wrong way, or headed down a rabbit trail. These were the times they realized the full benefit of traveling with a guide as experienced as Percival. He never hesitated. He had obviously been this route many times and never even needed to pause for bearings. The sights were all old and familiar to him and he just kept moving, looking back only occasionally to make sure his chicks were still in tow.

As they rounded one bend after another and the sun grew high in the sky, Vic started to feel the drain of the journey and his hard push the day before. He was still doing OK, but wondered how that boy could be faring. When the road turned slightly, Vic caught a glimpse of his face. The boy's face was flush and he was breathing heavily, but he was determined and his eyes were set on the trail ahead. Every step was important, even life or death for his father, and the mission was all consuming. Vic knew the boy would pass out before he asked to stop, and he was becoming concerned that it would soon happen that way unless Percival took a break. About that time they crested a small peak and to their right saw a small grassy nook with a waterfall tumbling down the side of the mountain. The water gathered into a pool before it continued on its way.

"We rest here." Percival announced, and no one argued.

After refreshing themselves with the cool mountain spring water, they all sat down on nearby rocks and Percival passed out some dried beef to chew on. It was salty and hard, but they were so hungry they would have eaten anything. No one said a word as they ate until Vic broke the silence.

"For an old man you're moving pretty fast, but us strangers would like to know how much father we have to go." Vic verbalized what the boy was thinking but was afraid to ask.

"Old man goin' too slow for ya?"

"Oh no, no. Not at all. Just wondering." The boy was relieved at Vic's reply.

"You two are about to set my all time record for the fastest trip up the mountain. At this rate we'll be there in another five hours, which means we'll be able to get our business done today instead of tomorrow morning. That should put us several hours ahead on the trip back since we will be able to leave the peak at sunrise instead of waiting for the merchants to arrive. The important thing is to make it there before the merchants close shop for the day, that way we can get our business done before nightfall."

Both Vic and the boy nodded but said nothing. It would be a challenge to keep up their morning pace, but both knew it had to be done. After what seemed like all too short a break, Percival stood again and, sounding far more chipper than anyone his age should have sounded after such a grueling hike, he piped up, "Everyone ready?"

Ready or not, they both gave the right answers. "You bet," said Vic, and the boy chimed in "Let's go," and they were off again.

Though still at break-neck speed, it seemed a little slower this time, and Percival took more backward glances to check on his travelers. How that man could keep up this pace at his age was beyond Vic, but he didn't have much time to think about it; his hands were full watching the trail with all its rocks, branches and loose gravel.

While they hiked, the only sounds they heard were the crunching of each other's steps and an occasional bird in the distance. It was a wild area but it was not the animals that concerned him. He knew those creatures could be around any corner, so he kept watch.

The first time he became concerned was when they stopped for water about an hour after their waterfall break. In the distance behind them, he saw a figure come out from behind an outcropping of rock where the trail hugged a cliff. When the figure came into view he darted back behind the rock. Vic stared at the spot for a few minutes but didn't see any further movement. It was too far away to see details, but what he saw was suspicious.

The second time he noticed something was when a flurry of birds suddenly took flight from the trail several switchbacks below them. He quickly looked back and thought he saw a shadow on the trail but never saw a person emerge. If there was someone there, he was gaining.

"Don't worry, Vic, you're overreacting," he thought to himself. That fear that had been gnawing at the back of his brain was doing its dirty work. Even on a normal day, he was always on the lookout for dangerous situations but after Blood Canyon, he was especially on guard. Those beasts were not to be trifled with and his instincts told him it was time to mention it.

Vic tried to put on his most nonchalant voice and asked, "So Percival, do many others take this path?"

Percival replied without turning around, "Not many, but more and more lately. Most travel with me, and some on their own, why do you ask?"

"It's probably nothing, but I thought I saw someone behind us on the path."

Percival stopped dead in his tracks so fast that the young boy almost ran into him. He turned to look at Vic.

"Tell me *exactly* what you saw." Percival was intently interested in Vic's comment and his command emphatic.

"Well," Vic spoke while trying to catch his breath, "The first time…"

Percival interrupted, "The first time?" He looked surprised.

"The first time I saw him was a few hours ago when we took that rest stop. I saw a figure on the trail behind, about half a mile back. Instead of continuing along the trail, he jumped back behind the nearest rock when I saw him. The second time was just a few minutes ago when we rounded that steep switchback. I didn't actually see him again, but saw a tall shadow and heard a group of birds flurry away." As Vic finished, Percival had a solemn look on his face.

"I'm glad you were watching, Vic, but it only means that our situation is more grave than I thought. It also makes the decision before us easier, though the road ahead will become much harder." Percival let out a sigh, then continued.

"Up ahead, there is a ravine and before we reach it, a fork in the road. The path to the right will come to the ravine and gradually descend its way down along the close side. It is mostly straight and the incline not too severe, but it is long. The trail travels to the north several miles to where the ravine is much shallower. At the bottom we must ford the river, then begin the trip back up the opposite side. In the end it will take us at least three hours, and possibly longer if the river is swollen. It is the way we usually go."

"The path to the left goes straight to the ravine and ends at a rope bridge. The bridge has been there since ancient times and was once well maintained by the King. Now, all that remains is the center foot rope and the two hand lines. At the bridge location, the ravine is about 40 feet wide. It would not be an easy crossing even under perfect conditions, but the conditions are usually far from perfect. Winds gusting through the canyon are typically around 25 miles per hour with gusts up to 40. A storm could make those numbers double. The planks and cross ropes are all gone. No one knows exactly how far down it is to the river below. The waterfalls nearby create too much mist to see the floor of the ravine, but I can say with certainty that no one who has fallen has ever lived to tell the tale."

"Crossing at the ravine is not easy or safe. Many have tried and died attempting it, but there is a secret. The bridge is enchanted, and that is the reason some people are able to cross safely even in the worst of conditions. On each side of ravine are stone monuments to which the hand ropes are attached, and between each set of monuments sits a center monument that contains the seal of the King who ruled many years ago. If you stare directly at the seal without looking down, you will not miss a step as you come across. I cannot explain why it works, but it has worked for me many times, so I know it will work for you too. If you look down, there is a very real chance you will not survive. Only one can cross at once, so the trip for the three of us would take fifteen minutes, far less than the three hours it would take to go around the long way."

"Ordinarily, I would not bring anyone that way. The risk is simply too great, but today I was going to present you with a choice since time is of the essence. Our decision has become easier because I fear the figure Vic saw behind us was a Sentry. I do not know why he is here, but I sensed his presence and Vic's sighting has confirmed it. I know that if we do not reach Lucid Peak before he catches us there will be a very difficult battle ahead, one that is far more dangerous than the bridge I've described. We could probably prevail, but the delay may mean that we do not reach the peak before the merchants leave for the day. Also, Sentries seldom travel alone, so there is a strong chance that another Sentry is not far behind. We would not all survive if there were two to deal with at once."

Vic had been taking all this in, and did not like the alternatives, but wanted to understand the full story. "You think the bridge would help us avoid the Sentry?"

"Yes," Percival explained, "the enchantment of the bridge will not permit the Sentry to cross."

"You sure put a lot of faith in the magic of that bridge," Vic liked the thought of saving a few hours and outsmarting the Sentry, but didn't much like the idea of falling to his death. "If any part of your story is wrong, we will quickly find out exactly how deep that ravine is."

"Or meet the Sentry's sword," Percival completed the thought for Vic.

"I say we take the bridge," the boy finally joined in the conversation. "My dad needs every minute he can get, and I don't know about you, but I couldn't last a minute in a fight with a real warrior. I know a few things about magic, and I know that I trust Percival." He looked straight up at Vic. "If he says it will work, I believe him. Don't you?"

Again, the boy had gone straight to the heart of the matter. Vic did trust Percival, even though his head kept saying he was a fool to even listen to this old man, let alone follow him across a dilapidated rope bridge. But there was no denying it; Percival had been right every time and this was probably the only way. Their decision was easy and painful at the same time.

"Yes, I do trust him, and that is the way we must go." Vic knew they had little choice. "We better get moving."

In a few short turns, the fork in the path was upon them. It seemed so innocent. No signs with directions, no warnings or guide posts, just a simple fork in the road. Now that they knew the meaning of the fork, the very sight of it turned their stomachs in nervous anticipation. At least their anxiety would be over soon. Less than a quarter mile later, Vic heard the distant sound of roaring water, and shortly after, the ravine was upon them.

10. Crossing with Focus

The path led to a part of the ravine edge that was surrounded by a grassy meadow in front of the three bridge monuments. Hemmed in by trees and shrubbery that formed a semi-circle around the close side of the bridge, Vic could see the remains of a crude staging spot for those who wanted to cross the bridge. With a little imagination, one could see where soldiers of old would gather to guard the crossing of their companions across the bridge. Out of instinct, Vic turned his back to his companions and began scanning the semi-circle for any movement while walking backwards, his hand on his sword. Though a battalion of well armed knights might have felt quite safe out in the open, right now he felt more like target practice. After a quick scan, he turned back and caught up with his friends. "Let's make this quick," he prodded, "I have a bad feeling about this."

Percival was already standing with his hand on the center monument and squatting down to the boy's level, pointing to the other side.

"You see the monument just like this one on the other side? Do you see the King's seal on the center of the three monuments? That is your target. Fix your eyes on that seal and don't even so much as blink if you don't have to. I guarantee your feet will find the center rope as long as you do not look away. I'll go first to show you the way, and then I'll wait for you on the other side." He stood up and turned to Vic, "The boy should go next while you stand guard. I'll keep an eye out from the other side and warn you if something comes up behind you, but once you are on the bridge you will be safe from the Sentry. You heard what I was telling the boy, didn't you? Don't take your eyes off that seal, and I mean not for a second. If you do, I make no guarantees about what will happen, so if something happens and you have to look away, get your eyes back there at once."

Vic nodded. He could feel the weight of what Percival was instructing, but could not really understand the difficulty of what he was about to do. It sounded simple enough. Keep your eye on the seal. No problem.

Percival was the first to make the crossing. He grabbed the two hand ropes and checked his grip of both. He then checked to make sure he was centered between the two emblems, near and far. Then without looking down at all, he stepped out over the abyss and began walking across the rope bridge. He had the confidence of someone who had done this many times before.

For the first few steps, Vic couldn't help but stare at Percival's feet. When he did, he could see the ravine below and it was long and deep. He hated heights. He had always hated heights, but fortunately, Percival didn't miss a step. Each foot landed squarely on the rope as if it were as completely smooth paved street. He could see the wind blowing the ropes, and Percival's weight slightly bend down the bridge, but his step didn't waver, and neither did his gaze. As much as Vic wanted to keep watching, he was snapped back to reality by a noise in the bushes behind him.

Vic whipped around and put his back to the monument and the boy, half drawing his sword. His eyes tried to stare right through the bushes, watching for any movement or sign of life. At first there was nothing, no sign of movement at all. Then he heard a rustle in the leaves to his far right. He stared intently where the noise had originated and then he saw it, a low shadowy creature moving stealthily behind the bushes. He couldn't make out exactly what it was, but it was no higher than four feet high and by the almost total silence with which it moved, an expert hunter. A few seconds later, Vic spotted a set of eyes in the bushes. Those were not the eyes of a Sentry, but a mountain lion looking for its lunch.

For most, being stocked by a hungry mountain lion would not be a relief, but it certainly was for Vic. He had taken down animals of all shapes and sizes in the past, and was not the least bit worried about whether he could take down a single mountain lion if it were to attack. The Sentry was a different story. If these were anything like the ones he had seen in Blood Canyon, he wanted nothing to do with them. That boy better hurry, there was no way to tell how long before the Sentry caught up.

However, the cat did present a problem. With a predator in the bushes behind them, Vic couldn't help the boy at all. He shot a quick glance at him as he was readying himself for the crossing. If something were to happen to him, Percival would have to do all the helping from the far side so Vic could keep his eyes on the feline. It was not an ideal situation, but would have to do.

Vic heard Percival call out to the boy. Percival had reached the other side and was now telling the boy to start his crossing. That was excellent news, as the mountain lion was now moving closer to the path that would put him in easy striking distance. Vic glanced back at the rope. The boy had started across. A few more minutes and it would be his turn.

He turned back to the mountain lion just in time to see it crouching down as if to spring. Vic drew his sword fully, and it rang as it came out. The sword's song was enough to talk the cat out of its strike, and it began shifting its way toward the center where it would have a clearer path.

Vic looked back; the boy was half-way across. "Hurry up!" Vic thought to himself. He looked back at the big cat. This time there was no doubt about it, it was about to strike. Its eyes were hungry and intense. It had the same focus Percival and the boy had going across the bridge, only it was staring at Vic! It wouldn't be fun, but Vic was ready, until the unexpected happened.

The mountain lion heard something coming up the path, and then a moment later, Vic felt it. A cold wind blew down on him, much colder than the breezes that swept through the ravine at his back. The look in the cat's eyes changed from attack to fear. Without warning, it jumped out into the path in full view. It was a beautiful creature; golden brown with sinewy legs and a long thick tail, but its actions were hardly appropriate for the consummate predator. Turning from side to side as if looking for an escape route, this huge cat looked more like a scared house cat when a big dog was coming. It bolted off in plain view toward the bushes on the other side of the clearing and kept running until it was out of sight. It had no desire to stick around even for a moment. Vic had never seen a predator turn so quickly from the hunter to the hunted. A moment later, he knew why.

Someone, or something, was running down the path toward them and the steps were heavy, clanking with mail. They were fast gaining in volume and their tempo was a run, not a walk. It was the Sentry, and he too had found his target. Vic sheathed his sword and turned for the rope bridge. Ready or not, he was coming across. Like the cat, Vic had no intention of sticking around for a fight.

Thankfully, the boy was just reaching the monument on the other side, so the bridge was ready for Vic. He quickly ran through the instructions in his mind. Grab both handrails; Vic grabbed the handrails. Fix your eyes on the far side monument; Vic looked up. *Where was the far side monument? Where was the far side???* The breezes that flow through the canyon had brought with them a dense fog that had just settled across the bridge. It was so dense that for a few seconds, Vic couldn't even see the other side of the ravine. Now was *not* a good time for a fog to roll in! Without letting go of his grip, Vic turned his head to look behind him. Sure enough, it was a Sentry much like the ones he had seen in Blood Canyon, but this one had no cloak. It wore mail of black metal bound with dark leather and its sword was drawn. Its red eyes shone through the open face plate on its helmet. It ran until it arrived in the clearing in front of the bridge.

"STOP!!!" he heard a deep and gravelly voice barrel out from behind him. Vic froze while a chill ran down his spine. Where was that monument?? Finally! The fog cleared just enough for him to make out the monument on the far side. The minute he could see it, he stepped onto the rope bridge.

There had been so much stress and confusion with the stalking by the mountain lion, its quick departure, and the arrival of the Sentry that Vic had given little attention to the act of crossing itself. Now that he was in the middle of it, a whole new fear gripped him. There was a noticeable difference in the wind once he was over the ravine. Blowing mostly from his left to his right, the breezes would come and go, moving the bridge several feet in each direction. Though he didn't like the swaying, Vic was glad for the breezes because they kept the fog moving. So far, he had been able to see the monument on the other side, and through his peripheral vision, could see that both Percival and the boy had made it across. The trick worked for them, so it should work for him too, he hoped.

The traverse seemed to be progressing nicely until Vic heard the Sentry yell again, "STOP!!!" and this time, it sounded like he was only inches away. Vic felt a huge jolt on the left hand rope. What was going on? Percival had promised that the Sentry wouldn't be able to cross the bridge. Was he wrong? Was the Sentry coming? Another jolt. *He wasn't trying to cross the bridge, he was trying to cut it down!* Vic had to know what the Sentry was doing. If he was crossing, Vic would be attacked from the rear and that simply wasn't how he wanted to die. He just couldn't help it, he HAD to know, so he planted his feet, and turned his head around.

The next three things happened so close to simultaneously, time seemed to stand still while they happened. Out of the corner of his eye, Vic saw the Sentry with his sword high in the air swinging at the rope with all his might. A blue flash of light emanated from the rope when the sword hit it, but it didn't make even a dent in the rope. Vic felt the strike reverberate along the rope, so he knew there was incredible force applied that would ordinarily have sheared straight through the old ragged rope, but this rope was obviously different. It had taken three direct hits so far and showed no damage at all.

The next thing he noticed was that the Sentry was NOT looking at the rope. The Sentry was looking directly at Vic! When trying to cut through a rope, one would expect to aim carefully, so as to hit the same spot with each stroke. This Sentry didn't look at the rope at all. It was almost as if he knew that his sword would have no impact on it. So then what was the point of hitting it? Of course! It was the only thing he could do to Vic while he was on the bridge – try to distract his focus, and that is just what he succeeded in doing! Vic fell for the ruse, and now he was going to pay for it.

The third thing that happened was that his feet immediately gave way. He was strong enough to hold himself up with his arms, but the hand ropes were too far apart to move forward at all. The most he could do was keep himself from falling without the support from his legs, and even that was an incredible challenge.

Immediately after he turned, he heard Percival yell out to him. "VIC, DON'T LOOK BACK!!!" but it didn't take Percival's urging to make correct his focus. He already knew what he had to do and was trying to do it. He turned his head back around to where the monument had been, but patches of fog had again blocked his line of sight. He held himself with his arms and continued to move his legs around, trying desperately to find the rope that had been there just moments before. Another jolt on the rope by the Sentry, this time on his right hand-hold. There was no way Vic was going to look back now. He knew that the only way he would survive was to find that monument through the fog. He strained his eyes staring into the grey mass trying to find it. The few seconds that passed felt like hours until finally, the fog cleared again. Instantly when he spotted the monument, his feet found the rope below. He wasn't about to look down at the rope though, he had learned his lesson. The Sentry continued to strike at the ropes on either side, but Vic was focused on that monument and nothing would break his gaze. The farther across he got, the less he could feel the effect of the

Sentry's strikes and soon enough, he set his feet on solid ground again and landed in the arms of Percival and the boy.

Once on land again, he turned around to see his assailant. The fog had returned, but he could faintly make out the Sentry leaving the clearing and entering the trail, no doubt to try and catch up to them the long way around. Fortunately, they now had a solid lead. As long as nothing like this happened again, they should reach Lucid Peak long before the Sentry caught up.

11. An Unexpected Visitor

The next day at the dress shop, Catherine couldn't keep her mind on her work. She even started sewing a sleeve on upside-down until Bethany pointed out the mistake. Fortunately, she fixed it before the tailor came by to check on her work. Usually Catherine would have been telling stories and coming up with new adventures for them after work, but not today. She had been uncharacteristically silent. Bethany had been keeping an eye on her, but Catherine was so distracted it was like watching a toddler in a crystal store.

"Cath, stop! Look what you're doing!" The spindle of thread that should have been on her lap had rolled halfway across the room. "That gypsy from last night really got to you, didn't he?"

Catherine sighed and got up to clean up the mess. "I guess he did, but more than him, it was what I saw. I can't get those images out of my mind. I've never seen anything like that before. Everything looked so real, and then it really happened. If I could control it at all, I could do a lot of good."

"Maybe so, but that gem did strange things to you too." Bethany went back to attaching petticoats to a yellow chiffon evening gown. "You looked so tired after he left. I'm not sure it's safe."

"Look who's talking! You were the one who reached right out and grabbed it without thinking about anything else! I must admit, though, it really drained me. I'm glad I was OK when I woke up this morning. I wonder who Eunice is going to bring over tonight."

"Someone else who knows how to use the coursite, maybe?" Bethany asked as she got up to get another length of material for her piece.

"I don't think so, but that's what I've been wondering about all day." Catherine was staring out the window as she said it.

"So I've noticed!" Bethany flashed her a smile.

The ladies finished their work and headed home for the evening. They burst into the house hoping to find someone waiting, but there wasn't. The two dinner guests for the evening were a pair of traveling goat salesmen. Not exactly the kind of conversation the ladies were hoping for. They got to hear all about the milking process, the virtues of goat cheese and even the problems with mating purebred goats. Catherine nodded behind blank eyes. "Really? Goats?" Bethany got up to refill their drinks and on her way back to the table pretended to make a silent "baaaa" sound from behind them. It was all Catherine could do to maintain composure. She faked a cough to cover her laugh, then kicked Bethany under the table when she sat down again. Would this ever end?

They kept looking to the door, but their gypsy friend never knocked. When the meal was over, the guests left and the ladies cleaned up as usual. They had all but given up when Bethany had an idea.

"Why don't you use the gem he gave you to try to see them. Maybe they're still coming. This will be a good test to see if it still works!"

Catherine gave herself a smack on the forehead. "Duh! What was I thinking?" Catherine hopped up and ran into the dining room. She returned with a small leather pouch and pulled up a chair beside where Bethany had taken a seat. Catherine gently removed a clean white cloth from the pouch and set it on her lap. She gingerly unwrapped the cloth to reveal the gem she had tucked inside. There was no need to spend any more time in contact with the stone than necessary, so Catherine made sure that the gem stayed on the cloth and didn't come in contact with her skin. She spread out the prized package on her lap and they both stopped to look at it.

"It sure is pretty." Bethany was the first to speak up. "Now let's see if it still works. Fire it up. Do your thing. Let's go!"

Catherine nodded and picked up the gem. Like the night before, a tingle ran from her fingertips all the way down her spine. It made the hair on the back of her neck stand up and gave her a quick chill. She closed her fingers around it and shut her eyes like before. The images swirled for a few moments, and then as before, things came into sharper focus.

First, Catherine saw a bright summer day with a young boy and girl lying in the grass looking up at the clouds. The scene looked familiar to her, but she couldn't place it. After a few seconds, it faded away and the images swirled again.

The second set of images she saw was what she wanted. Catherine saw Eunice standing outside a large barn-like building with two armed guards at his side. At first she thought he was a captive in their custody, but as she watched, she realized that they weren't paying much attention to him. It looked more like they were waiting. Eunice then began pacing back and forth and it all made sense. They were all waiting for someone, or something else. Bethany interrupted her vision.

"OK, out with it! What do you see?"

"Yeah. Sorry. Well first I saw two kids in the summer time. I don't know what that was all about, but it disappeared. Now I see Eunice, and two armed guards. They are all waiting for something, or someone. It's hard to tell what. It looks like they are in front of a barn of some kind, but it's dark. It might be that barn down the street from the dress shop."

"That's Sanders' barn," Bethany interjected, "on the north side of town."

Catherine continued, "Looks like the door is opening and there's lots of light inside, and people too. It might be some kind of meeting. Someone came out and is talking to Eunice. He's tall and looks important. Oh look, they mounted horses and the four of them are riding away together. They're leaving the barn, and it is definitely Sanders' place, I could read the sign as they rode by."

"That's great! They're headed back into town. They should be here in a few minutes, unless you were seeing something strange. How do you know you weren't looking at the past, or the future? Eunice said that it can do that sometimes."

"I'm not sure, and I really don't know how I can tell, but that's what it looked like. I guess if I'm right, we'll know for sure in a few minutes."

Catherine packed away the gem and tied the pouch to her side. She wanted to keep it handy in case they wanted a demonstration.

The ladies cleaned up the last remnants of the dinner and made the house as tidy as possible before Eunice and his guest arrived. They had told Aunt Mabel the whole story, but she seemed to think it was their imaginations run wild more than anything else. Mabel was upstairs tending to the beds for the evening when they heard a knock on the door. Bethany jumped out of her chair and answered it.

As the light from their parlor lamp stretched out into the darkness, the shape of two cloaked figures materialized. One was short and one was tall, with more figures in the background. Catherine rose to meet her guests as the short one pulled back the hood of his cloak, revealing Eunice's funny little face with a huge grin.

"Good evening, Miss Bethany, I believe you were expecting us?"

"Oh yes, do come in."

Two guards remained outside and the tall man with Eunice joined the ladies in the parlor. Eunice stepped forward to provide the introductions.

"Miss Bethany, Miss Catherine, this is Lord Dramon. He is the baron over this whole region and one of the most powerful barons in the land. His men provide protection for most of the villages in this area and he collects the taxes. He also commissions the judges that administer justice. In short, almost everything that goes on from here to Broad River Valley falls within his jurisdiction. Lord Dramon, these are the ladies we spoke about."

Lord Dramon pulled back the hood of his cloak to reveal a full head of jet black hair. He was probably in his 40s, but it was hard to tell. His features looked young, but at the same time he looked experienced beyond his years. Catherine thought he was really quite handsome, but also sensed a blend of fear and admiration; almost like a panther, beautiful but deadly. His voice matched his appearance perfectly. It was clear, yet measured and respectful.

"My ladies, thank you for allowing me into your home this evening. I was very interested to hear for myself of your special talents with Eunice's coursite. It has been a busy day and I'm sure you would like to get along with your evening, so please forgive me if I dispense with the formalities of small talk and pleasantries. If you would be so kind, please tell me about what you saw while under the influence of the gem."

Bethany turned to Catherine to continue.

"I'm the one who sees things through the gem," Catherine was not used to being nervous, but this time she was. Her mouth was dry and she had to consciously try to keep from talking too fast. "I don't understand exactly how it works, but when I touch the gem, I see images. I can't really control it. The images come out of the fog and then are perfectly clear. I see people, and places, but I don't know where or when they are. For some reason, Bethany didn't see the images as clearly as I did. I don't really know why, but when I touch it, the images come."

"So what have you seen lately?" Lord Dramon was kind, but obviously not yet impressed.

"Well, when you were delayed in arriving, Bethany had the good idea that I should touch the gem to see what it showed me. I did, and though I can't control what it shows me, this time I recognized the scene right away. I saw Eunice with two guards standing outside of the Sanders' barn." At the mention of the Sanders' barn, Lord Dramon went from mildly interested to intently listening. Catherine had certainly gotten his attention.

"A few minutes later, you came out of the barn and met them, and then mounted horses and left to come here. Is that right?"

"It seems you saw us with surprising clarity, Miss Catherine. How did you know it was Sanders' barn?"

"I saw their sign as you rode out the gate."

"I see." Lord Dramon paused for a moment and then resumed. "Ladies, would you mind excusing us as we retreat to the doorway, I need to speak with Eunice in private for a few moments."

"Certainly."

The two men stepped back and Lord Dramon moved close to Eunice and bent his head down to the gypsy's ear.

"Have you ever seen anyone else with this ability?" Dramon asked.

"Never."

"Did you tell anyone else about her?"

"Only you, my lord."

"Can you teach her to control it?"

"I have no idea, but I can try."

"Very well. You and the girl must come with me to the festival. I cannot have this talent fall into the hands of my enemies. I will need to make several stops on the way and must leave tomorrow morning. I will pay you handsomely but you must tell *no one* of the journey or her abilities. It is absolutely imperative, and your life depends upon it. Do you understand?"

Eunice did not miss the forcefulness of those last words. "Of course," he replied.

"Then I will see you tomorrow. Go."

Eunice immediately turned back to the ladies, "I must be off, but will see you soon. In the meantime, I leave you in the care of Lord Dramon." Eunice bowed and swiftly departed, leaving only a swirl of dust from the closing door. Lord Dramon again approached the ladies and spoke directly to Catherine.

"My lady, you have a gift, and as far as I have seen, it is unique. I believe you can put this gift to great use, given the proper training. I am leaving for the annual Harvest Festival in Petersberg tomorrow morning. Have you heard of it?"

"Why yes, it's the largest celebration around, with games and merchants and performers. I remember going once when I was very young but don't remember much more about it."

"I would be honored if you would join me for the trip. I've asked Eunice to come as well, so that maybe together we can explore this new talent of yours."

"Tomorrow?" Catherine was amazed and flattered. "I really don't think so, I have to work at the dress shop and if I went, who would help Aunt Mabel with the meals?"

Bethany was surprised to see Catherine shy away from an adventure. Catherine was always looking for excitement, so it was fun for Bethany to be the one doing the pushing this time. This was Catherine's time to see the world, and how better to go than with someone very powerful and important. She didn't want Catherine to let this opportunity pass by.

"Don't worry about a thing, Cath. I'll tell the dress shop that you had to leave suddenly on some very important business. I'll even work extra hard to get everything done while you're gone. Mother can take care of herself and a hundred guests just fine. She doesn't really need our help; she just likes having us around. You can't pass this up, Catherine. Go!"

"Well..."

"Catherine, I would gladly pay you to join me. We should return from the festival in around two weeks. For your time, I will pay you what you make in a year at the dress shop. If we are able to refine this talent of yours, you will be worth far more than that to me. Do we have an understanding?"

Catherine looked at Bethany, who nodded her approval. Catherine turned back to Dramon. "Lord Dramon, may I discuss it with my Aunt Mabel first? While I am staying in her house I owe her that courtesy."

"Certainly. I will be here tomorrow morning at sunrise to pick you up. Eunice will meet us here and we shall travel together with my security detail. I'll need to make a few stops along the way, so you'll get a chance to see the countryside as we go. You'll see the world in a whole new light when you travel at my side." Lord Dramon pulled his hood back over his head and bowed slightly, "Until tomorrow." He turned and went out the door without a sound. The girls stood there in amazement until the sound of the horses' hooves drifted away. Bethany was the first to snap out of it, "Let's go tell Mother!" and she ran through the parlor and up the stairs to find Aunt Mabel.

They found her tending the fire in her bedroom. Bethany was so excited she started recounting the story in reverse, which didn't help Aunt Mabel understand it, but by the end Mabel got the full picture.

Catherine had been silent through most of Bethany's monologue. When it was through, Aunt Mabel turned to Catherine. "So what say you, lass? Is this something that turns your fancy?"

Catherine looked down a moment, then back up at Aunt Mabel, "Yes, and no."

"Lordy, that ain't gonna help much!"

"I know, but it's the truth. I think this would be a great opportunity to do something incredible. I probably won't ever get a chance to do this again, and I love adventures so I want to go, but I don't know him at all. Something about him makes me nervous. I can't explain it."

"I'll tell you what it is, lass, it's power. The man has power to do whatever he wants, and he knows it. Not many around here are willing to try and stop him. I'm glad you noticed. Power like that *should* scare you because you're never safe around it. 'Course these days when are you safe? At least you won't have to fear anything else on your trip, his security detail will protect you. All you need to fear is him."

"That doesn't make me feel much better about going. Maybe I should stay."

"Child, I didn't say that. Truth is, you'd be smart to go with him nicely while he's still ask'n nicely. Seems to me you'll be going either way unless you run home to your father right now. He's the only one I know who would stand up to Dramon, and you're the only reason he would do it."

"Hmm. Then I guess I should go."

"Yes, you should. I'll send word to your father to let him know."

"Thank you, Aunt Mabel."

Mabel gave her a hug and a kiss on the forehead. "You're a good girl Catherine Claybrooke." Aunt Mabel paused. "But you probably shouldn't tell him your family name."

Catherine looked at her quizzically, but Aunt Mabel was quite finished. "Now run along, you have packing to do!"

The girls ran out of the room until Bethany stopped Catherine in the hall.

"I can't believe how boring you two are! Aren't you excited? You're going to the festival!" Bethany could barely contain herself.

"With a baron!"

"And his security detail!"

"And learning to use magical powers!"

"I can't believe it!" Then Bethany's smile faded when she remembered that she wouldn't be going. "You have to make sure to tell me *everything* when you get back. I want to know *details.* Don't forget!"

"I won't forget. You'll get to hear absolutely everything."

Bethany gave Catherine a sad kind of smile. "I'll take care of everything while you're gone. Let's go pack."

It was late before the girls finished. Catherine was excited, nervous and scared all rolled into one. She had never been farther from home than Rochester, and leaving made her thoughts drift toward Vic. He should be on this adventure with her! She remembered all the fun they had together growing up, and remembered that he was always there to get her out of trouble. Where was he now? Would she see him while she was traveling? That would be so nice. Lord Dramon was the scary part and Aunt Bethany's words rang in her ears, "That man has power to do whatever he wants..." That wasn't right. How could one man have amassed so much power that not even the other barons would resist? He obviously had great interest in her learning to use the gem. Would this lead to other exciting places would they visit together? Could she really learn to see the past, the future and the world? The questions kept swirling in her mind long after her head hit the pillow and her lamp was out. She didn't know why, but she knew her life would never be the same again.

12. Lucid Peak

Finally! After several more hours of hiking, Vic, Percival and the boy crested the last ridge and arrived at Lucid Peak. Though they did see the peak itself, clearly the highest point in this part of the ridge, the area Vic focused on was the trading area at the foot of the peak. That was his destination.

From where they stood, the path led down through some ancient stone markers that had once been an archway, and then up into the Lucid Peak trading area. Each of the stone markers contained the emblem Vic would never forget. He had stared at it with all his might crossing the bridge: it was the King's seal. As they passed through the ancient archway, the path opened up before them into a wide green meadow. The meadow was about a hundred yards square, bordered on the right and the left by sheer cliffs at least 300 feet high. Tucked away on the far side of the grassy meadow was the trading area. The rock walls carved by no human hand provided the perfect protection from the tempests outside and an easy way to keep watch for enemies, animal or human, that would disturb the traders. Scattered rock ruins spoke of walls and magnificent structures that once filled the gap between the cliffs, now long gone. There were no formal guards at post, only the comfort from company kept them safe.

There were only a few people at each station and some vendors sat alone behind their tables. This was the place they had been seeking, and now was the time for each to find what they had come to acquire. As they approached the trading area,

Percival imparted some final words of wisdom before they began.

"The vendors here change on a daily basis. Not all are trustworthy, so choose carefully whom you deal with. You will know it when you have found the one you seek. Until then, do not think twice about the others no matter how good their story seems. Many travelers have bought a lie at the end of their long journey and found themselves swindled out of all they brought, or they return home with some worthless trinket, if they arrive home at all."

Both nodded in understanding as they approached the first table and Percival turned to face the first merchant.

"Water from the fountain of youth," he proclaimed, "step right up and buy your own bottle. One sip a day and you'll never grow old." The boy looked up at Vic and smiled. Percival was right again!

Love potions, beauty cream, invisibility cloaks, you name it and someone there was selling it. Some choices were obvious, though some vendors had items that were quite creative.

"Fire boxes, get yourself a fire box." Vic was too curious and had to find out what this one was about. The merchant pounced on Vic's curious look. He held up a small wooden box about the size of an orange and opened its lid. As he did, a small flame burst to life. "Light this box once and you'll always have flame with you, see?" He closed the box and fastened the latch, then tossed it to Vic. When Vic unfastened the latch and pulled the top open, he saw the small flame burst back to life. Inside the box, he saw a small sponge like material soaked in oil and a wick protruding from the top. The mystery was why the fire didn't go out when the box was closed. He closed the lid and latched it shut. It wasn't even warm on top. He opened it again and there it was. Like the first time, the fire burst back to life.

"Could save your life on a cold night," he said, "isn't your life worth 20 pieces of gold?" Vic closed the lid again and tossed it back to the vendor. "Thanks anyway," and he turned to catch up with Percival and the boy.

As Vic approached the table where they stood, he found them already deep in conversation. Behind the table sat an old woman, her skin leathery from many days in the sun and long black hair, with grey running through it. Vic sensed that she was very old and wise.

"Forty-seven gold pieces, and not one less," she said. "The recipe you seek is expensive to make and I must be compensated." The boy looked down at what he had in his hands, and then looked up at Percival. He obviously did not have what the woman wanted for her cure, and Percival did not seem to have an answer for the problem. When he realized the Percival was not going to be able to help him, the boy turned to Vic.

"Mister, I know you don't really know me or my dad, but you've just got to help me. We've made it so far, and I just KNOW I can make it back and my dad will get well, but I only have 30 gold pieces. I'll pay you back no matter how long it takes, and we have things back at home we can sell. Please. I have to get back to my dad. Can you help me?"

Vic was moved, but he had virtually no money of his own left. Most of what he carried was money given to him by Catherine's father to buy the seeds. So far, he had not found the seed merchant, but he knew that their money wasn't his to spend. Instead of facing the difficult situation, Vic tried to diffuse it.

"How do we even know this woman is the right one? Do we really know she can be trusted?" Vic directed the question toward Percival, but was clearly within the woman's hearing.

"You have doubts, my warrior friend," she looked at Vic, "That is good. Ask your friend Percival what he knows of me, and he will tell you that my words alone are worth more than the price you pay. However, do not doubt long, because the boy's father will not last under that tree if he must wait for you. Your seed vendor will not arrive until tomorrow."

Vic looked at Percival with an inquisitive look on his face, wondering if Percival had told her all the information she knew about him. Percival shook his head no. He had told her nothing.

"Not arrive until tomorrow? I've come a very long way to meet him and was told he would be here. How did you know I was looking for a seed vendor, and are you sure he will be here?"

"Oh, he'll be here, but you will probably check with every vendor between these cliffs twice until you believe that he is not here today. When you wake up in the morning, he'll be here."

Vic was disappointed and amazed. He looked to Percival for support, but Percival only nodded slowly.

"It seems I have little choice but to wait."

She smiled and added one final thought, "Your seeds will not buy you love, but they will lead you to what you need to know, if you are ready to hear."

Now Vic was more interested than ever! He hadn't told any of his companions about his feelings for Catherine, or the reason he had come in search of the seeds. This woman's comment was not only more than he had told her, it was more profound than he had even realized himself. She was no ordinary woman, to be sure.

"OK, I see you are something special, but I can't give you the money I have for the seeds. It is not mine to spend."

"It is not yours to spend, true enough," she replied, "but not *all* you have is for the seeds. Has it been so long, that you have forgotten? The boy's price has already been paid by another, and you are merely the messenger."

What was she talking about? Paid for by another? Then he remembered the bag of coins Angela had given him at the inn. He had been so distracted by all his recent adventures he had completely forgotten. He searched through his sack and there it was at the very bottom. He pulled out the satchel and held it in his hand. He hadn't even counted it.

"I'm not sure how much is here, but whatever it is, you can have it," and he set it on the table.

The boy's eyes lit up. He immediately opened the satchel and spilled its contents onto the table. Five, ten, fifteen, seventeen gold pieces, exactly. "Oh thank you!" he exclaimed, and threw his arms around Vic.

Not sure exactly what to do or say, Vic flushed and slowly returned the embrace. "You're welcome, but as you heard, I am just the messenger. "

"We have all done our part," the old woman said as she scooped the coins into the fold of her skirt and then into her money sack. "Now for your remedy."

She cleared the table and placed a clean white cloth upon it. It was made of beautiful silk, and perfectly square, hemmed all the way around. Then she reached into her large sack and pulled out several bottles of powder, a few pressed leaves, a flower, and a flask of liquid. Carefully, she took the first bottle and poured out a deep red powder into the middle of the cloth. She spread it flat with her finger. On top, she sprinkled a fine white powder, but not near as much, only enough to speckle the red with its color. On top of that, she doled out some of a deep brown substance with the consistency of fresh soil, and then took the leaves and after tearing them into very small pieces with her fingernail, she placed them on top of the powdered mixture. The sap from the leaves began to drip out onto the dry substances as the leaves lay atop the mixture. She then cupped her palm and poured some of the liquid from the flask into her hand and added it to the mixture. Finally, she took the flower and squeezed it hard in her hand, crushing it, until a single drop of clear liquid dripped from the bottom of her fist onto the concoction. With a small stick, she combined the ingredients until they made a wine colored paste. As she mixed it, the smell of the flower seemed to grow more intense until it was almost overwhelming.

"It is finished," she proclaimed, and she folded the cloth into a small packet and wrapped it tightly. "Place the paste under his tongue once each morning until he is cured. Do not open the cloth until you are ready to deliver the remedy, as it will begin to spoil once it is exposed to air."

The boy took the packet and nodded in understanding. He turned to Percival, "Can we leave yet? I really want to get back to my dad before it is too late."

"It isn't safe to leave tonight," Percival replied, "but we can leave at first light tomorrow morning. We will make good time, do not fear."

Vic was happy for the boy, but concerned too. He had a job to do too, and was very concerned about having to go down the mountain alone. They had been going so fast on the way up, he had not been paying close attention to the landmarks and junctions he would need to know to find his way back down without mistakes.

Percival turned to Vic. "In three days, I will return. I will leave the boy and his father at our resting place and bring the friar up to meet you here. If you are still here at that time, we will all go back down the mountain together."

The plan sounded good enough to Vic, so the threesome headed off to find somewhere to rest for the night. Percival headed straight toward the western wall of the canyon. Nestled up against the wall of the canyon were two columns of wispy smoke drifting upward until they disappeared into the rock and sky above. Vic wasn't sure what time it was since there was no way to see the sun from deep in the canyon, but he could tell from the bite in the air that nightfall was close.

As they approached the first camping area the trio was greeted by suspicious glances from a motley crew of strange travelers. Each had setup his own "camp", consisting of little more than a blanket or cloak on the ground, all placed as close to the small fire as possible. Since they were the last to arrive at Lucid Peak for the day, it was no surprise that they were also the last ones to find spots around the campfire. There was room for one person left at this campsite, and the crowd made it clear from their stares that they would not welcome three people trying to use that one spot. Vic nodded to Percival and glanced over to the next campfire.

At the second campsite, there was more room than the last, but not by much. Unfortunately, the fire was in worse condition, and probably wouldn't burn for long before flaming out for the night. Someone had to go for more fuel, but none of the current residents seemed the least bit interested in gathering more wood. Each was quietly eating what food they had packed for the night before turning in. Vic motioned to Percival and the two stepped back from the campsite.

"There is only room at this campsite for two, and you and the boy need to leave early tomorrow. You have a long trip ahead of you and need your rest. There's room at the other campsite for me and I can afford to miss some sleep. You two settle in and I'll be back in a few minutes with some firewood."

"Thank you, Vic, you truly are ready for this trip. I wish I could be around tomorrow when your purpose for coming here is fulfilled." Percival turned to the boy and motioned to the open spot by the fire. "We'll camp here, go ahead and set out your things." The boy nodded and headed to the fire.

Percival continued going over plans with Vic as the boy headed off, "We will be back here in three days, but I do not think you will be here when we arrive. Our paths go different ways, but we will meet again. Prepare yourself for tomorrow and remember what you have seen and heard. All will become clear soon enough."

Again, Vic was more confused and amazed by Percival then helped. "I can't pretend to understand all that has happened, and sometimes I think you're just a crazy old man, but what you say seems to come true. I really hope so, because I would certainly appreciate some clarity right now." There was something special about Percival and Vic knew that he owed him more than he could ever repay. "What ever happened to that Sentry that was chasing us? Shouldn't someone keep watch in case he finds us?"

"Like at the ravine, the seal of the King protects us. The Sentries cannot pass through the ancient markers, but beware when you leave the area. They have a keen interest in making sure you never arrive at your destination, so I expect you will see more of them. Stay on your guard."

"I will." The two shook hands. By the time Vic returned from gathering the firewood, the boy was asleep. "Thank you for everything, Percival, and safe travels."

He stepped away from the fire and into the darkness. The only light and noise was from behind him. The world was bathed in the moon's bluish white glow, but the moon itself stayed hidden by the tall canyon walls. Before returning to the first campfire, he wanted to take one last look around for that Sentry. He scanned the whole trading area for any other movement and saw nothing. Then he traced the path back to the ancient archway and stopped in the field where he could see up the trail they came in on. All looked quiet and still until he looked to the ridge where he had first laid eyes on this canyon and the Lucid Peak trading area. There, standing on the trail was a dark silhouette. It was too far away and too dark to tell whether the figure was facing Vic or facing away, but the figure was not moving. It was the Sentry. He stood there still as stone. Vic couldn't see his face but somehow knew that he was staring right at him. Percival was right again. Seeing him gave Vic a chill, but it was also reassuring. He was safe here, and that was a good feeling, even if such an intense evil was waiting just outside. He took a deep breath and turned back. He would worry about the Sentry tomorrow.

As Vic returned to his campsite, one of the other travelers was cleaning up after making some stew and offered Vic the remainder. Vic smiled as he remembered Percival's stew from the night before. Though the flavor of this stew wasn't nearly as good as Percival's, Vic was glad to have something hot to eat, and it didn't have the after-effect either.

As he laid down to rest, his body was tired but his mind wouldn't stop turning. He couldn't believe he was finally at

Lucid Peak and tomorrow he would have the chance to buy the seeds he had come so far to get. It seemed like years ago that he left Tom Claybrooke in Mayport, and even longer since he had really been able to talk to Catherine. Would the vendor come? Would he be able to get past that Sentry to get home? Whatever happened to Derek? How did Angela know exactly how much money the boy would need to buy the remedy?

"I wonder if Catherine has ever felt this way."

After an hour he was still awake, and wishing he had some of Percival's stew after all.

13. More than a Bargain

When Vic awoke, it was later than he had expected. Sleeping on the ground after two hard days of climbing and hiking made him sore and every joint stiff, but he was in surprisingly good spirits. Mixed with the stress of the ravine crossing on the enchanted rope bridge was the thrill of knowing that the power of the King's seal was something the Sentry was helpless to combat. It gave him hope, and a renewed spirit. He sat up and took a great big stretch.

The sun was blocked from view by the tall canyon walls, but by the warmth and brightness of the day, Vic guessed it was mid-morning. He leaned back and looked over to the second campsite to see if Percival and the boy were still there. They were gone. Though he was glad for the extra rest, he felt like the party was already over and he had missed it. All the other travelers had also moved on, except one.

The remaining stranger was a man probably five years Vic's senior. His clothes reflected quality craftsmanship of leather and sturdy cloth, but they were well worn. From the looks of his bag and gear, he looked like an experienced traveler and he carried a full sword on his belt, unlike the merchants who usually carried only a hunting dagger. He was a few inches taller than Vic and his arms were thick and strong. His hair was bleached blond and his face was tan from many days in the hot sun. Vic didn't remember seeing him the night before, but he was gathering his things up and it looked like he had slept around the same campfire last night.

"Looks like you've had quite a journey, either that or you had a little too much to drink last night," he commented.

"Two days ago I was in Traveler's Junction. It feels like I ran straight up the mountain and it finally caught up with me." Vic rubbed the sleep out of his eyes to get a better look at him.

"Been to see the merchants yet?"

"No. My friends and I arrived yesterday, but I have not done my business here yet." Vic was hoping for some insights on the trading, and maybe a sense of where his seed trader would be.

"Great, I'm heading in too and could use the company. What are you looking for? Maybe I've seen your vendor. I've been here for two days now and had a pretty good chance to see what's around."

"Seeds. I heard there was a vendor selling some special ones and he would be here today."

"I do remember seeing someone two days ago, but didn't notice him yesterday. I'll let you know if I spot him. I suppose I should introduce myself. I'm Jason."

"Hi Jason, I'm Vic." Vic continued packing up his things while Jason waited. "What brings you here?"

"I needed to meet someone, but now my work here is done. Unless something comes up, I'll probably head back down the mountain this afternoon. Maybe if you're done with your business you could join me for the trip down. Two are always better than one on that path."

"You call that a path?" Vic smiled. "If I can find my merchant, I would be glad to join you. I have no desire to spend any more time here than necessary. The group I came up with had a great guide, but an injury too, and so I'll have to wait three days for my friends to return and then it will probably be a slow trip down. They aren't exactly the most agile group, if you know what I mean."

Jason flashed him a quick smile back and then pointed across to the far side of the plateau. "That's where I saw your seed trader two days ago. Let's see if he's a creature of habit."

The two made their way back to the strange bazaar of vendors and kept walking past booths until they reached a man removing several large sacks from a donkey. The beast looked tired and was glad to have his burden lifted. Jason was the first to speak.

"You the seed merchant?" The man's back was to the pair but he turned his head to size up his first customers of the day.

"Yep. You lookin' for somethin' in particular?"

"I am." Vic chimed in. We've got about 10 acres that used to produce great crops every year, but now it has been infected with some kind of disease and nothing has grown there for the past 4 or 5 seasons. We heard someone up here was selling a new type of wheat that could thrive almost anywhere. You ever heard of such a thing?"

"Heard of it?" the man chuckled, "That's what I've been pullin' off this poor donkey," and he tossed the last sack to the ground.

"Will it really grow anywhere?" Vic asked, excited to have found him so easily and that everything seemed to be going well.

"Almost. You'll need to water it and plant it just like any other variety, but it grows where nothing else will, so it sounds like a pretty good bet for your field. What's the weather like where you're trying to grow it?"

"It's in the lower plains. We have mild winters and warm summers, and have always been able to grow pretty much anything, until recently. So how much do you think I need? We didn't bring up a donkey so I'll have to carry it back down myself. If I can't carry enough, maybe we'll just have to start with a small crop for the first year and then plant from our own seeds next year."

"Next year? You obviously didn't get the full story on these seeds, my friend." The merchant sat down at his table and Vic and Jason did the same. "You can collect seeds from your first crop, but they won't grow until they have been seasoned for one full year. That's part of what makes them so resistant to attack. If you plan on keeping the crop going, you'll need to buy two year's worth today, one for this season and one for the next while the seeds from your first crop cure. Sorry to break this to you, but your load just got twice as heavy.

"That's the bad news, but here's the good news. All the seeds I have here are already seasoned, so they'll grow right when you plant them, and they are exceptionally small seeds, about half the size of normal ones. For a full crop, you need almost 50 pounds of seeds per acre, but I bet you can get away with a nice yield if you plant 15 pounds per acre at a bare minimum. I wouldn't recommend trying to carry more than 30 pounds on your back for as far as you've got to go. That'll give you two acres the first year, and you'll have to come back again next year if you want another two acres next year. Unless you want to buy this donkey from me, I think that's about as much as you can take."

The merchant reached into his sack and pulled out a smaller bag and a measuring scoop. He unfastened the top of one of the larger grain sacks and dipped the measuring scoop in. Instead of filling the small sack, he lifted the scoop and let the seeds pour back into the mouth of the grain bag so they could see it. The golden seeds shone in the sunlight and poured back into the bag like fine sand. Vic wasn't very excited about the news, but he had always known that size and weight would be a factor. The worst was that the seeds he bought would only give them one year of crop, and only for 1 acre. It was a painfully small profit for such a long journey, but at least it was a start. He took one more look at the donkey, and confirmed his earlier suspicion; that animal wasn't in any shape to make it back down the mountain in one piece, at least not the way Vic had come up. He would have to buy only what he could carry.

"I have to pass on your donkey. So how much for the seeds?"

"Two gold pieces per pound." The merchant closed up the bag and folded his hands on the table. "So how many pounds do you want?" As he spoke another man with a pack mule began walking up to the table, obviously to buy some of the same seeds Vic was interested in.

"Wow, that's pretty steep for seeds, don't you think?" Vic was concerned that Tom Claybrooke may not have given him enough money for the 30 pounds he was hoping for.

"Well these are special seeds, and my guess is that you wouldn't have come all the way up here if you had any other choice. It doesn't take much to see you aren't a farmer yourself, so let's just get this over with. I have other customers to help. How much did they send you with?"

Vic flushed. It was embarrassing for someone to recognize his ignorance about farming so quickly, but it was probably just as well. Vic had noticed that this vendor *was* a farmer just as fast as the vendor had realized that Vic wasn't. The vendor's hands were worn and calloused, and there was dirt in every fingernail. The fine dust from the seeds covered him, but he didn't seem to mind at all. He carried no sword at his belt, but had an old rusted blade strapped to the saddle on his donkey. This man knew his trade, and part of that trade was sizing up his customers. Vic wasn't here to save money or get a great deal, he just needed to return with the seeds. It was clear he had no great bargaining strategy, so he decided just to throw himself at the mercy of the merchant. Vic reached into his bag and pulled out the small satchel of money Catherine's father had given him and set it on the table.

"OK, you win. No games. Here's what I have, and I've been sent to come home with seeds for 10 acres. It sounds like I couldn't carry 10 acres worth even if I could pay for it, but I probably don't even have enough for 2 acres at your prices. To be perfectly honest, I have nothing more to offer. This whole trip was a favor for a friend who desperately needs the seeds, so that is what I have to offer. Do we have a deal?"

The merchant picked up the satchel and poured some of its contents into his hand. He wasn't so much counting as inspecting the coins themselves. There were gold, silver and copper coins, though mostly gold. From a quick glance he estimated value at around 50 gold coins. Usually, Vic would have expected the merchant to count out exactly what he had and then measure out a corresponding amount of seed stock, but that isn't what this vendor did. He put the coins back in the bag without counting the rest. He looked at Vic, then looked at Jason, then back at Vic again, then finally spoke.

"OK. I'll give you enough for 2 acres. If you need another year's supply, come back again next year and buy them. Now that you know my prices, you should be able to bring the right amount next time." He sealed up the satchel and threw it into his bag. Then he took the smaller sack and measured out thirty pounds of the golden seeds into two bags with his measuring scoop. When he was finished, he tied the top of each bag with a leather strap and then handed one to Vic and one to Jason.

"Happy planting. Keep them dry until you're ready to plant and they'll keep forever. See you next year." He turned away from Vic and Jason to greet his next customer.

Vic stuffed his sack of seeds into his traveling bag and it completely filled it up. His bag was much heavier now, but it would hold. He turned to Jason, "You mind giving me a hand on the way down the mountain? Looks like I have a little more than I can handle easily."

Jason smiled. "No problem. As long as our paths stay together, I'll be happy to hold on to a bag for you," and Jason stuffed the second sack into his pack.

It wasn't near what Vic had been hoping for, but it would have to do. He had the seeds, and now with Jason to lead the way, he had a guide too. If it wasn't for the strange encounters he had been having with those Sentries, he could have looked forward to a peaceful trip home. As it was, he was starting to become concerned about getting off the mountain alive. Jason interrupted his thoughts with the practical chores of the day.

"How about we get some food for the trip and then get under way. The day is still young and we could probably make some good time if we get started."

"Sounds good," Vic replied. They went their separate ways and then met back at the trail head a few minutes later.

"Ready?" Jason asked as he tossed Vic an apple. With a wave of his arm, Vic motioned for Jason to pass, "Lead the way."

Jason started heading back toward the main entrance and the ancient archway that provided their protection. With each step closer, Vic could feel the knot in the pit of his stomach growing tighter. His eyes were peeled on the ridgeline where he had seen the Sentry the night before, so much so that he tripped on mostly even ground. Jason looked back to check on him.

"Everything OK?"

"Yeah, just uh…checking out that ridgeline…making sure…uh."

Vic felt terrible leading Jason into such peril without at least telling him about the enemy that could be right around the corner, but he couldn't bear trying to explain the whole story. If that Sentry was still up there, Jason would find out soon enough, the hard way.

"Have you ever seen anything strange on the way up the mountain?" Vic asked Jason, hoping he already knew of the evil they faced.

"Depends what you consider strange, why?"

"Oh, never mind. I just had some pretty unusual things happen on my way here that I would prefer not to go through again anytime soon."

"I know that feeling for sure, but with the two of us, what could be out there we can't handle?" Jason gave Vic a slap on the shoulder and stepped ahead of him on the trail.

"Snap out of it, Vic!" he thought to himself. He had beaten countless soldiers in battle. Thieves and warriors, animals large and small, all had been taken by his sword, so why did this single Sentry strike such fear in his heart? He realized the answer. He was not prepared.

Every other battle he had encountered, he felt prepared for what lie ahead. He could analyze his opponent, weigh the odds, calculate defense and offense, and then execute his plan. With this foe, he didn't know where to begin. Vic had met an evil that he didn't have the tools to understand, but he knew enough to know that he could not face that evil again without greater training. A big piece of the puzzle was missing. Derek had it, and Vic wanted it. The enemy was strong, but Derek was stronger, and Vic wanted that strength too. Now with Derek nowhere to be found he didn't even know what the first step was to finding the answer, but he knew that if he faced a Sentry before he was ready, it would be his end.

They arrived at the archway and Jason went through, but Vic stopped cold. The protective covering of the seals stopped here, and he couldn't take another step.

14. Ruthless Ambition

Catherine had now been on the road with Lord Dramon and Eunice for two days. The three of them rode in a coach drawn by four horses. The driver who rode on top was a menacingly large fellow with forearms the size of Catherine's legs. He didn't say much, but she felt safer knowing he was up there. Two guards rode horseback in front of the coach, and two behind. At night they would sleep under the stars around the campfire and the four guards would take turns keeping watch. It was quite an operation, and obviously something they were very accustomed to doing, and as they traveled she could see why.

Since they left, Catherine had seen a great deal of countryside and was starting to understand how much land Lord Dramon actually controlled. During the two days they had been driving, they still had not left his region. She always thought the regional barons were something like local magistrates, loosely governing and handling disputes between local landowners but never extending their reach much beyond their line of sight. She had no idea any single baron had amassed so much land, and knew for certain that this fact was not widely known.

On the road, she had spent a considerable amount of time working with Eunice on her use of the gem. It quickly became clear that he had no idea how to help her, but it was nice to have someone else to work with. Using the gem was still quite draining for her, so she spent much of her time on the coach sleeping when they weren't working with the stone.

In her exercises she had seen all kinds of things, some of which made sense and some that did not. Often she would see details about the road ahead, and sometimes matters related to the nearby farms. The images she saw through the gem often seemed to have a relationship to her surroundings or things that were going to impact her in the near future. Although Catherine had no idea how to control what she saw, she was beginning to be able to control how long she viewed a certain scene, and to be able to see the scene from different angles. As she would concentrate on a certain portion of an image, it would become larger and more detailed. Through this method, she could focus her efforts on the areas of most interest. She still only saw images and could not hear any conversation, but she could usually glean enough from what she saw to gather the general nature of what was going on even though she couldn't hear the spoken words.

Another thing she began to understand was that Lord Dramon's guards were frequently not kind to the surrounding farmers, and that he was feared by the peasants more than loved. On several occasions she had seen images of Dramon's guards beating local farmers. Over what she could not tell, but it did not seem like the kind of behavior she would encourage of her servants. When those scenes would appear, she would either not describe what she was seeing or move as quickly as possible to another scene.

This particular morning, the carriage pulled up to a bustling marketplace. Catherine didn't know exactly where they were, but knew it was a coastal town because she could smell the sea and the fish for sale in the market. Wagons and horses were everywhere, and trading took up every square inch that wasn't otherwise occupied. As the carriage stopped, two guards approached them and Dramon dismounted alone. They were wearing swords, but no mail, and had matching hats with feather plumes. The first bowed as he arrived.

"Lord Dramon, we are pleased to welcome you back to Twin Harbors, is there anything we may assist you with?" His tone was conciliatory, but he was clearly uncomfortable at facing Dramon.

"I require an audience with your master. Is he here?"

"Yes of course, Lord Dramon, but he is in an important trade meeting. Would you like to wait in our pub? We have some of the finest chefs anywhere who will prepare anything you like."

"I'm aware of your culinary experts, but today I do not have time for them. I am not interested in your pub. Please tell Grithos I will wait for him right here."

The guard was agitated but didn't dare contradict Dramon. "Yes, my liege." He hurried off, leaving the younger guard standing there alone, fidgeting with his sword.

"Don't you have somewhere to patrol, or are you lost?" Dramon did not like waiting and liked being stared at even less.

"Yes sir, I mean no sir, I mean..." and he stumbled away as fast as he could.

Dramon chuckled and snapped his fingers. One of his mounted guards immediately dismounted and came to his side. They whispered a few words, and no sooner had they finished than Lord Grithos emerged from a nearby building with five servants behind him.

"Lord Dramon, what a pleasure to see you! What brings you to our thriving hub of commerce?" Grithos was a short, portly man with wiry hair and wire-rimmed glasses. His clothes had an air of luxury, but they didn't suit him. Catherine thought it made him look like he was trying too hard to appear rich.

"Only to check on your progress, Grithos. I am counting on you to deliver what I need."

"Of course, Dramon, of course. Ever since we found gold in the foothills outside of town, we can't keep the people away. They leave their farms, their friends, and their families to get rich, and many do! My business has never been better!"

"I'm so happy for you," Dramon said sarcastically, "but have they been taking you up on our offer? That *is* why I have provided so much support for your free trade, remember?"

"They have been, but not as many as I would have liked. We will redouble our efforts to make sure everyone has heard of our offer of great riches and power. How could they refuse?"

"Yes, how could they?" Dramon was unimpressed. He stepped closer to Grithos and looked down into his beady eyes. "And how could you?"

Grithos visibly shuddered. "Never, my lord."

"Good. I need every man you can deliver to the festival immediately. Get them there now."

"Now?"

"Yes, NOW."

"Yes, my lord."

Grithos turned to his servants and then they all scurried off in different directions. Dramon spun around and climbed back into the carriage. A moment later, they were off. Before long, Twin Harbors was a distant memory.

By afternoon, the road led them into a beautiful valley lined with vineyards that Catherine would enjoy between her sessions with the gem. It was late afternoon and a cool breeze greeted them as the sun was starting to set. She had spent close to an hour using the gem and was tired. As she took in the scenery, she was drifting in and out of sleep while leaning against the side of the bouncing coach. From time to time while she rested, Catherine would hear Eunice and Lord Dramon talking about various matters. It became clear Eunice wasn't only a traveling salesman, he was a local informer who helped Dramon keep control of his growing domain. Eunice and the others who worked with him would casually travel through various areas of the region and report back what they saw. Sometimes this would result in greater enforcement of local rules, collection of taxes, or letters written by Lord Dramon. As the coach traveled, they would arrive at places along the way where they were greeted by more of Lord Dramon's servants. Much of the time while Eunice and Catherine were working with the gem, Lord Dramon was writing letters. He would seal these letters and then give them to his servants manning outposts along the way. On one occasion, a rider caught up with the coach to deliver a message. He galloped alongside the caravan until the reply was ready from Lord Dramon, then reached out to the coach to grab the return letter and dropped back. He did all this without the coach stopping or even slowing. It really was quite an amazing operation.

Catherine had been resting and though her eyes were still closed, she began to hear the voices of her two traveling companions. What quickly caught her attention was that they were talking in hushed tones, almost a whisper. That only made her want to hear what they were saying more. Over the noise of the horses and the road beneath them, it was a wonder they could hear each other at all.

"I wish they would speak up a little," Catherine thought. Fortuantely, try as they might, the horses won. They couldn't communicate without speaking a little louder, and as they did, their words became intelligible to Catherine.

"They *will* agree. They have no other choice. With her at my side, there is no way they will be able to approach without my knowledge. They already know I have troops in strategic locations across their territories and at any time I could cripple their ability to manage their regions and trade. Add to that her ability to predict their actions and I will be invincible. This meeting was going to be swift in the first place and now, it will be over before it begins."

"But what if they don't believe you, about the troops or about her?"

"They are all barons with land, servants and fortunes to protect. They may not like what I have to say, but they have too much to lose to ignore it. If I cripple one but not others, their people will revolt and they will soon watch their puny little empires slip away. The time to reunify this kingdom has come, and they will serve me or die."

"What of the spies who have been attacking your Sentries? Do we know any more about them? My sources say that they are not working for any of the barons. Do you think they are random mercenaries or are they working together for some common purpose?"

"Do not waste your time worrying about them. They are remnants of a by-gone day and can see what is about to happen. We can simply wait until they reveal themselves, and then there will be no escape. They win because they attack my men while they are in small groups and use the element of surprise. We finally captured one and we would have discovered much more about their operations if he hadn't escaped, but no matter, it is only a matter of time until we eliminate them. They could never take on my forces in a frontal attack and survive. Unless they are able to win in open combat, my kingdom will take shape as planned, with or without their resistance. In a few days, my plan will be complete. That is all we need to think about."

The men were quiet for a few moments. By now, Catherine was wide awake, but kept her eyes closed and was concentrating more than ever on staying relaxed. She needed to appear to be asleep, no matter how alarmed she was by what she heard. They were silent for so long, she wondered if they were staring at her to see if she was awake, but she dare not open her eyes to check. To her great relief, the coach struck a rock and jostled them all in the compartment. It was enough of an excuse to finally wake up. She blinked as the sunlight reached her eyes and she rubbed her neck which had become sore from staying in the same position for too long.

"Nice of you to join us, my lady." Eunice was the first to address her. She felt a great wave of relief as she realized that her ruse had been successful. Now she needed to decide how to deal with a newfound fear. She had seen the ruthless ambition of the companions with whom she had entrusted her life. They were only a few days away from the festival and she would be there for several more days. She no longer felt safe with them, though she had nothing to fear as long as she appeared to be helping them. Dramon apparently placed great stock in her abilities and intended to use her as leverage to get the other barons to submit to him. He needed to keep her alive and cooperating, but now she knew he also would never let her leave willingly.

She was trapped, but not in immediate danger. Dramon's servants were everywhere so it was unlikely that she could get in contact with her father or her aunt to send help. If only Vic were here, he would know what to do.

15. The Long Way Around

Frozen between the pillars of the ancient archway, Vic struggled with his indecision. He didn't want to try to explain to Jason why he didn't want to cross the archway, but he didn't want to walk into the clutches of a waiting Sentry either. Half hoping for a miracle and half trying to think of what to say he looked up, and there he saw his answer.

In the distance ahead, dark clouds were forming high in the sky ahead. Though they were far away, they were just what he needed. Jason heard him stop and turned around to see what was the matter. When he saw Vic looking at the sky, Jason did the same and saw the storm clouds.

"Looks like we might want to take the long way around. Did you come up this way yesterday, or did you come up the long way?" Jason asked.

"This is the way we came up, and it was my first time so I really don't know any other way. One thing's for sure, I'll never forget that rope bridge."

"You crossed the rope bridge?" Jason seemed amazed. "You must have come up with old Percy, he's the only one crazy enough to try it. Everyone else is too scared to go that way. We all think he's nuts, but I guess if you made it, he can't be all that crazy."

"What difference does it make which way we came up?"

"You might be able to talk me into trying out that bridge, but those clouds look like a storm to me. A storm could make the only other way across that ravine much harder. If we don't take the bridge, we have to take the path down, ford the river, and then climb back up the other side. Just about any storm on that side of the mountain will make the river swell and the crossing becomes extremely hazardous. Even if we make it across, we still have to climb the other side with water washing down like a mini river as we climb against the current. There's another path that leads out of Lucid Peak on the other side of the plateau. It's a much longer trip because the trail circles around to the North, but it stays on the far side of the ridgeline and that stops most storms. If you don't mind going the long way, it should be much safer."

Vic tried not to show how relieved he was at the alternative. For the present, it was enough just to agree. "Sounds good to me," he replied.

Jason chuckled under his breath, and then turned around.

With that, much to Vic's delight, they did an about-face and headed back into the trading area. After a few minutes of walking back through the vendors, Vic spotted a small cave opening in the sheer walls of the cliff. As they first approached, Vic wondered if it would be big enough for them to fit through but by the time they arrived, he realized the opening was much larger than it had appeared. The shape of the rock around it almost completely concealed its size until you were right upon it.

Jason led the way into a long tunnel that seemed to be cut straight through the rock that formed the east side of the canyon wall. Though there were no lights in the tunnel, Vic could see daylight on the other side and the light from both ends made it easy for the pair to find their way. Halfway in, Vic noticed that there were torch holders hewn in the rock walls of the cave and that the walls were too parallel to have been made naturally.

"Who made this tunnel?" Vic asked.

"Good eye," Jason glanced back and smiled. "The King used to use Lucid Peak as a staging ground for troops many years ago. He didn't like the way the canyon had only two exits so he had his men carve this one out of solid rock. It took over a year to cut through the rock, but when it was done, it made Lucid Peak one of the most effective areas for clearing information and orchestrating troop movements on the eastern front."

"Speaking of Lucid Peak, where's the actual peak?"

"On the other side of the canyon wall there's another cave like this one, but it's in much worse shape. Time has done more damage to that side and the opening is harder to find than it used to be. That cave leads up a set of stairs to the real Lucid Peak, the highest point for miles around. The view up there is spectacular, but with the disrepair of the stairs, it doesn't get many visitors anymore. Back when this area was used as a staging area and information center, people used those stairs constantly. As the legend goes, that is where the King used to watch troop movements in the valley below, protected by some of his best troops on top and below. It would be virtually impossible for an attacking force to make its way through that small cave and there was no other way to the top of this most incredible of natural citadels."

"This is a pretty amazing place." Vic had never heard so many stories about the King before. Though his grandmother had spoken of kings and wars and fortresses, he always thought they were legends. Now seeing this cave hewn out of solid stone, there was little doubt that there was some truth to the old stories. He could see the craftsmanship of the tunnel. Its floor was smooth and level. The walls were parallel, though rugged, and the torch holders were evenly spaced on alternating sides of the tunnel. He couldn't see the ceiling clearly, but could tell that though it was not smooth, it was tall enough to carry spears vertically to facilitate quick troop movement. Just these accomplishments alone were amazing. Cutting a straight and level tunnel out of solid rock would have been hard enough and making a tunnel of this quality would have required extensive planning and foresight. Before Vic had even finished admiring the tunnel, they emerged blinking in the sunlight on the other side. There was no sign of the storm on this side of the mountain. They found themselves standing on a large plateau that had probably served as a gathering area for troops and for defending the position.

While Jason walked over to the edge to take in the view, Vic looked back at the mouth of the tunnel. As he had suspected, the King's seals marked the entrance and that was probably the extent of his protection. He turned back to Jason and scanned the horizon. Fortunately there was no sign of the Sentry on this side of the peak, at least not yet. He headed over to where Jason was standing at the edge of the plateau.

"This is the Eastern Wilderness. It extends as far as the eye can see," Jason waved his hand across the valley below them. It was a beautiful scene with thick forest in parts, a stream running down through the middle of the valley and wide areas of grass dotted with little white flowers. Vic could trace the path of a falcon soaring overhead until it disappeared into the few puffy white clouds on the far side of the valley.

"This was the scene of some of the bloodiest battles in the Great War. Many lost their lives here, but it was through their sacrifice that the King was able to crush the rebellion and save our land. He drove them back through this valley until Lucid Peak was too far from the front line to use as a staging point. He then moved the center of operation somewhere in those mountains on the other side," Jason pointed to a chain of mountains that formed the other side of the valley. "I've never met anyone who knows exactly where."

"You seem to have more information about this place than anyone else I've met. Answers have been hard to find lately and I seem to have built up a lot of questions. Do you mind if I ask a few?" Vic didn't want to wear out his welcome, but he was finally starting to put some pieces together and didn't want to miss the opportunity to learn more.

"No problem." Jason seemed happy to continue, "We have a long road ahead with plenty of time to talk. What's on your mind?"

"Why do the vendors meet here? It seems like it is terribly out of the way, at least for those of us who live in the lower plains."

"Some of the vendors come from the harbor down at the end of the valley, where the river lets out to sea. They can apparently travel in the Eastern Kingdom, and they are the only ones I have ever seen traverse the Eastern Kingdom and live. Some come from the coastal towns in the north. For them, this trip is easy. Many believe the Eastern Kingdom was totally uninhabited until the King drove the rebels eastward, out of the Western Kingdom. The war has been over for fifty years now and there are no obvious physical barriers to passage between here and the kingdoms on the other side of the range, but many believe the rebels still roam free in the Eastern Kingdoms and the King and his soldiers are still hunting them. The vendors who travel back and forth keep very quiet about what they see on the other side."

Vic was beginning to understand, "So this is a central meeting place, but we have always lived in one half of the world and never knew there was another."

"Right."

The two stood silently for a few minutes taking in the view and digesting all they had discussed. Jason finally broke the silence, "Let's get moving. I'd like to make it over that next peak before nightfall." Jason pointed to a peak at the top of the trail they would be following. They wouldn't be following the trail that led down the valley to the harbor, but the one that led back up into the mountains. It ran on the eastern side of the range but hugged the mountains closely. Presumably, the two paths either joined eventually or ended in their own towns that were joined by the main highway.

Either way, Vic was content to follow Jason's lead for the moment. It gave him the opportunity to keep scanning the horizon and the trail behind for any sign of the Sentry. Vic knew that sooner or later he would have to explain to Jason what he had seen and done, but he wasn't looking forward to it. It wasn't fair not to tell him, so Vic resolved to explain the whole thing when the time was right. For now, he tried to nonchalantly examine as much of the countryside as he could, but since every bush that moved made him jump, he knew it was only a matter of time before Jason started asking questions, or the Sentry showed up.

Unlike the path on the other side of the ridge he had followed with Percival, this path was well worn and easily visible. It also was not steep like the other one. It had a much slower elevation change, which also made it much longer. Even though Vic had never been there before, the path was plain enough that the two men were able to take turns leading. They also took time to pause whenever there was a good chance at picking fruit or berries, or catching an animal along the way. Their rations would sustain them if necessary, but fresh game cooked on an open fire would taste much better.

For all Vic's agitation, the remainder of the day was fairly uneventful, except for one strange occurrence. One of the times Vic was in the lead, he noticed the footsteps behind him stopped for a moment. Thinking Jason may have spotted a rabbit or some other possible catch he paused and glanced behind to see if Jason wanted to stop. What he saw was Jason leaning into some bushes beside the path. Instead of finding a rock or stick, he picked up what appeared to be a small scroll wrapped with red ribbon. It was similar to the scroll Vic had seen the boy deliver to Derek in front of the inn at Traveler's Junction. Vic asked Jason if he wanted to stop, but Jason said no, and they continued on. Vic never checked to see if Jason read it, kept it or tossed it back. In any case, Vic didn't see it again.

They continued to hike in earnest until early evening when they slowed down to find a place to camp for the night. They needed a place that provided shelter from the elements, was easily defensible from animals or criminals, and was not too far off the beaten path. It was Vic who finally spotted a possibility.

"How about there?" Vic pointed to a small clearing up ahead. The clearing was next to a rock wall where the side of the mountain was exposed. Separating the path and the spot was about 25 yards of grassy meadow. Trees grew on either side of the meadow, but the grass would give them some warning if anyone tried to approach. The sheer rock wall provided protection from the elements, something to lean against, and a natural barrier to prevent anyone or anything from sneaking up from behind.

"I couldn't have picked a better place myself," was Jason's reply. They headed over to take a closer look. When they arrived, they found signs that others had also chosen this as a camping spot as well. A small circle of rocks and some ashes were left by the prior tenants, from the looks of it probably no more than a week ago. There was also a faint circle of ashes about six feet to the left of the fire pit, signs of still others before them.

"Looks like we're not the only ones to get this good idea," said Jason as he kicked at one of the rocks forming part of the makeshift fire pit. "Part of our work is already done. Now all we need is some fuel and something to cook. You feel like hunting or gathering?"

Vic thought the chances of being able to catch something to eat with only his sword and dagger were not very good, so he opted for the task he enjoyed less but at which he was more certain to succeed, "I'll gather some firewood."

"OK," Jason replied. He dropped his sack against the rock wall and headed out to hunt. "I expect to see a roaring fire when I return," he yelled without even turning his head back.

It wasn't long before Vic had returned with firewood and a few long branches for a nice roasting spit and poker. Vic lit the fire and once it had taken hold, sat down to enjoy its warmth and wait for Jason to return, hopefully with something to eat.

While he waited, Vic marveled at the completeness of their temporary residence and the crude sketchings scrawled on the wall. The more he examined the area, the more perfect the spot became. It made him relax, even though he knew there could still be a Sentry out there looking for them. Even the wind protected them. The column of smoke coming from his fire hugged close to the cliff until about half way up. As soon as it reached the top of the trees, a strong wind blew it in a thousand directions. Would-be attackers wouldn't even see the telltale smoke column rising.

About an hour later, Vic heard some footsteps coming through the trees toward him. He jumped to his feet and grabbed his sword. Fortunately, Jason emerged from the trees blinking in the firelight with two rabbits in his hands.

"Dinner is served!" he announced with a grin, and tossed his two victims down on the ground near Vic. Jason dropped his things by the fire and sat down with a thud. "They may be small, but those buggers are fast, or *were* fast I guess I should say."

While Vic prepared their catch for roasting, Jason told of his most recent adventure. "My one piece of advice," Jason said after taking off his cloak, "is that rabbits can move faster than you think. It's also not a good idea to follow them into small places." Vic looked up from his cooking and noticed Jason rubbing the fresh scratches on his arm and picking small thorns out of his shirt sleeve.

As they finished their meal, they leaned back and looked up at the night sky. The mountain stars always amazed Vic. Now that the cool evening breeze had passed, the night was still and peaceful. The crackling of the fire was all they listened to for a while, watching the embers become one with the stars as they floated away into the night sky. Jason grabbed a straight stick they had been trading to adjust the logs. As he reached his hand nearer to the fire, the glow of the flames caught a reflection off a ring on his right hand. Vic thought it was strange that he hadn't noticed it before, even though it was large and had a very unique stone.

"So where'd you get it?" Vic broke the calm silence and pointed toward Jason's hand, "looks like something special."

Jason turned and smiled at Vic briefly as he kept turning the fire, "I was wondering when you would see it. You know some people never do."

"Really? It's fairly large, I'm surprised I didn't notice it before."

"It's not the size that matters, it's what it carries."

"You mean the stone?"

"This is no ordinary ring, and no ordinary gem. It's coursite, and the gem is hidden from those who are not ready to embrace its meaning. Are you ready?"

"Well apparently so," Vic was confused but amused, "or at least it thinks I am." Vic gave Jason an awkward grin.

Jason liked the way Vic was open, even though he knew that what he was going to share would come as quite a shock.

"I'm an enlisted warrior, a soldier of sorts, but not like any you've heard of before."

Vic chuckled, "you know, I think you've strayed a little from your squad then, because you're the only one around!"

Jason smiled back, "just because you haven't noticed the other soldiers, doesn't mean they aren't there. Remember how long it took you to notice the ring? Don't you think it's possible that others have been wearing the stone and you didn't notice them either?"

"Hmm. I guess so."

"And you know who the enemy is, don't you?"

Vic knew. "The Sentries."

"They serve the enemy. Right. You're farther along than I thought. Had a talk with Percival did you? I'm surprised you got anything out of him, the old codger."

"Well I didn't get much, that's why it was so nice to start talking to you; someone who spoke in complete sentences and filled in some of the blanks."

"We have different ways, Percival and I, but we fight the same enemy, and are on the same team."

"Percival is a soldier too?"

"Yes. One of the best. He's been leading people to the peak since before you and I were born. Without him, I can't imagine where we would be. I guess you could call him an ambassador of sorts. Almost everyone I know on our side made that same journey with him. We all asked the same crazy questions, and we all ate that terrible spiked stew."

"He gave you that stew too?" Vic couldn't believe it.

"You bet. Everyone gets it. I think he doesn't want to be bothered with all the city folk and their questions. By the second night, he knows everyone is so tired and talked out that they go right to sleep on their own. Once you've been up once with him, you'll take a pass on the stew the first night and just eat your own rations before turning in. He won't give you a hard time, as long as you don't mess up his plan."

"Funny, I never would have pegged him for a soldier."

"This war is not like any other you've seen, and those who fight are not like others either. It sounds like you've encountered the enemy before, so you've probably seen their power."

"I met one up close and personal. Too close in fact." Vic pulled back the collar of his shirt to reveal the top part of the scar that went across his chest. "It was almost the last thing I ever did, and I lost my first apprentice to them. I've never been the same."

"Too bad," Jason paused. "You're fortunate to have survived at all. Most people who meet a Sentry before they are ready don't live to tell about it. Don't you think there might have been a reason someone stepped in to save you?"

"Someone did step in, but how did you know that? I never really saw who it was; just a flash of light and a burst of wind and then I blacked out."

"That's right. Surviving that day had little to do with you, and more to do with me and my partner."

"You?"

Jason paused and looked off into the distance as he remembered the day.

"Trevor and I stepped in to save you on the road outside of Yorksville, and I was the one who made sure you were taken care of after the battle."

It was such an incredible tale, Vic wanted to say he was crazy and try to prove him wrong, but for some inexplicable reason, he simply knew it was the truth. They both sat quietly as the import of the words sank in.

"I guess I should say thank you."

"You're welcome, but I was just following orders."

"Orders?"

"Yes, orders. They come in a variety of ways. Sometimes it's a message from a stranger, sometimes a vision, sometimes a note on the ground."

"Like that scroll you picked up today along the path?"

Jason smiled. "You are observant, aren't you?" Jason reached into his side pouch and pulled out the small brown scroll that Vic had seen earlier in the day. It was no more than six inches long and was wound tightly with a red ribbon around it. From the looks of it, the seal had already been broken, so Jason had probably read it while they walked along the path. Jason stretched it out and read it to himself, then handed it to Vic. It read only "Beware the north wind."

"What's that supposed to mean?" It seemed like some kind of strange riddle to Vic, some puzzle to figure out. "Is it in code?"

Jason shook his head "No. It means exactly what it says. Beware of the north wind. I have no idea what will come, and no reason to be concerned until I feel it, but when the north wind blows, be on your guard. Instructions always come for a reason, and they are always right."

"Always?"

"Yes, always. Sometimes we don't know what they mean right away, and I have heard stories of a scroll being kept for years until it is completed, but they are always completed."

"How do you know when they are completed?"

"You'll see. I have a feeling this one will be completed soon. If not, I'll tell you all about it when it happens."

"So one of these led you to me that day?" Vic was quiet for a few moments. "What about my apprentice? What about him? Wasn't *he* part of your mission?"

The last few words had been delivered with some bitterness and not a little sarcasm. Vic didn't like the thought that Jason might have let his apprentice die. He didn't want to sound ungrateful for his own life, but he had lived with the guilt of that day for so many years, he had to know the truth.

Jason looked down for a minute, then continued, "I wish we could have saved him too. We were on Lake Stevens early that morning fishing. Just as we brought the boat in, a woman ran up to us from out of the trees near the lake. She was exhausted and dirty, and looked like she had been running all night. She was so out of breath and so thirsty she could barely speak. She handed me a note she had clenched tightly in her fist. I could barely understand her, but was able to make out that the scroll had arrived by messenger the previous afternoon, addressed to her husband. She didn't know why, but he had not arrived home the night before. In the middle of the night, she had a dream like none she had experienced before. A man in the dream told her to take the message to the lake by sunrise. She awoke with a start, and knew that no matter what happened, she had to go. She had run all night to deliver the message, and then collapsed in Trevor's arms.

"The note described you and your friend and said that you would be traveling from Mayport to Yorksville the next day. It finished simply with, 'Protect them.' I knew right then that we needed to leave immediately, but Trevor insisted on staying with the woman for a few minutes to make sure she was OK. I think it was those few minutes that cost your apprentice his life. Trevor knew it too, and he was never the same. I don't have any idea where he is now."

"You went from Lake Stevens to Yorksville in a few hours? That must have been a really fast horse."

"We didn't have a horse."

Vic's puzzled expression said it all, so Jason continued.

"Have you ever wondered how we are able to fight those Sentries?"

"More than wondered, it is the thing I want to learn the most. I've been trying to remember exactly what went on that day ever since it happened. I'd never been beaten up like that before. I can usually hold my own, but those guys were way out of my league. I don't like that feeling at all."

"Right. That's why we need some help, and that's where the Timekeeper comes in."

"The Timekeeper?"

"Yes. You see, I serve the King. The true King of this land from times of old. There is a whole company of powerful soldiers like me, some here and some with him far away. The Timekeeper is one of those who serves him from afar. He's a powerful sorcerer that does the King's bidding. He is constantly monitoring the land and bringing situations to the King's attention where his soldiers need assistance. While there are lots of ways the King can help his soldiers, often the way he chooses to intervene is to slow down time, just for you. He channels his power through the gem you are wearing right through your body. It's a very strange feeling. You have to experience it to really understand, but it is a very powerful asset when you're in a battle."

"So that's how you can move so fast!"

"Right. Actually, when it happens to you it doesn't feel like you're moving any faster, it feels like everyone else is moving slower. When watching it happen to someone else, it makes them appear to be moving faster. Make sense?"

"Yeah, but it seems pretty incredible to me. I would think you were crazy if I hadn't seen it myself."

"You mean that day outside of Yorksville?"

"No, it was a few days ago at Blood Canyon. I saw my friend Derek do some amazing things that night, but he took a pretty serious beating too."

"You know Derek?" Jason seemed surprised. "I haven't seen him for years and had no idea what had happened to him. We were good friends and partners for a while a few years back, but then we were called in different directions and have lost touch. He was always one of the best, so I'm surprised he took a fall. You say he took a beating?"

"Not until after he had taken out at least five Sentries. I could hear the screams. The first two I watched, or tried to watch. He was going so fast that it was hard to tell exactly what happened, especially in the moonlight. Reinforcements eventually came and he sent me away with the prisoner he had freed. By the time they arrived I was already pretty far away. He was doing well, but getting tired. In the end, he was on the ground and about to meet his end when a dagger came flying out of nowhere and took out his attacker. I never saw who threw it, but whoever it was had good aim. I heard the last scream a few moments later and knew that Derek would be fine."

"Wow. Sounds like you've seen more action than most already. I would be willing to wager it was Percival who stepped in at the end. He's pretty amazing with daggers and if he was in the area, he was probably the one who got the call to assist."

"Really? I never saw him fight, but I did notice that he didn't carry a sword."

The two were silent for a while as each thought about all the recent revelations. Finally, Vic broke the silence.

"Where is Trevor now?"

"It's funny, I don't really know. After that day he was never quite the same. We did a few more missions together, but he was never one to follow directions well and the next time he didn't make a meeting, I went on without him. That was probably at least six months ago and I haven't seen him since. Why do you ask?"

"A strange soldier of some kind gave me the third degree around the campfire on the way up to Lucid Peak a few days ago. He was in the traveling party on my way up to Lucid Peak and he knew things about Yorksville that I've never told anyone. In the end, he stormed off into the woods. I had already eaten my share of Percival's famous stew so I was in no condition to follow him, but the next morning Percival said something about him 'leaving the path.' I didn't really know what he meant, but it didn't sound good. Do you think that could have been Trevor?"

"Unfortunately, yes, and I'm not surprised. He was never willing to make the sacrifices necessary to be a good soldier. Like I said, he was probably the reason your apprentice died that day. If he had followed instructions, we might have been able to save both of you."

The fire crackled and sent sparks into the night sky. Again, Vic broke the silence. "So if the King's so powerful, why doesn't he just come back and take over? He could consolidate the kingdom and resume control."

"He will," Jason replied, "but he doesn't want to be fighting against the common folk when he does. He gave these people the land to care for it, but they have forgotten him. The more people become his servants now, the better the transition will be. He wants to make sure the people *want* him to return. He has no problem fighting the Sentries and those who control them, but the last thing he wants is to end up fighting against his own people. He wants to lose as few lives as possible, and the better job we do, the fewer will rise up against him. Inevitably, he will come back and those who reject him will pay dearly. The idea is that there are as few of those as possible."

"Why wouldn't they want him back?"

"Some parts of his reign will be hard for people to swallow. Some of the barons have given in to using a powerful tool to keep control of their subjects: greed. They've read the stories enough to know how the King ruled. In the old kingdom, the King established rules for fair trade and gave people the freedom to do what they wanted, but he also told people what *he* thought they should do. If they followed his instructions, things would be easy for them. If they didn't, things were harder."

"Easy for them? What does that mean?"

"If you followed his advice, then things went harmoniously. You would find things prepared for you, people would be expecting you when you arrived and everyone would be going in the same direction. If you didn't follow his suggestions, you were on your own. That's how local barons, like one particularly nefarious one named Lord Dramon, have been gaining power. He has been telling people that they are better off just doing what they think is best for themselves and letting no one tell them what to do. This generally sounds appealing to people and sometimes they are better off … for a while."

"I don't think I understand." Vic was trying to follow this bizarre world Jason was describing, but something was getting lost in the translation. Jason refilled his cup and tried again.

"Maybe an example would help. I once heard a story of a farmer who had been growing barley in his fields for many years. He knew the soil very well and his family had been farming this plot for generations. He knew when to leave it fallow, and when to rotate crops. He even stored water for irrigation. People from all around knew to come to him for his barley; it was the best anywhere in the kingdom. One year, the King sent him a message. It simply said that this year, he should plant sugar cane instead of barley. The farmer was indignant. What business does he have meddling in my affairs? We've been growing barley for generations and we're not stopping now. The farmer threw away the message and went on with his barley crop. The next year, his harvest was just as large as ever, and the same the following year. He was convinced that the King was simply wrong in his assessment and this became a well known "mistake" he had made. The King never recanted his instructions, but never said another word to the farmer.

"During the third year, right at harvest time, a freak fire broke out and ravaged through thousands of acres of forest and farmland in the farmer's area. His entire crop was lost, and the storehouse where all his seeds were kept was destroyed. As the fire was raging through his fields he went out with his two sons to their irrigation tank, thinking that if they could flood the fields it might possibly stop the fire. Instead, all three were killed when the winds changed suddenly and the fire blocked their path to the tank."

"That's terrible, but I don't see what that has to do with the King's instructions. The fire would have ravaged through the field no matter what he was growing."

"Sugar cane farmers usually let a new planting grow for the first three years without harvesting. When harvest time comes, the fields are intentionally set on fire. The fire spreads throughout the fields and burns away all the dead leaves and kills snakes hiding in the crop, but the water-rich stalks and roots are unharmed. After the fire, the stalks are cut down and processed, leaving the roots to grow again the following year. A single planting of sugar cane can last for as many as ten harvests. If they had followed the King's instructions, the fire would have been a welcome work saver and they would have already prepared the fields for burning. In all likelihood, he and his sons would have lived to see many more harvests."

"Wow. That's pretty amazing. So does the King predict the future?"

"No one knows how much he knows, or how he knows it, but we who follow him know that his advice is true and he has our best interests at heart. That farmer must have thought the

King was crazy, and for a few years, made lots of money from his fields. Replanting a new crop would have been hard, inconvenient, and expensive, but would have saved his life and his fortune. The King will never make you follow his advice, but in time you learn that his way is always the best way."

"So if he was always right, why didn't people follow his instructions? What would make someone turn against him?"

"Usually because they didn't like what he had to say. He would generally instruct that land be given to those who would make the best use of it, but sometimes the ones who were not using it wisely didn't want to give it up. It's easy to ignore advice when you can't understand the reason for it. He was never one to explain his reasons, just to make suggestions. That's his way."

Jason continued, "Last week I was in Wrigley, a small town on the road into the Capitol, when I received a scroll that said 'Get up and go to the Black Mountains. Travel alone. Leave at sunset.' That's all it said. So I settled my accounts with the innkeeper, ate a good meal, and then set out after sunset."

"Are you crazy?" Now Vic was more than amazed, "its suicide to travel that road at night. Every thug in the county will be having *you* for dinner, not to mention the animals in the forest as you get away from town."

Jason smiled. "I'm pretty fair with my steel," he patted the butt of his sword, "but this night I would not have to use it. About an hour out of town I met up with a band of traveling musicians. They had been playing at a nearby feast where the rum flowed freely. They made enough noise to scare away the animals for miles. I rode with them all the way to Traveler's Junction, the town where you and I first met."

Vic's mind raced. Traveler's Junction? He didn't meet Jason until Lucid Peak two days later. How did Jason even know Vic was in Traveler's Junction?

"We met in Traveler's Junction? Where?"

"In the tavern. You probably don't remember. You sat down next to me at the bar. I heard you tell your whole story to Percival. He really gives people a hard time sometimes, doesn't he?"

"You were at the bar?" Vic didn't remember much of anything about that tavern except his conversation with Percival. He did remember that the room was crowded, and that he didn't stay long.

"It was a busy night, and your mind was on other things." Jason continued, "I don't think you looked at me once."

"I'm very sorry to have been so rude. Usually my head isn't in the clouds like that."

"No matter, the important point is that we finally met. I had other business to attend to that night or I probably would have been the one called to help Derek. Apparently that was the plan...."

Jason froze and didn't say another word. He brought his finger to his lips and motioned for Vic to be silent. Vic noticed that the ring on Jason's finger, usually a soft blue, was now bright red and glowing brilliantly. Jason motioned to a nearby tree and said in a hushed tone, "Climb it, and don't come down until I tell you."

Vic didn't hesitate. He grabbed the rope from his pack and ran full speed for the tree. About two steps from the tree he heard Jason throw the knapsacks into the bushes and run for cover. Vic tossed the rope over the lowest limb and just as the other side came down he felt it: a chilling blast of wind came thrusting through the forest from the north. Fortunately he grabbed the other end of the rope just as it was about to blow away. A moment later, that same wind blew the fire out and everything turned pitch black. There was no question about it, the north wind had arrived.

16. Behold the Festival

It was an hour past sundown when Dramon's carriage finally rounded the bend into Petersburg, the little town that hosted the festival each year. After a long day of traveling, Catherine expected more than a handful of artisan shops in the town square. Small homes clustered around narrow cobblestone streets that reached out from the city's hub. Most of the year, the few residents went about their business without fanfare, but once a year, this sleepy town became the busiest place in the whole region as their streets became clogged with all the vendors, visitors and dignitaries.

There was no room for the festival in the town center, which actually had little to do with the festivities. The festival took over the entire property of Adam Davidson, the town patriarch, who was also the festival's progenitor. At one time, he had grown crops in his fields like everyone else, but now, he spent all his time and efforts working on the festival. The day after one festival ended he would begin planning how to make the next year's bigger and better than the year before. His entire livelihood came from what he earned off the festival each year and it truly was a sight to behold.

Catherine had never been to a county fair, and had never even imagined anything like this Harvest Festival, even in her wildest dreams. The coach pulled up near what appeared to be the entrance, and Catherine, Eunice and Lord Dramon disembarked. Though she didn't exactly notice where they came from, there were now four soldiers ready and waiting to walk into the festival with them. Simply the size of their group made people step back as they approached, and Catherine thought the large entourage surrounding Lord Dramon was intentionally designed to let people know that someone important was in their midst.

Before they even entered the makeshift entryway, she could hear the sounds of music and laughter wafting from the tents inside the festival. The smell of smoking beef and fresh baked bread were the next to greet her and they made her mouth water. The festival was a massive collection of tents of all different shapes and sizes. By lining them end to end around the outside, the back of the tents served as a natural barrier to those who would enter, forcing them to use the main entrance. The tents served as miniature kitchens, game booths, and even resting areas. Since guests came from far and wide, many stayed multiple nights. There was no way the town could handle such an influx of visitors, so many locals brought tents and pitched them to allow guests to rent a night in their tent for a fee.

Food and drink were everywhere. It seemed like every few feet there was a vendor with a keg selling whatever you could want to drink. In the first twenty feet, Catherine saw two men selling hard ale, one selling red wine and one with lemonade. Street musicians had staked out locations and were entertaining anyone who passed by in hopes of adding a few coins to their hats.

At first, Catherine could see no apparent order to the booths, or to the makeshift roads that led people through the festivities. Their path kept twisting its way through the vendors, performers, and even a traveling acting troop was in the middle of a performance as their entourage walked by.

As interesting as the vendors were to Catherine, she found those who attended even more fascinating. Young and old, rich and poor, tall and short, fat and thin, every stripe of humanity was there. Catherine saw a woman in a cat costume, complete with tail, followed by women in ball gowns like the ones she would make back at the dress shop. Some had gone to incredible effort to make their time at the festival fun, and it made Catherine feel unprepared. She wasn't really there to have fun at all, but it was certainly better to be walking inside the security detail right next to Lord Dramon, than to be on the outside looking in.

After walking through the festival for an hour, the intensity of the festival's sounds and smells became overwhelming. Catherine was glad when they came upon what seemed to be the center of the festival, with a single large tent. Much grander than the others, its ornate decorations gave it the look and feel of royalty, but on closer inspection, it was really just a roof suspended on poles with canvas walls. A large wooden table filled much of the space under the tent and was encircled by 15 large carved wood chairs. There was no one in them now, but Catherine could tell that they were there for some particular reason, as they seemed out of place among the frivolity of the rest of the festival.

It appeared to Catherine that the festival was organized in a figure eight shaped loop, and they were in the middle where both sides of the loop came together. The main entrance was at the bottom, and they had taken the path to the right when they came in, following the lower right leg of the loop. This large tent and wooden table was apparently the place where the two halves of the festival came together. On the opposite side of the center tent stood the only permanent structure she had seen since she entered the festival, a large stone wall towering over the tents, with a building behind. Catherine could see many smaller gabled windows peeking over the top of the wall, and one large tower. The moss and scarring on the stone walls told of many years of battles and weather. It was well over five hundred years old. The wooden sign at the gate welcomed them to the Davidson estate.

The guards led the group across the area to the large wooden front gate and rapped loudly. The gate was opened by a gentle middle aged man with leathery hands and kind eyes. His formal attire and diminutive mannerisms spoke of his job as the butler. As he opened the gate a breeze blew through and disturbed his thinning hair. He straightened it with his hand as he bowed slightly to invite them in.

"It is always a pleasure to welcome you to the Davidson Estate, Lord Dramon."

"Thank you, James. Is Adam here?"

"Yes, he has been awaiting your arrival. I shall fetch him right away."

James showed them across the courtyard and into the main house. Once inside, he left them in the front parlor and went to fetch his master. Before they even had an opportunity to sit down, the doors to the parlor flew open as a distinguished man entered the room. He was tall and slender and exquisitely dressed. Probably in his early sixties, he had a long pointed nose and sharp chin and every one of his uniformly silver hairs was perfectly in place. This was obviously Adam Davidson, and he gave them more than a warm welcome.

"My friends, welcome! The festival has been going for two days and I was afraid you weren't going to come! Lord Dramon, will you be using your usual room? Everything is prepared for you."

"Yes, that would be most appreciated," Lord Dramon greeted his friend with a handshake and pat on the back and then turned to face Catherine. "Adam, this year I also have a guest. Her name is Catherine and she will need a room as well. Eunice will be staying with the guards at the perimeter outpost and will be keeping me informed of the status of our patrols. Do you think you will be able to accommodate the request?"

"Why certainly, such a lovely guest is always welcome in my home." Mr. Davidson clapped twice and his butler appeared in the doorway. "James, please fix the second room in the South Wing for Lord Dramon's guest."

"Yes, Sir," he replied, and was off.

"The festival has been just wonderful this year," Mr. Davidson was always eager to boast about his pride and joy. "Attendance is at record levels. We have more vendors and more performers than ever before..."

"And you have taken in more revenue from their participation than ever before, I presume?"

"Of course, Lord Dramon, as any businessman should, I plan for the worst but hope for the best, and it looks like this festival will also be the most profitable ever. Thanks to your security, we are hoping to keep the mayhem to a minimum on the last day. That is always when I lose the most money; after five days of drinking and dancing, the guests tend to have a little too much fun. Hopefully, we will not have that problem again this year."

"It is my pleasure to assist, Adam. My guards are the best trained anywhere and I'm sure we will be able to handle any trouble that comes along." Lord Dramon sounded completely confident of his ability and after all Catherine had overheard, she knew he was right. "Believe it or not, Catherine is also part of my security detail. She has some very unique abilities that I hope will assist us in avoiding any unforeseen problems. I plan to keep her close by my side through the end of the festival."

"I could never imagine so pleasant a security officer," Mr. Davidson bowed slightly to Catherine. "If I had a security officer as lovely, I would keep her close to my side as well!"

"You are too kind, Mr. Davidson," Catherine replied in her most gracious tone. The door swung open again and the butler reappeared.

"Your rooms are ready, my lord and lady."

Lord Dramon was the first to respond, "Catherine, if you would be so kind as to go ahead with James, I have a few things to discuss with Adam before I turn in for the evening, and I've been to my room many times before. I'm sure you will find the accommodations delightful, and tomorrow we will see the festival in all its glory."

"And don't forget to pick out costumes for tomorrow evening," Mr. Davidson interjected, "We will be having our first masquerade party. It will be the party to end all parties; a sight to behold!"

"It sounds wonderful," Catherine replied, "then I bid you both good night."

As Catherine followed James from the room, she wished she could hear what they were talking about. She knew Dramon had big plans for their time at the festival and she hated that he was in charge of all the security too. At one point she had thought that if things turned out badly she would be able to escape into the crowd at the festival, but with him in charge of the festival security, there was no way she would be able to leave the festival grounds without his knowledge.

James led Catherine out of the parlor through two large doors that opened directly into an even larger entryway with a wide carved staircase that led to the second floor. At the top of the stairs, the hallway turned slightly and ran along the outside edge of the building, with a stone wall on their right and small cutout windows every ten feet or so. Abruptly, the hallway turned inward and the windows stopped. Shortly after, they arrived at the first set of doors; large double doors with candelabra sconces on either side. This was probably Lord Dramon's room. They passed by and James opened the next door into Catherine's room. It was everything she had hoped for. The room was large and beautiful, with tapestries on the walls, thick velvet curtains and a four post bed in the center of the room. A fire crackled in the large stone fireplace and the bed covers were turned down with fresh satin sheets.

"If there is anything you need, do not hesitate to ring." James pointed to a long red rope with a tassel on the end that dropped from a hole in the ceiling and hung down by the doorway. "Pulling the rope will ring your bell and summon the night watchman."

"Thank you so much, everything looks wonderful."

He bowed gently and backed his way out the door. "Good evening, Miss Catherine," and he closed the door behind him as he left.

"This is amazing!" she said to herself. "If Bethany could see me now!" Catherine chuckled at Bethany's imaginary twenty questions.

"What color was the bedspread? Was the carpet soft on your toes? How was the view? Did you pull the cord and call your personal servant? What do real satin sheets look like?"

"Geez, Bethany, get a grip!" It sure would have been fun to have her here. A room like this would have been much more fun to share with a friend, but today, thinking of Bethany only reminded her that she really had no friends here.

It was a scary thought and even though she was enamored by the beauty of the room and the curiosity of having it all to herself, she wished she could have heard the conversation Dramon and Davidson were having in the parlor. She *really* wanted to know what they were talking about. Catherine found herself walking back toward the door. Should she sneak back down the hall to try and hear what they were saying? She put her hand on the handle, but then stopped. James was probably out there somewhere and would see her for sure. Lord Dramon might be on his way back to his room already and if she stepped into the hall, there would be nowhere to hide.

"How silly of me!" she said out loud to herself, and turned to go sit on her bed. She had the power to see things through the stone. This would be a perfect test to see if she could direct where it took her and what she saw. Once she had made herself comfortable, she reached up to the pendant around her neck and grabbed the stone in her hand.

The feelings she encountered were becoming more familiar to her now. Eunice and Catherine had practiced a great deal on the coach, and she was becoming better at entering and exiting the visions brought on by the gem without feeling as dizzy or disoriented. In just a few seconds, she began seeing images. The first scene appeared to be a couple playing a game of chance at one of the nearby vendors in the festival. A court jester walked by and began performing magic tricks for them, but the game owner was not pleased with the distraction for his customers and it looked like a fight was about to ensue. This wasn't the scene Catherine was looking for, and she concentrated hard as if to say "NO" as loud as she could in her head. All at once, the scene changed. Her message had been received and the gem had moved her to another scene entirely.

The second scene was on the outskirts of the town and at first, the vision contained no people at all. It was a picture of the corner of a hedge surrounding one of the large farmhouses about a quarter mile from the town limits. The festival was on the other side of the town so this vision appeared to be nowhere near where she was. She was just beginning to wonder why she was seeing this vision at all when she saw two black cloaked figures on horseback come around the hedge. Instantly, terror gripped her heart. These two figures were like nothing she had seen before. She concentrated on the figures to get a closer look. As the scene moved in, she saw glowing red cat eyes piercing through the darkness under their hoods and noticed that one appeared to have scales on his hand. They weren't saying or doing anything, but they gave off such a pervasive feeling of evil it was difficult to describe. Both the men and their horses seemed larger than normal and were certainly more menacing. They pulled their horses up into a clearing and then, were met by two other figures of equal description. The scene disturbed Catherine a great deal, but she knew this too was not what she wanted to see. She again told herself "NO!" and the scene morphed again.

This time, she saw what she wanted. Lord Dramon and Adam Davidson were sitting at the parlor table with documents spread out in front of them. At the center of the table was a drawing of the large meeting table Catherine had seen in the center court earlier that evening. Though she couldn't hear what they were saying, she could make out symbols set around the table at the locations where she had seen the large wooden chairs. At first she didn't know what the symbols meant, but as she looked at each one closely, she ran across one she recognized. She may not have been able to place it if it hadn't been something she had seen earlier that day. While they were on the road, they would from time to time run into a squad of guards who served another nearby baron. Just that morning, they had encountered such a squad and on each shield, they had the same insignia painted in bright red against a field of white. The insignia was unique, probably a family crest, and Catherine remembered staring at it for quite a while as the guards up at the front discussed something. That insignia must have been the seal of the baron they were talking with, and his insignia was placed over one of the chairs at the table.

Catherine kept looking at the signs as she went around the table, and several seats later, she spotted another that corresponded with a baron whose land they had passed through several days before. The drawing appeared to be a collection of insignia, each representing a regional baron and their positions at the table. Some had been crossed out or were grouped together.

She kept mentally walking around the table in the drawing, looking at each sign when suddenly, one jumped out at her as if it leapt off the page. One of the insignia was the same as the family seal hanging on her wall back home! She had seen it a thousand times, and had even helped her father copy it onto parchment once. She couldn't imagine what it was doing here. Her father was no baron, and in fact, they had no baron governing the region where they lived. For some reason, everyone just lived in harmony together and worked out their problems among themselves. Other than the random attacks like the one that had nearly cost Vic his life, there was virtually no crime either.

Catherine pulled her hand from the stone. What she had seen was disturbing in numerous ways. What did her father have to do with this meeting, and would he be coming? Who were those evil looking horsemen outside the city and why did the gem lead her mind there? Too many questions filled Catherine's mind. If only Vic or Bethany were here to help talk her through it.

Catherine had seen enough for the night and needed to get some rest. Her mind continued to play the scenes over and over as she unpacked her things and dressed for bed. As soon as her head hit the down pillow, she was fast asleep in her beautifully soft satin sheets.

17. The North Wind

He had felt this way before. In Blood Canyon, when he first saw the Sentry in the distance, he had that same chill down his spine. There was no doubt in his mind they were here, but where? He was doing well getting into his hiding place, but the whole thing felt foolish and so very unlike him. He had never been one to run from a fight before, but now, any pride, strategy, or bravery were all gone. He climbed the tree like a scared cat.

"I'm not petrified, I'm just following instructions," he thought to himself. "Yeah, right. Who am I kidding? If Jason wants to do the fighting, that's fine with me," but it made Vic really want to move like they did. He was tired of running away.

He pulled himself up the rope and stared into the darkness below. With only the moonlight from above, it was hard to see anything. The tall trees cast shadows everywhere. Any one of them was large enough to conceal a man. For the first few seconds, the cold north wind continued to blow and the rustling of the leaves covered the sound of anyone approaching, and then it suddenly stopped.

Everything was deathly silent. Vic waited to hear anything, but there was nothing; absolutely nothing. With each passing second his senses became more acutely aware of everything around him. He began hearing distant sounds of the forest. As he strained to hear anything, every tiny sound seemed louder and louder until they roared like thunder.

Something moved off to his right. Was it a figure deftly moving through the shadows? It was too hard to tell. Leaves rustled in the cluster of trees beyond the clearing. Vic's eyes darted back and forth. A flash of moonlight reflected from something in the darkness. Was it a sword? No, it was just the shadows and moonlight playing tricks on him. He knew the Sentries were out there, but where? The game of cat and mouse had begun. Jason was out there too, hiding as silently as Vic was. Vic strained to see anything he could, but there was nothing. Seconds turned into minutes and there was no sign of anyone, let alone a battle. It was maddening. Was the note wrong?

Five minutes felt like five years and he was starting to remember why he never liked climbing trees as a kid. His arm was starting to ache from the strange position he had to hold it, and his right foot was falling asleep. He was about to call out to Jason when he finally saw something move that was so real it almost made his heart stop.

Two hooded figures emerged from the edge of the clearing just off the path he and Jason had followed earlier that day. They stood in direct moonlight so Vic was able to get a good look at them. They were Sentries without question. He could see the red glowing eyes of one facing him, and the scaly arms of the one facing away. They were large, menacing characters, both close to seven feet tall and of massive proportions. One stooped down to examine the dirt where he and Jason had left the road. They followed the path until they arrived at the fire pit where the pair had been sitting only a few minutes before. They were less than thirty feet from Vic's hiding spot in the tree, and Vic knew it would only take a few moments for them to find the knapsacks Jason had tossed into the nearby bushes.

They stayed at the campsite for only a few moments and then walked back into the darkness. Vic rubbed his eyes to try to get a better view. The strain of staring so hard in the moonlight made his eyes water. He blinked a few times, and they were gone, back into the shadows.

He expected to see them emerge into the clearing but instead, he spotted a small red glowing light, moving swiftly behind the trees. Was it Jason's ring? Just before they felt the wind blow around the campfire, Vic had noticed that the stone in Jason's ring had turned from a soft blue to a bright glowing red. This light was the same color, but Vic was surprised that he could see it from so far away. It was either brighter, or Vic's eyes had adjusted to the moonlight and the adrenaline had improved his eyesight. Whatever it was, it was moving fast.

A second of moonlight when he ran between the trees brought his profile into view. It was Jason. *That ring would give him away!* Surely they would spot the glowing light and that would be the end of him.

A few more seconds of silence followed. All at once the sound of a sword unsheathed, a flash of blue light appeared from behind the trees, and a shriek filled the night sky followed by silence again.

Almost immediately, a second figure appeared in the clearing. This time, his sword was out. His shadow was even taller than he was and it moved among the eerie blackness by the moonlit trees. The Sentry quickly scanned the area, and then a moment later, he was gone, as quickly as he had come. All was silent again.

Vic watched and waited. There was nothing but silence. The chilling wind was gone, but its memory was not forgotten. Ten minutes later he heard what may have been a distant scream but it was too far away to tell. He was not about to move until he was *absolutely sure* there was no one left down there. After what seemed like an eternity, with no sign of Jason and nothing but the forest to listen to, he decided to brace himself between some branches and go to sleep in his perch. He would investigate in the morning.

At the first light of morning, Vic awoke to a sudden panic as he realized he was still in the tree some twenty feet up from the ground. He gasped and grabbed tightly at the two nearest branches to steady himself. Once the initial shock of his strange awakening had worn off, he found the rope again and let himself down.

Feeling the earth beneath his feet was an unusually great pleasure. He yearned to sit down and enjoy it, but he couldn't. Vic headed straight for the campsite to see if he could find his knapsack. Nothing in it was irreplaceable, but it had essential supplies and rations that could really help in a pinch, and he needed to give those seeds to Catherine's father. That was, after all, the reason he embarked upon this crazy journey. After just a few minutes of looking, he found both packs and walked them back to the fire pit.

Now that he had found Jason's pack, where was Jason? Vic had not seen either Jason or the Sentry leave the clearing the night before, so they probably went straight through the forest. Vic walked carefully out to the clearing where the other Sentry had been struck down. There was no body and no blood.

If Vic hadn't seen Derek vanquish so many Sentries in Blood Canyon only a few nights before, last night would have been overwhelming. As it was, he knew what to expect, but was still glad it had been Jason out there doing the fighting. Though there was no way to be sure, Vic assumed the second Sentry had fled, and Jason had given chase. Vic would take care of breaking camp and getting ready for the day's journey.

When he was finished cleaning up and repacking their bags, he looked around for Jason. There was still no sign of him. Now what should he do? Vic examined the path in both directions and when he could find no indication of which way Jason might have gone, he decided it was time to get on the road, with or without him. Vic threw one pack over each shoulder and started off.

After walking about ten minutes, Vic saw something on the path up ahead. He hurried up to the spot and sure enough, there was blood on the ground next to a large oak tree. Bad news for Jason; Sentries don't bleed. The blood was still wet. It looked like someone had lost a lot of blood while hiding behind the tree. It had to be Jason, and with that kind of injury, he had to be nearby. Vic absolutely had to find him, and fast.

Vic scouted around for clues – any kind of blood trail or tracks. Everything seemed serenely calm and peaceful, with a slight morning breeze still blowing through the trees, but Vic didn't notice. He was haunted by the sinking feeling that any minute he was going to find a dead body instead of a friend.

At first, he found nothing, then finally spotted more blood. This time it was on the leaves of a bush about waist high and 25 feet off the path to the right. He immediately headed for the spot.

There was no path here, and Vic had to climb through brush and bushes. This was starting to make sense. If Vic had been injured and needed to get out of sight, this is where he would have gone – as far off the path as possible and somewhere covered by thick brush so he could hide. Up ahead he saw another stripe of blood on a tree. He was on the right course. He tried to quicken his pace, but it was hard going through the brush, which was getting taller and thicker by the minute. At first he had been worried about being found himself so he had not made a sound, but as he got farther off the path and he became less afraid of being spotted. He started calling out for Jason while he pushed through the brush. Finally, behind some big bushes over on the right he found what he had been dreading: there was a dark mass on the ground in the shadow of a large bush. It looked like a body.

Vic scrambled to the spot as fast as he could and sure enough, it was Jason, curled into a ball on the ground, but thankfully not dead. He was unconscious and pale, but alive. He was clutching a pearl handled dagger in his left hand. Vic threw down the packs and tried to wake his friend up. Jason moaned and then finally opened his eyes.

"Well, it's about time," he muttered.

"Hmm. Still have your sense of humor, eh?"

"What would I be without it?" He cracked a half smile and winced as he adjusted his position a little. His pant leg was torn off, but the bare leg wasn't wounded. The torn cloth was tied into a tight band around Jason's right arm, and was soaked with blood.

"How bad's the arm?"

"Can you put some blood back in?"

Vic chuckled, "I don't think it works that way."

"Then not very good." Jason's color was returning a little and he sat up some more. "Turns out there weren't two, but four. I took out the first one pretty easily. I thought the second one was running away so I followed him to finish him off. I caught up to him as he rounded a corner and met up with the other two. As I took him out, one of the other ones got a strike on my fighting arm and that's all it took. I was able to escape and take cover behind the huge oak tree by the path, but there was no way I could work my sword with my left hand, certainly not well enough to take two at once. Fortunately this dagger was stuck in the tree. I used it to climb up to the first branch and then pulled it out. As soon as it sounded like they were gone, I climbed down and then crawled under these bushes and bandaged my arm. When the bleeding stopped, I went to sleep and thought I would try and figure things out in the morning. Thanks for the wakeup call."

Vic got some water and food from the packs and then sat down. It wasn't much, but Vic knew Jason needed to eat. When they finished, Vic stood up.

"OK. Time to look around."

"No. Don't. We need to talk first. Sit."

Vic was a little surprised at the urgency in Jason's voice, but he agreed. "Sure What's on your mind?"

"Vic, I'm not sure if you're ready for what I've got to tell you, but you need to hear it anyway because we really don't have any other choice. You've seen my arm. I'm out of commission for a while until it heals or I get better with my left arm." Jason smiled and rolled his eyes. "My father always told me to practice with both arms, but I never listened. I could usually beat most people with my right, so why bother training on the arm I never used? Guess he was right all along. In any case, I can't protect you anymore and that was my job. If there's one thing I could tell about last night, it's that they had set a trap for us."

"For us?"

177

"Yes. Those other two Sentries were staying back on purpose to draw us out and I'm certain they planned to kill us both. They knew right where to look, and I think there will be more."

"That doesn't sound pretty."

"Pretty ugly, actually. I was going to travel with you for a while longer and explain more about Renatus and the stone, but we no longer have the luxury of time."

"Who?"

"Right. That's my point. You're going to have to come up to speed fast, or we'll both be dead. You want to move like I do?"

"Absolutely!"

"Then you need to know Renatus. He's the one with the power, and the plan. If you don't learn how to use his power, there is no way you will be able to defend yourself."

"I like power. I'm listening."

"It's not that simple." Jason adjusted his position so he could look right at Vic and sighed. "This is usually a much more graceful process. It makes more sense over more time, but we don't have time. So take a deep breath and stay with me, OK?"

"Stay cool and keep up. Got it." Vic smiled and gave Jason a thumbs up.

Jason continued, "I am a soldier for the King, a spy of sorts. He is the ultimate power in the land and is responsible for everything you see. He ruled this kingdom for thousands of years in peace, until the rebellion and the Great War. When he left to fight the war, he established the baron families to keep order until he returned, but over the generations, most people forgot his stories or started believing he didn't exist at all.

"So you're a spy for a really old king?" Vic could see Jason was serious but couldn't help poking a little fun at him.

"Stay with me, Vic!"

"Right. Keep up. Got it!" Vic wasn't sure he got it but smiled anyway.

"Remember when you noticed my ring last night? It wasn't the ring really, it was the gem. He uses the gem to communicate with his loyal followers and as a conduit of his power. Remember how you didn't notice it before? That's because you couldn't. It only becomes visible to those whose minds are open to meet Renatus. That gem is the mark by which his soldiers can recognize each other. To everyone else the gem is just a rock. To us, it is the key to communicating with Renatus. He is coming back and when he returns, we will be the ones to help him regain control."

Vic was serious now. He could feel the weight of what Jason was explaining. This really was a war after all.

"Search your soul, Vic. Deep down inside, you know something is wrong about this world and it's because he is not on his throne. He gave the world order and balance and without him, everything is off. You know what I mean?"

It didn't take Vic long to respond. "Exactly. I've had that feeling for as long as I can remember, and it has gotten stronger lately. So is Renatus the King?"

"No, he's the heir to the throne, and the commanding general of the King's forces. Renatus picks soldiers for the King's service very carefully, and I think deep down inside, you know that he picked you. That's why I was sent to protect you. You are destined to join me in the King's service. It is an incredible privilege to be called, but I must warn you, it is not an easy life. For the first time in your life you will know that you have a cause to live for. I know you've been without direction for a long time, but that's all about to change. You will be part of a magnificent and powerful plan for the re-conquest of this land, but you will no longer be the master of your own destiny. You will follow his instruction without hesitation like the lowest of slaves. At the same time, you will be the most free you have ever been because every day you choose again to dedicate your life to his service. You will know with confidence that choosing to follow his commands is the best decision you have ever made. You will be serving the true and rightful King. I wish we had more time to discuss things because I would love to answer all your questions, but I fear we are at great risk here. So what do you think? Will you join me? Will you learn the ways of the gem and become a servant of the King?"

Vic had known something like this was coming for a while, but didn't think it would come so fast. All this business about a King was intriguing. If there really was a King, Vic would love to actually meet him. It was a thrill to think about the scroll from last night, "Beware the North Wind." Mere minutes after they felt the wind, they were attacked. Without that warning, they both would have been dead for sure. It came from a general who was watching out for him. What a life.

It had its advantages, but he wasn't so sure. Vic had been a mercenary for a long time. He was a soldier for whoever would pay him the most, so it wasn't much of a stretch to get a new employer, but this sounded more like becoming a slave than taking on a new job. Vic valued his freedom and that was the part of this whole arrangement that still had him puzzled.

"What exactly do you mean by 'become his servant?' I don't mind having him hire me as a soldier, but it sounds like you mean more than that."

"Oh, yes," Jason replied, "it is much more than that. You will have to pledge yourself, your life, and all that you have to his service. He will not accept those with divided loyalties. Either you serve him one hundred percent or you don't serve him at all. He may not ask for your money or possessions right now, but if he ever asks you to give them to someone or do something with them, you must obey without hesitation. In exchange, you will never have to worry about another meal or another harvest. You will learn to feel his power flowing through you when you battle, and you will take your place at his side. This is the destiny you always knew you were to fulfill. It is not a part time commitment, it is a lifetime commitment. I can now say without a doubt that I would rather die in his service than betray him. It is the most thrilling life I could ever dream of, and you can have it too, if you are willing."

"What about my family and friends? Will I ever see them again?" Vic's thoughts unavoidably turned to Catherine. She meant so much to him, but she was far away in more ways than one. Even if he didn't take this commission he may never see her again, but he certainly hoped he would. This choice would forever alter their future together. Would he have to get someone else's permission to see her? He didn't like the sound of that.

"Though you don't know him yet, his Majesty knows you well already. You have a very special role to play in his plan to retake his kingdom, and his enemies know it. That is why you have been so relentlessly followed and attacked, and that is why he sent me to protect you. Some people say he knows you better than you know yourself. I'm not sure how he does it. Maybe through some deep magic or through a network of spies, but however he does it, he knows far more about you than you can imagine."

"He has also been watching out for you for much longer than you realize. Why else would he have sent me to Yorksville to save you? You have met more of his soldiers than you think. Each agent is recruited for a unique skill set. He knows your skills, relationships and desires. They will shape what he will have you do. You do not abandon everything you love to become his soldier, you begin using those loves for his benefit, and yours. Remember the story of the farmer with the sugar cane? With his foresight, his suggestions are better than our best ideas even when we have no idea why. Isn't that a better way to live?"

"Yes. It really is, but it sounds like it requires a lot of sacrifice."

"More than a lot, it requires that you sacrifice everything."

Vic thought about his life. For years he had been going from place to place doing odd jobs. He always got a sense of satisfaction when he helped someone, or protected someone, but he knew there was more. That is why he was so glad when something seemed to be happening with Catherine, but now she seemed so far away. Would he ever see her again? Did she still care for him? He didn't know, and maybe never would. The burning questions that had plagued him ever since Yorksville were finally being answered. As wild as the stories Jason told him were, deep down inside he knew they were true. He had seen the glow of the gem in the dark of night and he had watched his friends vanquish the Sentries that had almost killed him. He wanted the power they had, and his life was nothing special to hold onto anyway. If he was ever going to do something as crazy as this, now was the time. He had no idea what Jason was *really* talking about, but he didn't care anymore. He knew what he had to do.

"I'll do it. I don't know why, but I trust you, and what you are saying just seems right."

"Vic, it's the right choice, and you won't regret it. I promise." Jason smiled through his pain.

"There is a problem though. Vic, you're going to have to take over my mission, the one I had after this one. My first task was to escort you to the cave. That is where we are going next, but after that, I was supposed to escort a Watcher to the annual Harvest Festival."

"A Watcher?"

"Yes, a Watcher. You see, coursite has different effects on different people. To you and me, it acts as a communication device, a warning beacon and a conduit through which the Timekeeper can slow time for us during battle. It also does many other things you will learn of later. For Watchers, it acts more like a window. A Watcher can use the stone to see things. Sometimes they see things nearby, sometimes in the past, sometimes in the future. Most Watchers don't really have much control over what they see. Some think the King shows the Watchers what he wants them to see and others think it is purely random or guided by the Watcher's subconscious mind. Either way, they only get to watch; that's why we call them 'Watchers.' What makes a good Watcher is their ability to interpret what they see; whether it is in the past or in the future, and whether it is nearby or far away."

"As the Watcher's skills become honed, the person becomes more and more valuable. In battle, a good Watcher can be the difference between life and death. If you have a Watcher with you, you can defend yourself from attacks before they have even begun. You can out-flank your enemy and out maneuver them. It helps us get where we need to be to avoid getting hurt. There is a Watcher who lives in Clavis, a village at the mouth of the valley that starts just over the next ridge. He is actually quite young, only 17 years old, but he has been practicing his art for the past six years and has become one of the best. My mission was to deliver him to Petersburg for the Harvest Festival. We don't know exactly why, but the King has sent an unusually large number of soldiers to the Harvest Festival this year. Something is going to happen there, and we must be ready."

"Now that my arm's no good, there's no way I can protect him, and that was my job. Once you align yourself with the King and become his servant, I suspect you will be given the job to escort this Watcher to the Harvest Festival safely."

"Me? I really have no idea what I'm doing."

"You don't need to know any more than you already do. He knows what you can do, and if you have the skills, he will send you. The challenge is to integrate the skills you already have with the power the King gives you, and follow his directions carefully. As I said before, his instructions don't always make a lot of sense, but following them can mean life or death and you never know when. You will be a formidable warrior indeed. All you need now is to meet Renatus. Are you ready?"

"Meet him? He's here?!?" Vic ran his fingers through his hair and brushed the dust off his shirt, noticing the blood from Jason that had stained his sleeve. "I guess I'm as ready as I'll ever be."

Jason laughed, "I wouldn't worry about what you're wearing. It won't be that kind of meeting."

Vic was worried that Jason would be too weak to stand, but he got up without much trouble. Instead of leading Vic back to the trail, Jason took them deeper into the brush for another 200 yards. It was rough going, and Vic could tell Jason was not himself yet. They had to stop to rest several times, but each time he would pull through, and keep pushing deeper into the brush. Finally, behind some large rocks and a thick patch of trees, a path appeared from out of nowhere. Jason smiled when he found it, even though he was obviously in pain too. Whoever used this path didn't want others to find it and if it wasn't for Jason, Vic never would have. Vic looked back toward the main path through the mountains and it was nowhere in sight. They were well hidden from view. As they headed down the path, it began a slight descent, which made the going easier. Vic broke the silence.

"So how do I learn to use this gem and its powers?"

"You know, you really won't have to do much learning. It happens almost automatically. Your job is to let it work through you."

"Let it work through you?"

"Yes. Take the time shifting for example. It isn't something you control, it is something that is controlled from the outside. I don't know how it works, but when it takes effect, you'll feel it. As long as when you feel it coming you adapt to it, and don't let yourself get trapped in the slower times, you'll be able to move as fast as it lets you move."

"Is there any way to speed it up or slow it down?"

"No, and you can't turn it off either, so be careful. Sometimes it turns off before or after you think it should."

"Not sure I like the sound of that."

"Yeah, it's a pretty strange sensation the first time, but you'll get used to it." The path rounded a corner and a small valley spread out before them. "Great! We're almost there."

Jason continued, "I don't know if you will be given my assignment to take over, but just in case, here's what I know. David Flannery is the name of the Watcher I was going to protect. I'm sure it will not be difficult to find him once you get to the village. It is a pretty small place. Once you're finished in the cave, I'll show you the way to the village."

"The cave?"

"Yes, that's where we're heading now. It is where everyone goes, as far as I know. Anyone who pledges allegiance to the King starts in the cave. You'll understand when you get there. Because of its unique geological characteristics, it is the only place in the kingdom that I know of that can let you experience the true power of the stone. Think of it as a rite of passage of sorts."

"This is sounding stranger the more you talk about it. Is this a hazing? Are you sure about this?"

Jason smiled, "The little boy needs some help? Afraid of the dark are we? Don't worry, you're in good hands. In fact, in the future you will wish you could return to the clarity and power of the cave. Enjoy your time there. I will be right outside waiting until you return."

"You're not even coming in?"

"It's not my turn, it's yours."

The two continued down a winding path to the bottom of the canyon and then on its floor for about a quarter mile. Finally, they approached a very rocky area near the bottom of a waterfall and Jason motioned for Vic to stop. The path ended at the water's edge, but before they arrived, Jason stopped and pointed to some jagged boulders strewn off to the right of the path. The boulders were quite large and became more dense farther from the path and nearer to the cliff from which the water fell.

"Through there is the cave. Climb over and through the rocks until you reach the side of the cliff next to the waterfall. You'll have to go alone from here - there is no other way to the cave, and as much as I would love to go with you, I cannot make it today. You will find the entrance on the bottom of the rocks, so when you get close to the cliff, start looking for a way to climb down through the rocks instead of staying on top. I'll watch you from here and point out which direction to go, but you won't be able to hear me over the noise of the water. Got it?"

"Sure. Will you be OK out here?"

"Yes. Even though I'm not strong enough to wield a sword yet, I don't think I'll need to use it here."

"OK. Thanks for everything, Jason."

Jason nodded and then motioned toward the rocks. "The cave is calling for you. It's time for you to go."

18. The Cave

As Vic hoisted himself up onto the first boulder, he could see why Jason had no intention of coming along. The boulders were large, and not always next to each other. In some cases, the jumps were considerable. Sometimes it looked like there was a path between the boulders on the ground, but each time he thought he spotted one, it would dead end. It would be pretty hard to get back up if one fell down, so Vic was careful not to lose his footing as he moved along the top of the often wet rocks. As he began nearing the cliff, he looked closer at the ground for the path Jason had mentioned. After several looks back to Jason and his pointing left or right, Vic finally spotted what looked like a path between two rock formations that might actually be a cave entrance. When he arrived, he dropped down from the boulders and examined the opening. Sure enough, it was only about four feet high at the opening, but inside it appeared to open up considerably.

He entered and paused for a moment to let his eyes adjust to the dark. Climbing over the rocks took more care than exertion, so it had kept him distracted. Now that he was in the cave, he felt the anticipation about what this cave would hold. A bat burst out of the darkness right in front of him and flew by his head into another part of the cave.

"Fly away, bat" he said to himself, "Sounds like a pretty good idea right now!"

He pushed forward deeper into the cave. He wasn't even ten steps in and he could already feel a chill. Outside, it had been a clear, warm summer day. In the cave, the air was cool and dry, but something smelled different than he expected. Instead of the musty and stale smell that usually comes from an enclosed cave, Vic caught a faint whisper of another scent; something more like incense but not nearly as heavy or pungent. He took a big sniff. What a fascinating smell. It had an amazing pull and made him want more. It drew him farther into the cave with a longing to find its source. He kept moving.

The next thing Vic noticed was the light. As he plunged deeper, the sunlight from the cave's entrance waned. He expected to find pitch blackness deeper into the cave, but it never got fully dark. There were no torches along the walls for light, and no obvious light source up ahead, but he could still see the curvature of the walls. A soft blue glow permeated the cave. As his eyes adjusted to relative darkness, he began to see his surroundings more clearly.

The cave was narrow at its mouth where Vic came in, and then widened into what can only be described as a large room.

By now, the glow and the scent had grown strong and there was no mistaking their source. Embedded in the walls of the cave were precious stones. They looked similar to the gem that was mounted in Jason's ring, but this was like nothing Vic had ever seen before. It was the stones that were the source of the soft blue glow, and of the wonderful fragrance that he was now growing accustomed to.

"You're late." A stern voice cut through the silence. An old man in a long brown cloak emerged from the deeper parts of the cave. His white hair and beard looked blue in the strange light.

Vic instinctively put his hand on his sword and prepared for the worst.

"I was beginning to think you wouldn't come, Victor," he continued. "We never can tell which ones will come and which ones won't, but I did not expect you to shy away from the challenge."

"You knew I was coming?"

"Of course, how else would I have had your gift prepared in time?" The old man turned slightly backward and yelled, "Fetch me the box," and at that, a small boy seemed to appear from nowhere and ran back into the cave.

"My apprentice," the man nodded to where the boy had just been. "It will take time, but he will learn the way of things...just as you will." His eyes twinkled as he looked at Vic. "First, your gift."

The boy returned with a rectangular wooden box. It was hand crafted, carved from a single piece of wood with great care and was exquisitely beautiful. The old man took the box and opened it. Although Vic could not see inside, he heard the man moving around items in the box until he finally removed something and handed the box back to the boy.

"Ahh, I remember this one." He looked back at Vic, and then back to the item in his hand, "With so much potential, you indeed have much to learn."

The old man held out a wrist guard for Vic to see. It was made of treated leather and beautifully embossed. In the center, a beautifully cut gem was mounted. It appeared to be one of the same glowing blue gems that were running through the walls of this cave and emitting the eerie light that filled the room.

As Vic reached for the band, the man snatched it away.

"Not yet," he said sternly, "it was made with you in mind and only you can wear it, but before I give it to you, you must meet the Master. We must go deeper." He turned toward the darkness from which the boy had emerged. "You have an appointment to keep," he said to Vic without turning back.

The old man lead the way into the cave, with Vic following next and the apprentice close behind. The farther they went, the more gems Vic saw embedded in the walls. All gave off the same strange blue glow and the light grew brighter as they plunged deeper into the cave. By now the gems were all around the floor, the walls and the ceiling of the cave, and there were no shadows anywhere, only light. Vic also realized that although the light had initially been dim, he had no need to strain his eyes to see. On the contrary, he now began to notice himself squinting as the light became brighter with each step.

Finally, the old man motioned for the group to stop and all three abruptly halted. "This is the place," he said with finality. The place he had chosen to stop was an area where the cave had widened a bit, and they had entered a space the size of a small room. To the right, thick roots of what had obviously been a great tree still protruded from the walls and then reached right into the floor. The man pointed to the roots and addressed Vic, "this is where the meeting will take place."

Meeting? What in the world was he talking about? There was no one in the cave but the three of them, and he was supposed to be pledging himself to the King. Was Renatus hiding inside this cave? It seemed like a strange place for royalty, but Vic had heard of stranger things. He was surprised that there would be no guards, no army stationed outside for protection, just an old man and his boy. Nevertheless, Vic wanted answers more than anything and was willing to go along with whatever the old man had in mind.

"I suggest you take a knee and grab hold of that root, you will need it for support."

Vic was starting to get an uneasy feeling about what was ahead, but was still ready to play along, so he shot back, "and then what?"

"Then," the old man continued, "reach out and grab hold of those gems where the formation comes out from the rock. When you're through, let go of the gems and you'll come back. Don't worry, we'll help if you run into trouble."

Come back? Run into trouble? Now Vic was really starting to wonder if this old man was crazy, but there was no way to find out except to follow his instructions. Vic chuckled under his breath at what he was about to do. He took one last glace toward the mouth of the cave to see if there was anyone there who might see him and laugh. He knew there would be no one there, but it made him feel a little better to see only the strange blue light of the cave ascending up the path where he had come, and the old man's apprentice standing nearby. Then, despite his better judgment, Vic went down on one knee and took a firm grasp of the root with his left hand. He raised his right hand and then before touching the gems, paused for one last look at the old man, as if to check if he was doing it right.

The old man smiled. "That's it, now go on," he prodded, and Vic did as he was instructed. He took a full hand hold of the gems that were sticking out. Since they were still affixed to the walls, they were quite secure, but Vic immediately felt their power.

The gems themselves were cold and hard, like any other precious crystal, but he only noticed that for a second. Instantly, a wave of energy flowed out of the rock and right through him. Every hair on his head stood straight up, and he began to feel light headed. Vic closed his eyes. The tingling of the energy was soon replaced by a heat coming up through his right arm and moving through his whole body. He gripped tighter with both hands, to regain his equilibrium. When he did, the root on his left stayed steady like a rock, but the harder he squeezed the stones on his right, the more energy and dizziness surged into him. Vic closed his eyes to fight the spinning of his head and as he did, he began to see colors and sounds that were clearly not from within the cave. First he heard people talking, hooves at a gallop in the distance, and a door slamming. Then he saw a sea of colors that began to take more definite form. Blurs became shapes and lines, and gradually became human forms. As the shapes became clearer, he heard someone say "Look! He's almost here." It felt like he was coming back from unconsciousness rather than entering into it. He struggled to make sense of what he was seeing and hearing, and with each passing moment, more of the scene began to make sense.

The talking in Vic's hallucinogenic room quickly subsided after that first comment, and the forms gathered around Vic in a semi-circle. He still couldn't quite make out the faces or the room, but there was no question that what he was seeing and hearing was not within the cave.

As the room began to take shape, Vic could see that he was in a large stone building with tall windows and a wooden floor. There was no blue glow like in the cave, rather a soft yellow light from a nearby fireplace licked the walls with shadows and patterns. The figures surrounding him were now coming into focus, and they were quite a formidable bunch. There were seven in all, some in long cloaks and traveling attire, and some in finely woven chain mail. As things were becoming clearer, three approached him and the rest fell back. The man on the left was the first to speak.

"Victor, can you hear me?"

Vic tried to open his eyes, or his mouth, but found that he couldn't. He tried to move his head, but couldn't move that either. He was somehow paralyzed over his entire body, and he began to panic. This was not a feeling he enjoyed in the least, and curiosity or not, he was not going to stay in this place in this condition.

"Victor, relax. Let the words out. Don't fight it. Let us know what you want to say."

Let the words out? How am I supposed to do that when I have no idea what's going on! Vic still couldn't talk or move and was becoming more frustrated with each minute. It was smothering. Was he doing something wrong? Maybe he should let go of the gems so he could ask the old man how he was supposed to communicate.

"Don't let go, Vic," the voice continued, "Tell me why you can't speak."

"I can't move," Vic thought to himself without even really trying to talk.

"Say that again," the voice replied.

"I CAN'T MOVE," Vic thought again, only this time he thought it more like he would have said it: angry, frustrated and loud.

"Again!" the voice commanded.

"I C-A-N'-T M-O-V-E M-Y M-O-U-T-H," Vic replied, thinking this was the last time he was going to try before giving up, but this time, it was different. Somehow, Vic had heard his own voice, even though his mouth didn't move.

"And finally, now, you see that you don't have to." This time, the voice was much closer, and relaxed.

"I...guess...I...don't." Vic's words were deliberate and unnaturally spaced, but at least he spoke them, or thought them. He wasn't really sure if his mouth was actually moving or not. He thought it probably wasn't but he couldn't tell.

"The first time is always the hardest. It is hard to believe that we can hear you and understand what you are saying when you don't use the voice you have used all your life, but we can. Just relax and think the words clearly and they will be as clear here as they would be using your mouth back home."

"Where am I?"

The figure on the right spoke up next; his voice was gruff and course. "You're in the command center. We conduct the war from here. All the operations start and end from this room, and that's why you are here. You know that, don't you?"

"Yes. I don't know much about a war, but I know that I'm here to enlist. I have always known something was out there, but didn't know what. Strange things have been happening more and more lately, and I had to know why. Thanks to Jason, I'm starting to understand a little, but I still have much to learn. All I know is that the King has the power I need, and I want it. I'm ready to join his ranks."

The figure in the middle had been silent up until this point, and finally the two others looked to him and he stepped forward a little. As he did, Vic noticed that he was somehow different than the others. He glowed slightly, and his body was slightly translucent.

"Vic, this is my army you are joining, and you will be taking your orders from me." His voice was somehow clearer than the others, as if he was whispering right next to Vic's ear. "I am

Prince Renatus and everything that happens in this war does so at my direction. Are you sure you want to become one of my soldiers?"

"Yes, I think so."

Renatus paused, then replied "I am sorry Victor, but that is not enough. Though this may be the first time you answer this question, it will not be your last. You must continue to answer this same question every day for the rest of your life. Your life will never be the same. Once you feel my power flowing through you and the thrill of being part of a beautifully orchestrated plan, you will never understand how you lived before, and you will never be able to go back. There will be times when you will not understand my instructions. You will feel strong desires to return to things from your past that you loved, and my instructions will direct you elsewhere. The road ahead will not be easy, but I will be watching you, just as I watch all of my soldiers."

"Vic, you must be sure. When you hear my command you cannot hesitate. You must obey without question or you risk your own life, and the lives of other soldiers in the field. Though you are strong and skilled, your greatest strength is your ability to act in concert with my other soldiers and your greatest weakness is when you lose communication with me. Is this what you are ready to commit to, both now and each day for the rest of your life?"

Vic turned his eyes down for a moment. Was he really sure this was what he wanted to do? Hearing it this way made him realize the finality of what he was committing to. He had always been on his own; never really been part of a team before and the idea was exciting to him, but losing his autonomy was also hard. As hard as the choice was, he was ready for the challenge. Now that he finally understood, there was no going back.

"I am." The decision was evident in his tone. "Now that I know the truth, there is no one else I could ever serve."

"Good. Victor Bremerton, I hereby commission you as a soldier of the King. You are his, and he will protect you. Welcome to the team, Victor. Unfortunately, you will have little time to train. My enemies are organizing and you will be a key part of the strike force that will stop them. You are uniquely suited to the task, but you must learn to hear my voice quickly."

The figure to the right spoke up. "The coursite stone you will wear on your wrist will give you the ability to communicate with us here, but because it is much smaller than the gems you hold now, and you will have an environment full of distractions, it will be much more difficult to use in the world outside the cave. Visions like this one will only occur when the gem's power is strong. In the field, you will likely only hear my instructions. When there is danger nearby or we are focused on you, it will begin to glow. The stone is hidden from those who are not ready to see it, so the glow will not give you away in battle. Now that you have been here, you will learn to focus the power of the stone to hear us. Remember how you are communicating with us today and use the same technique in the field. It will always be easier to communicate if you eliminate distractions and calm your mind before touching the stone. Once a year, you should return to this cave to refresh yourself and experience the intensity of the stone. It will help you focus your mind when you are in the outside world and teach you to better communicate through the stone."

The figure on the left finished the thought, "We use the gem as the gateway between us. We use it to communicate, and to send power through you. We may use it in ways you do not expect, and it affects people differently. The way you use the gem will mature with time. One of the most powerful ways it can help you in the short term is when the Timekeeper uses it to slow time around you. You have seen this before, but when it happens to you, do not become alarmed. When you feel the sensation beginning, you must allow the power to flow through you. Catch the wave as it comes and then continue to move in the wave of accelerated time. We will push you forward as long as you need it, or you can drop out when you wish. It is difficult to explain, but you will become accustomed to it with time."

"It is time to leave now. Good luck, Vic."

Vic nodded and bowed his head slightly, then let go of the stone. Instantly, he felt himself falling and everything around him began to spin. He couldn't tell whether he was really moving or it was just the sensation of movement, until he felt himself hit the cold, hard, earthen floor of the cave. The apprentice was there to help him up, but compared to the room he had been in, everything was so dark in the cave that he couldn't see a thing. It took some time for his eyes to fully adjust to the dim blue glow of the gems that provided the only ambient light. The apprentice helped Vic get into a sitting position against the wall of the cave where there were no gems and then the man and boy waited for Vic to regain his composure. The old man was the first to break the silence.

"Now you understand."

"Could you hear us?"

"Only the grunting and complaining at the beginning. We thought for sure you were going to drop out before you even got started."

"I almost did."

"But you didn't. That's what is important." The man brought back his ornate wooden box and opened it up. "Now you are ready for this." Inside was the leather wrist guard Vic had seen before. This time the man let him take it. He examined it as best he could in the dim light. It was beautiful indeed, and the coursite gem mounted into the leather was perfectly cut for both beauty and strength. On the back, a leather strap joined the two pieces together and was tied in a way that let it be tightened with one hand. Vic put it on and pulled the strap tight. It felt like it was custom made for him and fit perfectly.

"Thank you."

"Wear it well. If you ever lose it or damage it, come back here and we will make things right. Are you strong enough to stand? Your friend is waiting outside and you need to go."

Vic nodded and the apprentice helped him up. His legs were a little weak, but he was soon feeling more like himself again, except for a lingering tingling feeling that seemed to permeate his very being. The trio said their goodbyes in the larger room at the opening of the cave, and Vic walked outside, blinking in the sunlight and excited about the adventures that lay ahead.

19. Your Watcher Awaits

Jason was resting against the trunk of a large oak tree when Vic returned from the cave. As Vic approached, Jason motioned for him to hurry and come under the shade of the tree.

"There was a scouthawk above a few minutes ago and I don't know if it's still around. The Sentries use them as their spies in the air. They look like turkey vultures without the red head. No one I know has ever seen one up close, so that's what we call them. If you see one, run for cover because a Sentry will probably be close behind." Jason gingerly stood up and began gathering his things. "So how'd it go?"

Vic pulled back his sleeve to reveal the new wrist guard on his arm. Jason smiled, "I see it went well. Welcome to the team."

"Thanks, but now I feel like I'm walking around with a target on my back and I don't know what I'm doing yet. They said I don't have a lot of time to learn, so let's start with the training right away. You're all I've got, so what am I supposed to do now?"

"Fortunately for you, I've got that part covered. You see, the most important thing to learn is how to communicate through the gem when you're *not* in the cave. That is a key way you get your instructions and assistance, so the better you are at using it, the better off you will be. It will take practice, but you will get it with time. While you were in there, I had a chance to spend some time with the gem. I'm sure it wasn't as exciting as yours, but I did hear clearly enough to confirm that you need to take over my mission where I left off. As I suspected, you need to escort David to the festival. I'm going to stay with his family in town until my arm heals. There's someone else in town who knows how to use the gem to speed up the healing process. As you'll learn, the gem affects everyone differently. I know where to find David and I'll introduce the two of you. Together, you two need to get to the festival."

As Vic and Jason headed down the mountain, Jason explained more about how the stone worked, how battle with Sentries was different than battle with normal foes, and how best to communicate with the stone. By nightfall, they were entering Clavis, the sleepy little town that was home to David Flannery and his family. They made their way through the cobblestone streets until they stopped at a humble home near the center of town.

David's mother greeted them at the door. She was a kind woman with olive skin and dark hair. David and his father were not yet home from the foundry where David helped his father and was learning the family blacksmithing trade. She welcomed them warmly and invited them in. Vic thought it was strange that she didn't ask any questions, it was as if she knew they were coming and expected them. Once inside, she quickly noticed that Jason had been injured and the three sat down while she tended Jason's wounds.

"Looks like a nasty sword wound. You're lucky it isn't infected yet."

Jason winced as she peeled back the shreds of his shirt that were caked with dried blood. "Actually, I was fortunate to live through it."

"Were you taken by bandits?" she asked, tending to his wound but not looking up when she asked. Jason paused before

he answered, scanning David's mother for a sign of whether she
was friend or foe. At last his eyes fixed on the small gems lining
the elegant bracelet she wore on her wrist. He knew he was with
a friend.

"No. They were Sentries." She looked up at him
immediately and her eyes began to well up with tears.

"Please take good care of my son, he's only a boy." Tears
began to stream down her face. "I know he has to go, I've known
for a long time. He has a gift, we've all seen it, but I'm so afraid
for him. If they can do this to you, a trained soldier, my poor boy
won't have a chance." Her words flowed uncontrollably as her
emotion for her son poured out. "He's no fighter. His father
could fend for himself but poor David, he's more like me, and I
could never fight with anyone, I just couldn't. I wouldn't know
what to do, and neither would he."

Jason let her words rest for a moment before he answered,
"But you know he's strong, only in a different way."

The very thought of her son's unique abilities helped her to
regain her composure. "Yes, you're right. He is special. Why, he
told me once that he was even moved by the stone. He closed his
eyes sitting in one location and woke up in another. Everyone
else thought he was crazy, but I believe him. He makes a
connection that the rest of us can't."

Jason's teeth bit down hard and he clenched his chair tightly
as she poured alcohol on his wound. Vic could see he was in
intense pain, but you wouldn't have known by his reaction.
David's mother needed to air her feelings, and he let her
continue without interrupting.

"I know he's part of a greater plan, but I still wish I could go
with him. He still has so much to learn about the world. We've
taught him everything we could think of, but he's never really

been anywhere and there are so many evil people out there. Promise me you'll stay with him until he's safely back home? Promise me you will see him safely back home to me?"

"Actually, Ma'am, I'm not going. As you can see, this arm is in no condition for fighting, but Vic here will be going with him. Vic will do his absolute best to take care of David and bring him home, won't you Vic?"

"Of course I will, Mrs. Flannery," Vic replied, "I'll make sure he makes it to the festival in one piece." Vic sounded sure of himself, but inside was still wondering how he was going to be able to protect himself let alone someone else.

"I don't know what I would do without him," she continued. "He means so much to me."

"I'll take good care of your son, Mrs. Flannery," Vic assured her, "and I'll do everything I can to make sure he gets home safe."

"Thank you," she said as she finished putting new wrappings on Jason's arm.

"Don't worry Mrs. Flannery," Jason chimed in, "I'll be staying here in Clavis while I recover, and I've got Vic's seeds. He has to come back!" He smirked and patted his pack. "Now Vic, you better make sure you don't forget to bring him home if you ever want to see your seeds again!" Jason poked Vic with his good elbow.

"I won't forget," he said as he patted the same spot on his own pack, "I'm carrying a reminder with me every day."

The gentle joking helped Mrs. Flannery relax. When the bandaging was done, she looked up to Vic and said again, "Thank you."

Just then, the door flew open and Mr. Flannery came in with David right behind. They were both laughing and talking about something, but they quickly became quiet when they saw their two guests.

"You've come for David?" Mr. Flannery asked straight away. Jason nodded in the affirmative. "Son, it's time. Go grab your things."

David nodded to his father and ran off down the hall as his father had instructed. They had obviously been expecting this call, and they were prepared. David returned only seconds later with his traveling bag all packed.

"Take good care of my son, OK?" Mr. Flannery gave the boy a pat on the back. "Aw, Dad," David complained as he gave his Mom and Dad a hug.

"Now son, remember where your strengths are, you hear? Don't ever let them get near you."

"Right, Dad. I know what I'm doing."

"I sure hope so, dear," his Mother said as she caressed his temple and fussed with his coat.

"Don't worry, Mom, I'll be just fine," David tried to console his mother. When they had finished their goodbyes, he turned to Vic. "OK, I'm ready."

"Looks like you've been ready for a while," Vic replied.

David smiled, "We didn't know when you were coming, but I knew you would come. I saw you right here, in this very room, and then leaving with you, almost seven months ago. Everything since then has been getting ready so I would be prepared when you arrived. Let's go."

Vic was impressed. David had been planning for this very day for seven months? There was obviously much riding on this mission if such extensive planning had gone into making it happen. Even more amazing was what he saw. "He saw me?" Vic thought, "even yesterday I had no idea I would be here but he has known for seven months?" It made him feel guilty that he had been preparing for less than seven hours.

Vic and David headed out straightaway. As they reached the edge of town, they spotted a caravan of others who were leaving a party, and bringing the party with them. The noise and laughter of the large group would scare away any animals or attackers, so they seemed like perfect traveling companions. Vic and David didn't really introduce themselves, but stayed with the tail end of the caravan and enjoyed the safety from their numbers and torches. As they walked, Vic and David used the time to get to know each other.

"So how long have you been seeing things with the gem?" Vic asked.

"My first time was when I was eleven. My father let me pick up a gem at the county fair. A traveling salesman had one in his collection of assorted items and my father recognized it right away. The minute I touched it, I saw a stampede of buffalo coming down a hill. I didn't know what I was seeing and immediately pulled my hand away and told my Dad what I saw. He said to touch it again and see if the vision came back. I did, and saw them again, only this time it looked like they were coming up on the edge of the fairgrounds where we were. I yelled, 'Dad, they're here!' and pointed up the road. Sure enough, there was a cloud of dust quickly approaching the fairgrounds. My Dad immediately yelled 'STAMPEDE!' and the whole place ran for the hills. Seconds later, the buffalo ran through and trampled all the booths. They would have killed anyone left in the middle. Thanks to the early warning, no one was hurt, but most of the goods were destroyed. They gave me the gem as a reward for saving everyone in the fair. Ever since then, I've kept it and practiced using it. About a year later, Dad took me to the cave and I became a soldier too, like both my parents."

"Can you control what you see?"

"Not really, I can just change the scene to a different one. I've always believed Prince Renatus controls what I see. There are some things I've noticed, though. I usually see things near me first, especially if they are going to cause danger. Then the circle broadens, and I see others in danger that are relatively close to me. I have to keep using it and concentrate to see things farther away, and wait even longer to see things in the past or future. Unfortunately, those are usually so out of context that I can't tell what I'm looking at very well. I usually just write them down and hope that someday they make sense."

"Wow. What an amazing ability."

"It's neat, but sometimes it can be quite painful. I saw our family dog get killed by a mountain lion. I really loved that dog and it shook me up. Once I knew what happened, I wanted to know where. It took a while to find the spot, but once I got in the general area, it didn't take long to find his remains. It was very sad. I guess I'm glad to know what happened to him, but sometimes it's better not to know."

"So how long does it take for you to see something?"

"It used to take a while to get into focus, but now I see things right away. The biggest problem is that I have to close my eyes to see things, so I really have to stop moving and I become pretty vulnerable unless there is someone nearby to protect me. I've always known that one day I would have a protector so I could use my skills in the field, and I can't believe the day has finally come."

"Well, if I'm not mistaken, we have quite a battle up ahead. Jason said that there have been many other soldiers with orders to meet at the Harvest Festival this year. That's where we're going and where I bet your services are needed most."

The two walked for a few minutes in silence. Vic was hoping David's abilities could help him anticipate attacks, since to be honest, he was concerned about his ability to protect David and needed all the help he could get. "It sure won't hurt to have you along the way, either," Vic said as nonchalantly as he could. "Is it easy for you to check and see if there are any threats nearby?"

"Easy enough, but it probably isn't as easy as just watching for your stone to glow, don't you think?"

Vic had forgotten it did that. It was strange for him to think about it now, since the last time he saw it glow it was on someone else, and now *he* was the one wearing the stone on his arm. He turned his arm slightly to see the gem. It was dark in the moonlight, but Vic thought he could see a faint blue glow as the moonlight gleamed off its cuts.

"I guess so," Vic replied, "but this is all sort of new to me, so don't let me miss it if it starts glowing, OK?"

"New to you? You're supposed to be protecting me!" David was shocked by the comment and instantly more tense than he had been a moment before. "How long have you been a soldier in the King's army?"

"That's really two questions." Vic wanted to put David at ease, but knew he needed to tell him the truth too. "How long have I been a soldier? Since I was a boy. I probably started when I was a few years younger than you are now. How long have I been in the King's service? About one day. You see, Jason was supposed to be going with you on this trip, but he was injured last night. We were traveling together and he was taking me to the cave to meet Prince Renatus. When I did and took the pledge, he said my first assignment was to escort you to the Harvest Festival, so here we are."

"I see. So it's really your first mission too."

"Funny, I've been on so many other missions over the years that it doesn't feel like it, but in a way, you're right. Just don't laugh at me while I learn, OK?"

David laughed, "No problem, Vic. Just get me there in one piece and I won't complain about how we get there."

For the next two hours, they traveled along at the back of the caravan until the group reached its destination. It was a small cattle town that smelled of manure. Not exactly where they would have chosen to stop, but it was now the middle of the night and neither wanted to continue to travel at night without a group. They found a small inn and woke the innkeeper. Begrudgingly, he rented them a room for the night. The room wasn't much, but they would be on the road at dawn so it would have to do.

20. Caught

The morning light streamed in through Catherine's window. She had slept so soundly that she didn't remember waking up even once. She rubbed her eyes and went to the window to see for the first time what the festival grounds looked like in daylight.

As she opened her curtains, the sun wished her well as it bathed the tent city with morning light. Though people still moved around in the festival grounds, it was a much different kind of movement than the night before. Instead of frivolity and fanfare as guests wined and dined in a festive environment, a few young boys picked up trash along the main paths and vendors attempted to clean and repair their booths from the night before. It was much less glamorous now, but still had a business about it that made Catherine eager to see more of what was out there.

She dressed quickly and went down the stairs to find the others. She found James in the kitchen who explained that Lord Dramon and Adam Davidson had left early with some business to attend to. She was to get ready to leave, and they would return for her around noon. Lord Dramon planned to spend the day taking her through the rest of the festival. Realizing there was nothing for her to do right now, she sat down to have some breakfast.

James served her in the formal dining room as he would all other guests, but it felt strange to eat alone in the cavernous room, so Catherine brought her breakfast into the kitchen to eat with James and the cook. She found James helping the cook clean up the morning meal. Catherine scooted a stool over to the counter and plopped down with her plate. James stopped just long enough to smile and acknowledge her, then continued with his work. The cook was rather gruff and not at all talkative, but seemed to be glad she chose to join them. While she ate and they cleaned, she made small talk with James. They discussed the weather, the crowds for the festival, and many other matters of little consequence until the cook finished his cleanup and left James and Catherine alone in the kitchen.

When they had stopped talking for a few moments, James began again, "My lady, until the others return from their business, do you have other plans?"

"Well, no, it doesn't look like I do."

"I suggest you visit the northern gardens. They are quite beautiful this time of year and there are many places for quiet reflection. It isn't far from the house and I will come fetch you when Lord Dramon returns."

The garden sounded like a wonderful idea to Catherine, who was already tired of being cooped up in the castle. "That would be perfect," she replied. When she finished her meal, James showed her out to the rear portico. As they left the building, she realized again what a massive structure the castle really was. The large stone building wrapped around in a U-shape and from the back of the building, a high wall extended to form a second U that held the garden. The trees and bushes led through a winding path all the way to the back where a steep hillside formed natural protection for the back side of the castle. Along the sides of the path were benches that made perfect places to sit and take in the beauty of the surroundings.

James walked her as far as the first set of benches. "As long as you stay on the path, you are welcome to go wherever you like in the garden, but do not leave through the gates in the wall unless you have a protector and guide. It is dangerous out there, just as it can be in here. You deserve someone to protect you. I wish I was that person... who could take you out...but I am not..." His voice trailed off.

"Thank you James, this will be lovely."

"One more thing my lady," James paused and looked down, almost as if he was embarrassed to tell her something, "well, umm... I ...."

"Yes?" There was a tense silence while James tried to compose his thoughts, "There is something I need to ...something you need to..." until finally a look of exasperation came over his face.

"Oh, never mind. Enjoy your morning," and James scurried away back to the house. Catherine shrugged, and then turned to examine this wonderful garden.

The flowers were in full bloom and the array of colors and scents was amazing. She had seen wild flowers and beautiful meadows, but she had never been in a landscaped place of such beauty where the flowers were neatly arranged and the trees all grew in perfect order and size. She made her way to a stone bench in the middle of the garden and sat down. The sun was just peeking over the wall and she found a place in the sun where she would keep warm.

After a few minutes of relaxing, Catherine began to wonder where Lord Dramon was and what his important business was. She reached for the gem and thought this would be a good time to see what it came up with.

As she began to feel its effects, the first thing she saw was a young boy cleaning in the festival. He looked familiar to her somehow, but she couldn't place where. She watched for a few minutes as he went from booth to booth picking up trash and talking with the booth proprietors. When she had seen enough, she gave the mental "NO!" that usually changed scenes and sure enough, the picture began to change.

This scene was entirely different. She saw two warriors in light chain mail and with their swords drawn. Over their faces, they wore partial helmets that concealed most of their faces from view, but they were young and strong. They were making their way through fields in a sparse section of the forest, carefully criss-crossing a road to avoid being seen. The men then moved into what looked like the shadow of a building, and came upon a rusted iron gate. The gate was tall and arched, but made a tight fit in the building so that they could not get through. The two soldiers spoke together in what looked like a hushed but very agitated exchange. Moments later, they were off, running along the side of the building until they reached a tall ivy-covered wall. Catherine was fascinated by the operation, so she kept watching. They continued along the wall until they came to another gate that looked like the last, but unlike the previous, this one opened when pulled. As they pulled the gate open, Catherine heard a faint squeaking sound. One of the soldiers stood guard at the outside of the gate, while the other quickly ran inside.

"How interesting," she thought to herself, "I've never been able to hear anything I've seen through the gem before." The scene changed slightly and followed the soldier that had entered the gate. He was now running full speed along a path, passing row upon row of flowers and perfectly planted trees. Catherine thought it looked like he was running through a garden much like the one she was sitting in, until suddenly, she realized it WAS the garden where she was sitting and there, in the vision before her, was a young woman sitting on a bench and he was heading directly toward her!

Catherine screamed and jumped off the bench just in time to see the soldier jump right over the bench. He spun around to face Catherine with his sword still drawn. He didn't stop to catch his breath.

"Head for the back gate," he commanded. "Do you want me to carry you or do you want to run?"

Confusion and fear flooded Catherine's mind. "I can run," she replied after a slight hesitation.

"Good, then let's go." He sheathed his sword and turned to leave, but Catherine wasn't finished yet.

"But I'm not going to!" At the same time Catherine said it, she kicked him as hard as she could in the shin just above where his boots ended and screamed at the top of her lungs. He just stood there with a shocked look on his face, amazed and confused by her actions. He was still standing there when they both heard a very high pitched whistle. It was coming from the direction of the garden gate from which he had come. It was his partner warning that guards were approaching. The whistle woke the soldier from his shock and he turned and ran for the gate. In no more than three seconds, he had already covered the entire length of the garden and was just about to exit when the gate was suddenly and forcefully slammed shut with a crash. He was running so fast there was no way he could stop and he ran into it at full speed. Catherine heard a great crash and saw her attacker bounce off the gate like a rag doll and crumple to the ground. The gate was then opened from the outside and she saw a large black cloaked guard enter the garden. This figure was just like the one she had seen from her vision the night before and the red eyes and scaly arms were even more frightening in person than they had been in her vision. Right behind him was Lord Dramon and then a second large black cloaked guard. Dramon spoke to the guards in hushed tones. They responded by picking up the soldier and dragging him outside the garden through the now opened gate. As they left, two of Lord Dramon's regular guards entered and the trio began coming toward Catherine.

"Are you all right?" Lord Dramon hurried to her side.

"Yes, I think so."

"I heard you scream just as we were entering the front of the house. We came straight to the garden gate and found it open. We heard someone running toward the gate, so we slammed it to try to stop whoever it was. Obviously, it worked. I should never have left you alone."

"I can't believe I let it happen," was Catherine's reply. "I was actually using the stone and saw him coming into the garden, but I didn't realize it was me he was coming after until it was too late."

"That is why I need you to see this whole area; you must be able to recognize what you see so we are better able to defend ourselves next time."

"Yes, I think that would be a very good idea."

"For now, let's go inside and rest. Then from now on, you will stay right by my side."

The Timekeeper opened his eyes and looked up at Renatus. "They have failed, and Philip was captured. She was not prepared."

Renatus shook his head. "Did Andrew escape?"

"Yes."

"Instruct him to track Philip's location but not interfere. Andrew will lead a team to rescue him when the assault begins."

"Yes, my Lord."

"This will make things more difficult for everyone, and puts her in much greater risk. Now her life depends on Vic arriving on time. Is he still on his way?"

The Timekeeper closed his eyes for a moment and again touched the massive crystal in front of him. "Yes, for now." He put his hand back on the stone for a few more moments and then looked up.

"He has some important decisions to make."

21. Detour

When Vic opened the front door to the inn, he was hoping that the smell of manure in the air from the night before would have passed. No such luck. He looked at David and they both had the same expression, "PEW!" They were in a hurry anyway, and the smell made them pick up the pace. Neither one felt much like breakfast. Soon enough they had climbed the road leading out of the valley where the cattle, and the smell, lingered, and they were greeted by a cool refreshing breeze that brought the scent of cleaner skies up ahead.

"So how far is it to Petersburg," David asked. "That's where the Harvest Festival is, right?"

"Right. If we make good time, it's about four days from here. We could do it in two if we find some horses. I've never gone this route before, but Jason told me it is straight on this road until it ends. Sounds pretty simple to me."

"Do you think we'll have any trouble?"

"It's hard to say, but I was hoping that if we lay low we should be OK until we get closer to Petersburg."

The two walked along the road in silence for a while until they heard a coach in the distance coming from behind them.

Vic stopped and turned around the minute he heard it. "What a break! If we can catch a ride, we'll save a lot of time, even if they don't take us all the way there."

As the coach caught up to them, Vic waved to them and they slowed down. It was a rather large coach, and was well decorated, though not particularly posh. It had room for six comfortably on the inside, and room for three more on top, one next to the driver and two facing the rear. It was driven by four large horses that were obviously well fitted to their harnesses. It looked like a great potential ride.

"Interested in a few more fares?" Vic yelled up to the driver.

"Always!" The driver was a clean cut, friendly looking man with a large hat to keep out the sun and a leather vest. He appeared also to be the owner of the coach and thankfully, was in it for the money. "We got room for one on the inside and one on top with me, if that'll suit ya. Where ya headed?"

"Petersburg, for the festival."

"Well you're in luck, so are we. Two silver pieces each will take you all the way there. We'll make stops along the way, and food and lodging are on your own. You in?"

"Absolutely." Vic reached into his pouch for some money and motioned to David to get inside. "I'll take the top. I like the view as lookout better anyway."

"You won't get any complaints from me!" David climbed up the steps and opened the door. There were two happy couples and an older gentleman laughing and drinking inside. Their celebration had already begun, and David thought it would probably continue all the way to Petersburg. Not a bad way to travel, he thought to himself, and plunked himself down near the left window facing backwards. There was a bench for two facing the rear, but Vic chose the empty seat next to the driver instead.

As the driver sized him up, he commented, "Looks like I'll do well with you up here to keep a lookout."

Vic smiled. "We'll be just fine."

"Yaaah!" The driver cracked his whip and they were off.

Vic sat back in his chair and couldn't be more pleased. Things were going even better than he had planned. At this rate, they would arrive in Petersburg at least a day ahead of schedule, probably by late tomorrow, and they would be much fresher than if they had walked the whole way. He might even be able to have David use the stone to make sure they were not in any danger. It would be easier to use it on the coach than if he had been walking and had to stop every time they wanted to see something.

"So you said we will be stopping tonight? Did you have somewhere in mind?"

"Yes, we'll stop in a little town called Chesterton. It's about ten miles past Rochester and gets us over the top of the hills. The ride tomorrow is downhill for the rest of the way and should put us into Petersburg by late afternoon."

"Did you say Rochester? Will we be passing through Rochester?"

"Why yes, you know of it? I was planning on taking a rest stop there, and then heading on to Chesterton before nightfall. When we arrive in Chesterton, I'll leave everyone in the town tavern, and then pick you up in the morning at the same place. There are several places to stay in town and it is fairly remote, so no one should have a problem finding a room for the night."

Vic had never been to Rochester, but remembered the name as the town where Catherine's aunt lived, and where Catherine had gone to stay. Was this a sign that he should go to see her? It didn't matter, Vic just *had* to see her. David was in good company now, he would be just fine. Vic could probably even meet Catherine in Rochester, and then rent a horse to meet David in Chesterton and be there before morning when they left. Maybe Catherine would even come along. Vic simply couldn't pass up the opportunity to see Catherine if he had the chance. If something happened at the festival, he might never get to see her again. She was his closest friend and he had to tell her about the cave, his mission, and what he had become.

"You mind if I take a little longer in Rochester and then catch up with you tomorrow morning at the tavern at Chesterton? There's someone I need to see while I'm in Rochester. It shouldn't take me long, but I'll miss that leg of the journey."

"Suit yourself, we ride at half past dawn, so as long as you're there, you can come along. Don't be late, or I'll sell your seat. It's a pretty good view from up here!"

What an interesting turn of events; Vic would even get to see Catherine on this trip! He fondly remembered back to when they had talked that night under the stars. He wanted so much to make things right with her, but he still didn't know what to say. In any case, he couldn't say it from hundreds of miles away and wasn't about to miss this opportunity. Unfortunately, his own promise to David's mother kept ringing in his ears. He committed to stay with David all the way to the festival.

"Would you mind making sure my traveling companion finds a place for the night? He hasn't been out much. I'll probably catch up with him before he even leaves the tavern after dinner but just in case, can you keep an eye on him for me?"

The driver looked at Vic a little surprised, but conciliatory, "Sure, I'll make sure he doesn't get stuck at the tavern." At that point, laughter came from the carriage below and the two heard David's voice as he told a story to the other riders. The driver continued, "...but it looks to me like that boy can take care of himself just fine."

Vic was relieved. David would be taken care of, and he could spend the evening making things right with Catherine.

The rest of the trip to Rochester seemed to fly by. Vic's thoughts were far away as he remembered everything he could about Catherine. She had pierced his very soul and he couldn't help but think about her. Finally, they arrived in Rochester and everyone disembarked.

"How was your trip?" David asked Vic when they had both disembarked.

"Bumpy, but good. That driver's a real character and the view was nice. How about you?"

"I don't know if this group will ever make it to the festival. They've had so much to drink already they could stop to party right here and wouldn't know they hadn't arrived!"

"That's what I thought. I heard the laughing once in a while. Did you get a chance to use the gem at all? I would love to make sure there is nothing dangerous around."

"No, I haven't yet. Got some sleep on the way, but that's about it." David looked around to see if they were alone. The stage was just departing to a nearby stable to feed and rest the horses before they got underway again and the other passengers were wandering into town to get in some shopping and eating before the next leg of their journey. "You never can be too careful, even with a protector." David smiled at Vic, and then closed his eyes and pulled his hands up to his mouth as if he wanted to blow into them for warmth on a cold day. It was then that Vic noticed for the first time where David kept his stone. It was on a ring he wore, and when he brought his hands to his face, he gently put one hand on top of the ring and covered it up, then closed his eyes. Vic had never seen this kind of thing before and was fascinated to watch. David's eyelids flickered a little, like someone who was having a dream. After about thirty seconds, he lifted his hand and opened his eyes.

"Nothing to worry about. There are quite a few people in the town square and a few riders down the road, but nothing that looks threatening."

"You saw all that?"

"Sure, and quite a bit more. I saw a blacksmith working in his foundry, three children throwing rocks into a stream and a dog barking at a bird's nest. None looked important, and so I just moved on. That's the way it works. More than half the challenge is simply sifting through the images and deciding what is worth looking at and what isn't. It can also be a challenge interpreting where and when the scene you see occurred. There are always clues that can help you interpret. For example, a scene at a different time of day can be the first clue. If the lighting is different, then you know it was a different time period than now. Other clues help you sift through things but it is still a challenge. I still wonder why I see certain things, but in my opinion, it is not near as important to know what everything means as it is to recognize what is really important."

"That is truly amazing." Vic had never heard or seen anything like this before. "I noticed that you just barely rested one hand over your ring and that is all it took to bring on the visions. Is it that sensitive?"

"Yes, it really is. If I make more contact than that it has a very serious effect on me. At one point I was even transported to a different location! I was curious one day and spun the ring around on my finger and then made a fist. When I woke up, I was out in the woods about two miles from my house with a headache like you wouldn't believe. For a while I thought I had gone into a trance and staggered out there, until my mother told me that she had found my room locked from the inside and when I didn't answer the door, they came in through the window to see if I was all right. I wasn't there, so they started looking for me and found me waking up and in a stupor. It was not a fun experience, and that is the last time I ever gripped the stone like that."

"I know a little about what you mean. They had me grab the stone in the cave. It didn't have near that much of an effect on me; it must be something in your blood."

"I suppose. Whatever the reason, I can tell you with some certainty that there are no immediate threats around us right now."

"Well that's good to hear, because I was thinking about taking a little detour. This girl I used to know, well, that I was pretty close to, is staying here in Rochester. I would love to stop by and see her for a few minutes before going on. The driver said he would be stopping in a little town about ten miles up the road for the evening. I was thinking maybe…"

"I could go on up ahead without you and you'll catch up tonight?"

"You read minds too?"

"It hardly takes a mind-reader to know that you won't want a third wheel around when you're trying to catch up with an old girlfriend! Sure, I'll be fine. I'll tell the bartender at the tavern to let you know where I'm staying. Just meet up with me in the room when you get there and we'll continue tomorrow morning together."

"That would be really great. She means a lot to me and I really want to see her if I can."

"OK, go on and find your friend. I'll hang out here in the city square and then be on the stage to Chesterton in a few minutes." David gave Vic a big pat on the back, pushed him off toward the town square and yelled to him as he left, "Give her a big kiss for me."

Vic shot back a grin and then disappeared into the crowd.

22. Knowing the Truth

Once Catherine had recovered her composure and the guards finished sweeping the area to be sure there were no other attackers, Lord Dramon came into the parlor where she was sitting.

"Do you feel strong enough to get going? I would very much like for you to see the area before this evening and we have much to cover."

"Yes, I'm feeling better now." Her hands had stopped shaking, but she couldn't help thinking about the confused look on her attacker's face. The more she thought about it, the more she thought he seemed surprised when she screamed, almost as if he expected her to be glad when he arrived. Why would he be surprised that she screamed? Isn't that what he should have expected? She didn't understand, but that look on his face stuck with her. Maybe it would make more sense after they had interrogated the guard. She decided to ask Lord Dramon about it.

"Did I see that you were able to capture my attacker?" The two walked outside of the castle into a large courtyard where the stages and horses were kept. Four guards were coming toward them with two extra horses in tow.

"Yes, we were. He should provide us with some valuable information."

"That's what I was hoping. I would like to know why he was trying to kidnap me. I've never seen him before and I can't imagine why someone would attack me."

"I expect that word of your talents has spread more quickly than we anticipated, or it may simply be one of my enemies trying to take someone close to me. You will find that many are jealous of my power and would take it if they could. By harming those close to me, they believe they can control me. It will not be the last time rogue elements try to attack us, so we must always stay on our guard. That is why I find your talents so valuable. If you can help anticipate the next attack, my guards can stop anything. It is the element of surprise that gives them their greatest advantage, and that is what you can take away from them." Catherine remembered how foolish she felt when she realized that the vision she had been watching was her own attacker. She had done nothing about it, but she wasn't going to let that happen again. Newly inspired to prepare for the next time, she was eager to observe every detail of the festival.

They mounted their horses and rode out of the large gates on the side of the courtyard. The guards turned left into the tent city, leading them up into the part of the loop where they hadn't been the night before. Catherine looked closely at everything she saw, the signs, the booths, the trees and the hills in the background. She studied everything that might give her a clue as to where the visions she saw could be coming from. The group marched on in silence, slowing only when something blocked their path or for Lord Dramon to point out something to Catherine.

After the better part of an hour, they returned to the center of the festival again, this time on the far leg of the figure eight from the castle. Instead of turning inward, they turned outward and exited the tent path through an opening Catherine had not noticed before. Now they were on the backside, where the world was much less glamorous.

Pack animals were tethered to tent stakes and supplies were strewn everywhere. Craftsmen were repairing or restocking their wares and servants sat in corners eating what they could get their hands on before the evening crowds returned and they would work well into the night. Debris was everywhere and birds flew in to pick through the garbage for their own dinner.

"I'm sorry you have to see this side of the festival," Dramon said to Catherine, "but if there is an attack, this is where they will most likely strike so it is something you must recognize."

Catherine nodded and kept examining everything. She made a mental note of every image should could. There was really no protection for the back side of the tents, so it made sense that this is where an enemy would attack first. The field where the festival was situated was large and the festival was tiny in comparison, so there was a considerable amount of flat ground between the festival tents and the hills and trees in the distance. Previously plowed for crops, the earth was mostly thick soft dirt with long straight furrows that ran the length of the field. Though it had few large rocks or obstacles, the thick soft dirt would make it difficult to run through and impossible for a carriage to drive on. A horse could probably make it through, but not without considerable effort. As a result, the guards protecting the tent city could see their attackers coming from this side for quite a distance before the attack arrived. The field formed a sort of natural barrier around the festival, even though there appeared to be nothing between the hills and the tents.

As they rode around the very top of the festival tent path, they came to a wooden tower with a guard in it. Unlike the others, this one was an archer with both a traditional bow and crossbow at his side. The platform of the tower was about fifteen feet high and gave him a decent vantage point to see the area, and the height also gave some protection from attackers. He saluted Lord Dramon as they passed by.

The castle side of the tent path was very different. Much closer to the hillside, there was a road that ran along the edge of the hills between the tent path and the hillside. As they came around the corner, Catherine could see the castle wall in the distance, and as they got closer, she began to recognize the images she saw when she was sitting in the castle garden.

"This is where they came from."

Lord Dramon ordered the guards to halt. "You saw this area?"

"Yes. I saw them running from tree to tree along the side of the road until they came to that gate up there. They tried the gate but it was locked. Then they moved around the back to the other gate."

The group began progressing again. As they rounded the back side of the castle, they came to the second garden gate.

"This is where they came into the garden."

"How did they get through the gate?"

"It looked like it was slightly open, but it was hard for me to tell, the angle was not good."

"Hmm. We shall have to look into that," Lord Dramon replied.

They finished working their way around the castle perimeter, and then continued around to the festival entrance. By the time they returned to the castle, they were all tired and hungry, and the real festivities were just starting. Lord Dramon advised that they would be eating at the festival tonight and would be leaving in half an hour. Catherine decided that was just enough time to return to her room to freshen up before leaving, so she headed upstairs. Even though the sun was still setting in the western sky, only a little light came into the hallway at this time of day and the lamps were not yet lit. After the attack earlier, she was a little nervous about the darkness. She paused at the end of the hall, "C'mon Catherine, get a hold of yourself. There's nothing here." Who could get to her inside the castle in the upstairs hallway? She continued down the hall to her room and was relieved when she finally arrived. Just as she grabbed the handle to her bedroom door she felt someone grab her arm. She jumped, and turned quickly. She was startled to find the butler James.

"Miss Catherine," he began, "I'm sorry if I alarmed you, but I absolutely must speak with you and there is little time."

"By all means, James, please come inside." Catherine opened the door to her room and they both entered. The flickering light from her fire and the setting sun through her window gave the room a strange orange glow. Just the presence of the light calmed her nerves and they went into her room and sat in the large overstuffed chairs in front of the fireplace. As the light reached James face, she could see that he was quite concerned and not at all himself.

"Miss Catherine, I've been weak, and did a terrible thing today. It has been so long since I was asked to do anything truly important, when the time came, I was simply too afraid to do my duty. Now the life of a good friend is in serious risk and I must do what I can to make things right. Do you understand what I'm saying?"

Catherine processed his words for a moment, but really had no idea what he was talking about. She could tell he was upset, so she tried to use her most gentle tone when she replied, "I'm sorry James, but I really don't understand yet. Maybe if you explain it again, I will."

James took a deep breath and swallowed hard. "This morning in the garden, I was supposed to tell you. I was supposed to explain everything. I brought you there as instructed, but I got scared. I couldn't tell you. I didn't know what you were going to think, so I went back inside and hoped things would turn out for the best, but they didn't. They went terribly wrong, and it's all my fault. Oh, Catherine, whatever am I to do?"

"James, what are you trying to say?" Her voice started to rise as she asked. "Did you have something to do with the attack this morning?" James was such a kind and gentle man, she found it very hard to believe he was a traitor, or had anything to do with something so sinister, but she was starting to get concerned.

"Catherine, I was supposed to tell you. I was supposed to explain that the soldiers would be coming to *rescue* you and that they were friends you could trust. Oh, Catherine, it was such a simple task, but I was afraid. I was afraid of what you would say, what Lord Dramon would do to me if he found out. Mr. Davidson would be forced to fire me for sure, and then what would my family do?"

"What did you say? You said *rescue* me? From what? What in the world were they coming to *rescue* me from?"

"Why, Lord Dramon, of course. With your amazing abilities, you must have seen his true character by now, haven't you? He is very powerful, but intensely evil. I have watched him come here every year for eight years, and each year his plans are more sinister and more grandiose. This year is rumored to be his biggest plot ever, and you play a key part. I don't understand it yet, but I know that we need to stop him and the best way to do that was to take you away. Don't you see, Catherine, you have the ability to stop him by yourself. He trusts you, and now that

I've failed, you have to do it. When the soldiers come back, you have to let them get to him. That is the only way to make things right now. They may be able to send someone else to help take you away from here, but now that I've ruined the best plan I may have sealed both our fates."

Catherine's head was swimming. Could Lord Dramon be evil? Yes, she knew that he was at least ruthless. She had heard that much herself on the coach on the way here. He was powerful, of course, she saw how the people cowered before him, but that didn't necessarily make him evil, did it? Could she betray him and let the soldiers reach him without her warning? No. She would be essentially killing a man in cold blood and that was not something she thought she could do.

"It was you who opened the gate, wasn't it?"

"Yes, it was me. That was supposed to be your escape route. Oh, Catherine, can you ever forgive me?"

She was still too confused by everything to answer, but she knew that James only had her best interests at heart. Maybe he had been deceived by strangers. In any case, he obviously felt terrible for what he had done and her heart went out to him. She reached out and grabbed his hand.

"James, I really don't know what to think right now. You need to give me some time to think about everything you've told me. I won't tell Lord Dramon anything about our conversation, and you will keep it a secret too, won't you?"

"Oh, of course Miss Catherine, but there isn't time! Tonight, barons from all across the western kingdom are coming here. Tomorrow night, they are scheduled to meet at the center table in the festival. Mr. Davidson has asked me to make arrangements for everyone, so I know it to be true. Lord Dramon's plan will take shape tomorrow, and he must be stopped tonight. There is no more time or I wouldn't have come to you like this!"

Catherine was starting to get frustrated with this conversation. What was she supposed to do? She was just along for the ride. James wanted her to harm someone who had been kind to her, she just didn't see how she could do it, and this pressure was not what she needed. This time, she spoke more firmly.

"James, I don't know what I'm going to do, but thank you for telling me these things. Please don't do anything you will be sorry for later. I'm sure everything will work out just fine." Catherine rose from her chair and walked to the door. "I think you should leave now."

"Of course, Miss Catherine." James obligingly rose from his chair and headed for the door with his head down. As he walked by, a slight glimmer at his waistline caught her eye. It was his pocket watch, and it seemed to have a sizeable stone mounted on the outside of the casing.

"Wait, James, that gem you have there, on your pocket watch, is that coursite?"

"Why yes, Miss Catherine, I'm glad you saw it."

"What business do you have carrying around a stone like that? Do you see things in the gem too?"

"No, Miss Catherine, that isn't what I use it for. In fact, I clearly should use it more often. Someday when we have more time, I'll explain. For now, know that the gem is useful for many more things than you are yet aware of. Please be safe."

"I will," she replied as she showed him out the door and locked it behind him. The hallway was well lit now by lamps, and it reminded her that Dramon would be calling any minute to leave for their evening meal. She hurried to change her clothes, and spent a few seconds fixing her hair and washing her face and hands. When she was finished, she rushed downstairs to the parlor where she found Lord Dramon impatiently pacing.

"Catherine, you're late." His face was stern and cold, a very different look than she was used to seeing.

"I'm sorry, Lord Dramon, the time escaped me."

"I do not appreciate being kept waiting, even by a beautiful woman."

The compliment was flattering, even though given as a scold.

"It will not happen again," she said, and bowed slightly. Dramon's face changed and returned to his usually cordial smile.

"Very good. We shall be off." The pair headed to the festival and soon found themselves immersed in the sights, sounds and smells of the evening.

Throngs of people were everywhere; even more than the night before. Catherine made out dialects from at least three other regions. She had never seen such a variety of life in one place, and there could be no better time to be at the festival. Dramon spared no expense to show Catherine a good time. Any game she wanted to play, any food she wanted to try, any musician to hear or drink to sample, all were hers. Finally, after they had spent several hours enjoying all the festival had to offer, Dramon took Catherine to the watchman's tower they had seen earlier. He motioned to the nearby guards and they promptly lifted a ramp to the platform so Dramon and Catherine could easily walk up. Unlike the guard, who was facing into the blackness of the great unknown, Dramon and Catherine held the rail facing toward the festival. From there, they could take in the whole scene.

"Have you enjoyed the evening?" Dramon asked Catherine as they both gazed over the bustling festival.

"Oh, of course! It has been wonderful, like nothing I've ever done before."

"Catherine, there is nothing about this place that I don't control. I've seen every part, and made most of it come about. I'm the real architect of this place, though Adam might say otherwise. He would have been nothing but a two-bit farmer with a small town market if it wasn't for me. I brought him thrill and excitement, and that brought the people. Now the festival is known across the land, but it is not all fun and games. There is much danger here and the truth is, you wouldn't have had near as much fun if you hadn't been at my side. They know me here, and if you are with me, you're treated like royalty. With me, there is nothing you cannot have, and no one who can hurt you. This is my domain, and soon it will stretch from here to the Southern Sea. I want you by my side always. Will you stay with me here at the castle for the rest of the festival, and then come to live at my estate when it is over? You will be my special assistant, and maybe someday, something more..."

Catherine didn't know what to think. Was this some kind of proposal? She certainly had enjoyed her evening, but wasn't ready to make any kind of life-long commitment. After everything James had said and what she had seen and heard, she had some serious reservations about Dramon's character. She could not afford to fall out of his good graces, but wasn't ready to leave all her friends and family yet either.

"I'm flattered," she said as she could feel herself blushing, "and I will certainly stay with you through the end of the festival, but then after that, I need to return to Rochester to see my aunt and cousin again, and then back to my family in

Mayport. There are many loose ends I would need to tie up before leaving everything I have ever known to join you." Loose ends seemed to be a good way to describe Vic, but she was really just looking for a good excuse not to have to make her decision with Dramon now. She waited on pins and needles for his answer, hoping not to arouse his anger. She had seen his temper before and did not want to see it again.

Dramon nodded and turned back toward the lights of the tent city, "A sensible choice, as always; exactly what I should have expected. We will enjoy ourselves through the festival and then I will have my coach take you to Rochester, but I cannot wait for your answer forever. If you are not willing to join me, I will find another. Please consider my offer and when you decide, write me and I will send for you." Even though he said he would find another if she wasn't willing, his tone showed he didn't think there was the slightest possibility in his mind that she would say no. It was almost as if that option wasn't really available to her at all.

"Thank you for understanding, and for the most generous offer." A cool breeze passed through them that made her shiver. Dramon noticed the cold and put his cloak around her.

"It is time for us to go," he said as he signaled one of the guards to bring the ramp back up. "Tomorrow will be an important day and we need our rest."

23. The Enchantress

A few minutes after Vic disappeared into the crowd at Rochester, David was back on the stage and heading toward Chesterton. Vic found no such luck. His evening kept getting more and more disappointing. First he went to the dress shop where Catherine worked, but it was closed. Next, he went to Catherine's aunt's house, which was almost never vacant. It too was as quiet as a tomb. Everyone in the tavern knew of Catherine and her cousin Bethany, but no one had any idea where she was. No one had seen her around for the past few days. When it started getting late, Vic was fortunate to find a rancher who had a place in both Rochester and Chesterton and rented a horse for a one way trip to Chesterton. He was feeling guilty for having left David alone, and all for nothing since Catherine wasn't even there.

The trip by horse took longer than Vic had expected. Thankfully there was a full moon so the horse could see the road, but there were several unmarked turnoffs that made him stop and wonder which way to go. Several times he took the wrong road and had to backtrack. By the time he arrived at the tavern, the doors were long since locked and closed. He pounded on the innkeeper's door, only receiving a gruff yell to "go away" in return. This detour was obviously a big mistake. Vic found the rancher's stables and tied his horse up outside, then walked out to a hill that gave him a clear view of the front of town. It was rocky on the ground so it didn't make for a very nice place to sleep, but he would make the most of it. Vic took a drink from the river, chewed on a few bites of jerky, and then sat down under a tree to try and get some sleep. As he adjusted his bag to use as a makeshift pillow, he felt the sack of seeds inside he had purchased at Lucid Peak. He was glad to have something malleable to use for his head, but it reminded him how far off course he was. He should be delivering the seeds to Catherine's father. He should be protecting David. He wished he was with Catherine. Instead, he was alone trying to get comfortable on the cold hard dirt. If he had found Catherine and Aunt Mabel he could have at least sent word to Catherine's father about why he was delayed. Instead, all the time and effort he had spent trying to find Catherine was a complete waste. Hopefully morning would come quickly, and David would be fine.

David wasn't fine. He turned the corner and dove into the shadows. His lungs burned as he tried to suck in enough air to run again. He could hear her calling his name as she ascended behind him. There was nowhere to go but up, so up he went. It was a dead end, but hopefully not literally. He was trying to think clearly, but knew he was in a panic. Where in the castle was he? By the number of stairs and the gradually narrower circle, he guessed he must be in the western tower. That was a problem. Though some of the towers had passageways onto the castle wall, and some had outside stairs there was no other outlet on this one and no other way out. He couldn't face her again; her power was too great.

The last time he looked into her eyes he thought he would never be able to look away. He could feel the soul being sucked out of him. He had heard of her victims before, some said they became drones that did her bidding. Others said she kept them in her dungeon and used them as slaves. In any case, they disappeared. All were probably young and naïve at one time, strong men who thought they could overcome her gaze. Now they were gone, and she was coming for him. If only he had realized where he was a little sooner, maybe he could have avoided this whole mess. It all began shortly after he arrived at the tavern.

Everything changed when she walked in the door. She was so beautiful every male in the place was looking for her attention. She was gorgeous, and she knew it, and she knew how to use her seductive power. She casually circled the room, greeting, flirting and teasing everyone she wished, until she came right over and sat down next to David. He was only passing through, what did she want from him? She said that she had a large home that was always filled with travelers and offered him a room for the night. He couldn't take his eyes off her, and before he knew it, they were in her carriage rounding the last corner to the castle, and what a castle it was.

Against the evening skyline, it towered over everything else in the countryside. It had a wide entryway with the gates propped open. Flowers lined the path and you could see straight into the courtyard, where a footman was waiting for any who would come in. A small wooden sign by the front gate read "Visitors Welcome." The fine calligraphy on aged wood had obviously been there for many years. There were quite a few horses tethered in the stables just inside the castle wall, and there were several coaches in the courtyard. Obviously, others had accepted her invitation as well. This should make for an interesting evening.

As the beautifully ornate main doors to the castle swung open, David was greeted by the sounds and smells of food, drink and frivolity. All present were in high spirits and having a grand time. Beyond the entry and coat room David was escorted into a cavernous dining room. Around the entire perimeter were long banquet tables laden with a huge feast. In the middle, guests danced to the music of minstrels that strolled the room. Many seats were taken, but many were empty as well, and all were eating their fill. Luscious displays of fruit and vegetables, venison, turkey, fish and beef, fresh baked pastries and breads adorned the lavishly decorated tables. Everything looked wonderful, and it was all available for the taking. "Rest and enjoy yourself, David," she said as she motioned to the tables. After a long day of traveling, David was famished. She didn't have to offer twice.

After several helpings of everything that looked good, the day began to wear on him, and his eyelids grew heavy. His gracious hostess had been working the room here in much the same fashion she had at the tavern; enjoying everyone's company as much as they enjoyed her attention. When she came around to David's spot, she leaned over his shoulder from behind and whispered in his ear, "Would you like to see your room now?" Her scent was intoxicating and her voice inviting. "Yes, please," he replied. David bid his new friends goodnight and excused himself from the table. Together they left the noise of the festivities behind them and began down the halls of the great castle.

The hallway was lined with beautiful artwork and weapons of war. "Who are the people in the portraits?" David asked. "Guests," she replied. Before he could ask for more specifics, she stopped and motioned to one of the doors. "Here we are," she said as she opened a tall doorway into a very large bedroom. The room was clean and artfully decorated, with a fire raging in the corner, large dark wood armoire and dresser, beautiful paintings on the walls and a tall canopy bed with a thick down comforter.

"Please, make yourself at home," she said as she helped him remove his coat. He took off his side bag and placed it on the beautifully crafted side table near the door.

Just as he was about to bid her good night, she grabbed his hand. David turned to face her and looked into her beautiful green eyes. "Won't you join me for a few minutes in my room? I have something I would love to show you." Her face was so soft and her expression so alluring he could not resist. As he opened his mouth to decline, he heard himself say, "Of course," and then she turned to lead him out. She continued to hold his hand, and looked back as she reached the door. "Come along" she said. And he did.

With every step, her enchantment over him grew stronger. They turned back down the same hallway, and continued farther into the castle, away from the banquet hall. The sounds of laughter grew fainter and the light of the wall torches became accented by moonlight that streamed in through high windows above. At the end of the hall was a grand entrance, double doors of massive proportions that seemed to stretch to the sky. As she approached, two guardsmen with spears turned to open the doors. Just before the guard's shoulders covered the center of the doors David caught a glimpse of an emblem – a great seal that marked the doors and he froze. He knew that seal and instantly his heart filled with dread. The hair on the back of his neck stood straight up and suddenly her hand in his felt cold as ice.

This was Widow's Castle. How could he have missed it? All the signs were there, but he didn't see them! He knew what it looked like, and knew that there was a beautiful woman who enticed men to her castle, and that they never returned. That was the seal on her door, and he was in her castle! Two steps more and it may have been too late. It already may be too late. He stopped cold and dropped her hand.

"David, what's wrong? Come with me." She looked deep into his eyes and put her hand on his cheek. Her hands were so soft, her eyes so dreamy and the magic of her enchantment so strong. He couldn't break her gaze and felt himself being drawn in. Fortunately, he had already realized the danger that surrounded him and knew that he was about to make a huge mistake. He closed his eyes tight and spun around. Now all he could do was run.

For some reason, the hallway was no longer straight. He was not sure whether they had taken turns while he was under her spell, or if the hallway had actually changed while he was distracted, but he immediately knew he was lost. He ran as fast as he could. He didn't care where he was going, as long as it was away from her. First the hall turned left, then right, then left again. It was like a maze. Suddenly, he was in a large parlor with stairs on the other side. Stairs could be good, maybe they led to a balcony where he could get out.

She was calling to him, "David, why did you leave so suddenly? There's nothing to be afraid of...."

He ran up the first flight of stairs and dove into the shadows. It was the Western Tower.

Vic awoke with a jolt. His adrenaline was pumping but he didn't know why. His hand went to his sword next to him. It was still there. It was cold in the dampness of the night, but it was there. He looked around. There was no one in sight, and not a sound in the forest. The moon was high in the sky, which meant it was sometime in the middle of the night. Why had he awoken so suddenly? Something was wrong. Very wrong. He glanced all around, staring into the dark shadows of the trees around him. There was nothing anywhere. Everything was completely quiet. Then out of the corner of his eye he caught the glow. The gem in his wrist guard was glowing white hot. He immediately got out from under his cloak and swung it onto his back. He struggled to remember what Jason had told him about how to communicate with Prince Renatus through the stone. He had never actually done it before, but fortunately, Jason's instructions came back to him. He went down on one knee, closed his eyes, and grabbed the stone in his wrist guard.

At first he wondered what would happen. Jason had told him that sometimes the message took some time to come, sometimes the voice was distant, and sometimes it did not come at all. But this time it was immediate, clear, and urgent. "Get up. Go to the Widow's Castle. Western Tower. Go NOW."

Vic could feel the urgency in the message and he had this sinking feeling that the urgency was about David. He wanted to listen longer and revel in the fact that he had just heard a message through his stone for the first time, but he had no time to waste. He jumped up and started running toward the main road.

Vic had done work in this area before, so he knew of Widow's Castle on the outskirts of town. He also knew better than to ever go there! The stories he had heard about the castle and its mistress made him sure of only one thing: he should avoid it at all costs. Now he was heading straight there!

A run at night through the cool night air was usually not a problem for Vic, but this time something was different. He began to get the sensation that he was running under water. His legs seemed to be growing heavier and heavier as he ran. At first, he thought maybe he was getting sick until he began to feel the same kind of resistance to his arms swinging. Everything was putting pressure on him as he ran until finally, it felt like an intense wind was pushing on him and trying to slow him down. Whatever it was that was trying to weigh him down, he wasn't going to let it stop him. David was in trouble, and it was because of Vic's own selfish tangent. Vic kept pushing harder and harder against this force until finally he noticed that the gem on his arm was glowing even brighter than before.

"Relax and ride the wave!" He suddenly remembered what Jason had told him about time shifting. How could he relax while he was running at full speed? He didn't know how to do it, but he knew that is exactly what he needed to do. Without even slowing down, he stopped pushing against the force that was trying to hold him back. He was still running, but began to relax; like running down a gentle hill and all you need to do is keep gravity from taking you too fast. As he lengthened his stride and felt his body relax, everything around him began to feel more like a picture than reality. There was no one around for him to watch and it was too dark to see many details in the nearby forest, but he could tell that everything around him was moving slower. With each step he took, he sensed himself getting farther ahead, or everything around him was falling farther behind, depending on your point of view. Each step still felt like running, but through a giant portrait where everything around was in still motion and you were moving among them. It was the strangest sensation he had ever experienced, but it was hard for him to enjoy the experience when he knew David's life was at stake.

The night sky was cold, and by now he was moving so fast that his nose and ears grew numb and his eyes watered from the wind. Even as he left the edge of town, everything was quiet. Not a soul moved about and all the lights in the farmhouse windows were out. He came around the final bend and saw his destination looming large in front of him, and he was approaching fast!

The main gates to Widow's Castle were sealed tight, so he raced by them without even slowing down. Vic kept right on running around to the back of the castle, to the place where he could see over the wall and up into the Western Tower.

The tower was set back in the courtyard and was much taller than the castle wall, but the angle just allowed a passerby to look into the tower window from about twenty feet back. Vic ran straight to the spot from which he could see into the tower window and stopped cold. What he didn't anticipate was the sensation he felt when he entered back into regular time. The "wave" he had been running with hit him from behind with the same force as the resistance he had felt earlier. The impact almost knocked him off his feet and it pushed him several steps forward. He was able to recover his balance and take a few steps back, but it knocked the wind out of him. Stop gradually - a good thing to remember for future reference.

Now what should he do? He was here, but where was David, and what was he supposed to do next? He was staring intently at the sliver of light coming from the tower window when, for a brief second, he saw the profile of a face in the window. It was gone so fast it took a few seconds for him to realize it was David.

What was he doing in there? He knew better than this! He shouldn't have been anywhere near Widow's Castle. Vic felt like kicking himself, "and if I had done my job, he wouldn't be!" Vic was sure of it; David was in that tower, and he was in trouble. Vic looked up and down the wall. There were no openings except the back gate, and it was sealed just as tightly as the front.

Vic could try to find a way to get in, but David was in trouble. If he attempted to find another entrance it would be too late. David had to get out of there, but how? It took only a second for the idea to come to him. David's ring was the answer. If he grabbed it tightly, he could teleport himself right out of there. Though it might be painful and he didn't know where he would end up, any place was better than where he was. David's face appeared in the window again, and this time Vic got a better look. The panic on his face made it clear. He was already under her spell and his mind was clouded.

"Use your ring!" Vic shouted. His voice echoed against the wall, and sounded like an explosion in the still night sky. David would never hear him from so far away, but the castle guards certainly would. Vic had to do something else. David needed a wake up call; a message from the outside. How could he get David a message? There was no time. Vic saw another figure cross the window. It was the Widowmaker.

Think fast, Vic, think fast. An arrow, that's how he could help. But how could he hit her? The chances were slim to none from this distance, and even if he hit her, she would probably survive the hit and the damage to David would already have been done. Shooting to kill wouldn't work, but he had another idea.

Up against the castle wall was a lean-to shed that was used by those arriving or leaving the castle who wanted to tend to their animals. Somehow he knew there would be a bow and arrow there. He got to the shed doors and with one swift blow from his sword, the lock clanked to the ground in a blue flash of light. He pulled the door open and there they were. On a peg hanging against the wall was a bow and one arrow. Only one arrow??? It would have to do. He grabbed the bow and arrow and headed back to the spot were he could see into the window.

Vic quickly began to rifle through his pouch. He found some silver coins, a few pieces of jewelry he had won, some jerky he carried for emergencies, and oh yeah, what's this? A crumpled up piece of parchment he had picked up on the road last week. It was trash by all accounts, but for some reason he had felt compelled to pick it up. Now he unrolled it for the first time. It said "SIX EARRINGS, SIX PENCE". Vic read it again. It had what he needed.

Quickly, Vic tore off the excess parts of the note, leaving only the word "RING" from the middle and wrapped it around the head of the arrow. He strung the bow, aimed straight for the window, pulled back with all his might and released. Twang. The bow bounced back and the arrow was off, whizzing through the night sky. To Vic's amazement, it sailed straight through the window and stuck fast into the wood paneling on the opposite wall. Was he too late? Did the message get through? It was too far to see clearly, and Vic heard nothing. All he could do now was wait.

As David reached the top of the stairs, he knew he was in trouble. No matter how fast he ran, her voice sounded like she was just around the corner, and gaining. He was at the end of the road: a small, round room at the top of the tower. He looked around for a weapon. A sword, a dagger, a chair, anything would work, but there was nothing. The room was bare. Other than the wood lined walls, there was nothing in this room at all. Nothing but, a window!

His excitement for a split second was almost overwhelming. He ran for the window. "I don't care how high it is, I'm jumping," he thought as he ran across the room. But reality was much more sobering. It must have been 75 feet straight down onto the cobblestone courtyard. There was no way he would ever survive the jump. His excitement turned to dread as he heard her voice close in behind him. "David, come back with me…"

There was no place to go; nothing else to do. How could he possibly get himself out of this one? She rounded the last corner and looked him straight in the eye. He was caught and he knew it. Her gaze began draining the fight right out of him. Just as he was about to agree to anything she wanted, an arrow whizzed by and stuck fast in the wall. Under the arrow was a note, and on it there was only one word. "RING."

His ring! How could he have been so stupid! David pulled the ring around backwards in his hand so the gem faced in, and then squeezed the tightest fist he possibly could. The result was instantaneous, and David blacked out.

Fortunately, Vic didn't have to wait long. About ten seconds later, which seemed like an eternity at the time, Vic saw a flash of blue light come from the tower window. David was gone. He knew it. Vic had an inexplicable sense of peace, and the stone was dimming back to its ordinary soft blue translucence. The job was done and David was safe. Now it was time to go find him.

Vic went back down on one knee and put his hand over the coursite in his wrist guard. This time, he didn't hear a message right away and what he sensed was not as clear. Then all at once, Vic knew where David was. He got up and started running back to town, back to the tree where he had been sleeping just a few minutes before. This time, he ran like normal, without any enhancement, and it took forever! As he approached, there was David, passed out in the same spot where Vic had been sitting earlier. Vic checked him out and he was breathing normally, like he was fast asleep. His face was a little scratched, but he had no other obvious injuries. Vic wanted to wake him to make sure he was OK, but on second thought, decided it might be best to let him sleep. Vic lay down beside him and covered David with his cloak. It was cold and slightly damp on the ground, but it felt good to finally be able to relax. It was early morning by now and dawn would arrive sooner than he liked.

24. On Target

When Vic woke up, David was already sitting up and eating some jerky quietly next to him. Vic immediately checked the road where the coach would be pulling up. There was no sign of it and, though it was past dawn, he surmised that they hadn't missed the stage yet. Vic sat up and turned to David. He looked depressed, but Vic didn't really know what to say. He was so ashamed for having left him he wouldn't be surprised if David said he wanted to go straight home. David finally broke the silence.

"You shot that arrow, didn't you?"

Vic nodded slowly.

"I can't believe I got myself into that mess. I KNEW about Widow's Castle. My father had told me the story, and it was exactly like he said. I can't believe I didn't recognize it sooner."

"I can't believe I left you alone," Vic finally found the will to speak. "My detour was such a complete waste of time, I never should have been there in the first place. It was a distraction that almost cost you your life. I can't believe I was so blind and didn't see it."

"What about your girlfriend, did you get to see her?"

"No. She was nowhere. I searched the town and found nothing, then rode straight here. The gem woke me in the middle of the night and told me where to go. I knew you were in trouble. I'm just glad I got there in time.

"Me too," David seemed to relax at the realization that they both felt equally ashamed of what had happened. They both chewed on their jerky breakfast for a few minutes.

"From now on," Vic finally said with conviction, "we stick together!"

"Right!" David replied.

It was the first time either of them had smiled all morning. Although the experience had been something neither was proud of, it brought them closer together. There was a new bond between them, and it helped them grow up fast. Vic packed his things up quietly, but David didn't have much to pack. His cloak and side bag were still in the room back at Widow's Castle and as far as he was concerned, they were both gone for good. There was nothing particularly valuable in the bag, but he would probably miss his cloak soon if he did not get another. Vic noticed the look on his face and chimed in.

"Don't worry, we can get you another cloak and bag along the way. Gear is replaceable, people aren't." Just as they finished, they heard the sound of horse's hooves and wheels on the cobblestone streets. The coach was arriving and they were NOT going to miss it. As the coach arrived, the other passengers started drifting out of the inn where they had been staying. Vic noticed a few new faces in the crowd, and a few from the prior day that were missing. When the driver disembarked, he saw Vic and David and his face lit up.

"Well now, I wasn't expecting to see either of you two today."

"Any why not?" Vic retorted, slightly bitter at the driver for letting David end up at Widow's Castle after he said he would look out for him, "I said I would catch up."

"True, but most people are not so determined to get to the festival. There are many coaches going along this path this time of year and most people just catch the one that suits them best. Your friend looked like he was in for a good time last night given the looks of the woman who invited him over," David was angry and embarrassed by the comment but held his tongue as the driver went on, "so I didn't think he would make it back here in time for the early coach, but here you both are."

The driver scanned the rest of the crowd and started counting heads. "You two, and you two," the driver pointed to the new couples that had not been passengers the day before, "one of you couples are going to have to ride on top, so you better decide among yourselves now who's going up and who's going in."

As the two couples began to discuss among themselves, David leaned over to Vic, "Let's take the top, it will let us focus more on the task at hand and not be distracted by the other travelers."

"Good idea." Vic waved to the driver. "We'll take the top."

The two other couples turned to them with glee, and one of the men patted David on the back. "Good man," he said to David.

"Well that's settled then," the driver waved everyone toward the door, "let's get going!"

They were soon heading down the road again and making good time. It felt good to be back on target. Instead of just making small talk, they spent the time discussing various battle scenarios and how they would work together. Every hour or so, David checked the stone to see if anything nearby posed a risk. Each time the answer was negative, until just after they got back on the road after their lunch break. David checked again, but this time he reached out and hit Vic with his elbow while he was looking.

"It's evening, in a very festive environment; could be at the festival. There's some kind of masquerade party going on, and a battle at the same time. Yes, it's definitely at the festival. I can see the soldiers wearing gems. We are attacking from the dark on the outskirts tented area. There's a man inside who is directing the opposing soldiers. They are huge black cloaked warriors. The fighting is fierce. It looks like the party is still going on inside. The music must be loud enough to cover the noise of the battle. He is anticipating our actions and sending guards to cover the places where we are attacking. Both sides are taking casualties. Here he is, walking out of the tent where he was commanding the battle. He has donned his mask; a grey fox mask that covers his whole face." David paused, and then removed his hands from his face. "The image disappeared."

"Do you think it was the battle we're going to?"

"Yes, I do, and it did not look good. We need to take out the fox. He was the one controlling the enemy forces and directing where they go. I'm not sure how he was anticipating our movements, but unless we take him out, I do not think the battle will go well."

"Hmm." Vic pondered the vision David had just described. "This is important information we need to get to our commanders in the field as soon as we arrive."

The rest of the trip was mostly uneventful, but the vision left both of them on edge. The rest of David's checks came up empty. It was late afternoon when they finally heard the driver yell out, "Petersburg, dead ahead!" They both twisted around in their seats and there it was, the small town of Petersburg. Unfortunately, between them and the city were hundreds of horses, carriages and people walking. The closer they got to the town, the more congested the road became. That last mile took them at least an hour and by the time they arrived at the city gates, the afternoon was quickly becoming evening. As they entered the city, they could see that it was completely overrun with horses and wagons of all shapes and sizes. There was a horse tied to just about anything that wouldn't walk away and carriages and wagons parked everywhere except in the streets. With the setting sun, the glow of the tent city on the far side of town was already becoming evident, and that is where everyone was headed. It took a while to get through the city due to the crowds, but they finally arrived at the entrance and the driver helped everyone down. Vic and David were the last ones off.

"Enjoy yourselves, boys," he said as he closed the door and hoisted himself back into the driver's seat.

Vic gave him back half a smile, "I sure hope so," and he and David disappeared into the crowd of people pressing toward the front entrance. Vic grabbed David's elbow and directed him out of the flow of traffic and off into a dark alley behind a parked carriage alongside the entrance.

"Is this your idea of a shortcut?" David poked at Vic.

"You don't like dark alleys?"

"Love 'em. Spend the day here why don't we?"

Vic's one raised eyebrow told the story well enough.

"This time, you keep an eye out for me," Vic said to David, and he dropped to one knee and closed his eyes. He grabbed the gem on his wrist guard with his right hand and waited to hear something. Again, the message came quickly.

"Do not enter the festival. Meet behind the barn at the end of Clover Avenue."

The message was clear enough. Vic let go of the gem and stood back up. "Sometimes the best directions come from dark alleys." Vic smiled. "We need to find Clover Avenue. Let's go." David was right behind him as they left their strange hiding spot and headed back into the crowd. Vic scanned the people to find someone who looked less like a tourist going to a party and more like a local. He spotted a young girl carrying a pail of water.

"Excuse me, which way to Clover Avenue?"

"That's funny, you're the third person to ask tonight. Not many usually care about Clover Avenue during festival time. Down that street, and take your second right. From there, you can't miss it."

"Thanks." Vic tipped his head to her slightly and they ran off in the direction she pointed. As soon as they were out of earshot of the crowds, Vic turned to David while they ran, "Sounds like we're not the first ones here. That's good!"

When they found Clover Avenue, it was a typical small town cobblestone street with shops lining either side. There were less horses tied here than on the main road into town and most of the shops were dark. The street was barren; obviously everyone was at the festival. One way led back toward the center of town, while the other headed slightly downhill and then ended in a cul-de-sac. The message said at the "end" of Clover Avenue, so Vic turned toward the bottom of the hill. As they got closer, a large barn loomed in front of them. It was nestled against a hill at the lowest part of the street, and there was no one around, and no lights to speak of. The two slowed their run to a walk when they reached the barn and followed a path around the side, Vic with his hand on his sword. As they rounded the back of the barn they were suddenly greeted by five drawn swords held by five soldiers who jumped out of the shadows with their tips only inches away from them.

The one in front whispered, "Halt!" which seemed rather silly to Vic under the circumstances since there was really no where they could go. He had only partially unsheathed his sword at this point and now as he surveyed the group, he saw that each of them had a gem somewhere on his body, and all were glowing brightly. He re-sheathed his sword fully and brought his wrist guard up to his chest.

"We're friends," was all Vic said, and all the swords went down. Vic was amazed how well that worked, but knew that it was not the words, but the glowing gem that instantly built a bond between them.

"I'm Vic, and my friend is David. He's a Watcher."

"Excellent," the leader said. "He's finally arrived. Both of you come quickly. We have much planning to do and not much time."

Behind the barn was a small outbuilding with a light shining out from its single small window. There was a guard posted outside with his sword drawn. He opened the door as they arrived and ushered them inside.

The building was larger on the inside than it had appeared from the outside. There were at least 15 soldiers there. Each one looked different, carried a different weapon, and seemed to come from a different walk of life. The only thing they had in common was the stone somewhere on their body that linked them all to the common cause. An older man leaned over the only table in the room, which upon closer inspection, was really a few pieces of wood balanced on top of two sawhorses. He was hovering over a crude drawing of the festival area and town, and was obviously in charge. The man who had met David and Vic at first announced their presence.

"Marcus, the Watcher is here."

"Finally. You are much later than we expected and time is short. The meeting is scheduled to begin one hour after sundown and we have already lost half of that time. You are both new faces, so I will explain."

"Every year Lord Dramon attempts a bigger and bolder scheme at the festival. It provides an environment where he can do mischief and bring his forces together with enough commotion and innocent people that it is difficult to stop him. The festival is a place of debauchery and greed and that suits him just fine. Every year we assemble and try to put a stop to his plans and each year we have succeeded. Last year, his method changed. Instead of merely attempting to execute his scheme, he turned on us. His usual plan became secondary to killing as many of us as possible, and to some degree, he succeeded. Most importantly, he killed the Watcher who had been with us from the beginning, which has left us without eyes on the battlefield. We had grown complacent and forgot about the true danger of our foe. This year, we have no idea if the plan we see unfolding is the primary goal, or secondary, but either way, we must stop him. If you had not arrived, many more soldiers would have died I am sure. He and I have been battling wits every year, but the job has become consistently more difficult. As he hardens his defenses, he forces us to be more creative in our attacks."

"This year, barons have been arriving in alarming numbers. Our spies have counted at least 8 regional barons who have come to the festival in the past two days. Never before have so many barons gathered in one place, and we are certain that they will be assembling tonight at the meeting tent. We don't know what he has planned, but it may be to either kill them all or force them to submit to his rule. Either way, the results would be catastrophic. Is there anything you can add that will help our mission tonight?"

Vic spoke up, "David saw a vision earlier today that may relate. David, why don't you tell them about it."

David stepped forward. His knees trembled and his stomach turned as all eyes turned to him. Never had this many men turned to him for guidance. He felt important, but scared too.

"I saw a masquerade party at the festival, and a battle going on at the same time."

One of the other soldiers interjected, "I was on lookout earlier this afternoon and saw people holding masks as they entered the festival. At the time I thought nothing of it, but this is the first time I have seen people do such a thing, so it sounds like the vision was, in fact, of tonight."

"I agree," Marcus prompted David to continue, "go on."

"We were attacking in the dark on the outskirts of the festival. At the time I couldn't tell which side I was looking at, but now that I'm here, I recognize some of the men here from the battle. I saw one man near the center of the battle who was directing the opposing soldiers."

"Tall, with black hair and dark eyes?" Marcus asked.

"Yes, and clearly in charge."

"Without a doubt, you saw Lord Dramon."

"He left the tent and donned a grey fox mask that covered his whole face."

Marcus's eyes lit up. "That is our advantage. Now that we know his disguise, we can strike when he least expects it and we will again have the upper hand. I will not lose another Watcher, so you must stay here. Two soldiers will stay with you. Send

256

them into the field one at a time when you identify information that is valuable. They will deliver the information and return. We are still expecting two more groups this evening that will assist. When they arrive, send them to me at the forward command center, or where they are needed most. The forward command will be here," Marcus pointed to the crude map in front of them, "in the trees across the field from the festival."

Marcus turned to the other soldiers in the room, "If they advance on us across the field, we will circle back and come at them from the rear. Speed will be our advantage, but theirs will be numbers. Do not underestimate their power. They strike with blows no ordinary human could muster. Do not let them get behind you. We must continue to control the location of the battles."

"The bulk of our force must lure Dramon's forces away from the festival so that a strike team can penetrate and take out the grey fox. The teams I identified earlier will take the northern, western and southern flanks. Bradley, you and your men will lead the strike force, and Vic, you will accompany him. Your task is not to engage the primary force, but to make your way to the meeting tent and take out the grey fox. Follow our southern flank to the edge of the tent city and then break into the crowd. When you are in, blend in as quickly as possible and make your way toward the center of the loop. When you have succeeded, or the fox has escaped, light the main meeting tent on fire. The commotion will allow you to blend into the crowd and escape, and will indicate to us that we can call off the main assault. Whether you find the grey fox or not, make sure the meeting of barons does not happen. Our attack will begin when I take out the guard on the northern watchtower. When you see him fall, it is time to move. Is everyone clear on their assignments?"

All nodded in agreement. Marcus wished them all King's blessings on their journey, and they departed.

25. Showdown

As the troops left the out-building to take up positions, David immediately began using the gem to scan the area. Most of what he saw was people drinking and reveling in the indulgences of the festival. He also saw the guards at their posts, just where they had been drawn on Marcus's map. Apparently, their old fashioned spy work had served them well enough.

Then he saw something different. It was three men pouring something into wooden troughs sunk deep into the soil in the middle of the field. He couldn't tell what it was, but it looked like water. Some kind of irrigation maybe? It was too hard to tell. The scene changed and he saw the watchtower guard with an arrow intended to burn. It had cloth wrapped around the tip and he was soaking it in liquid. There was a torch hanging against the back side of the watchtower. David thought that was strange, since a torch on a watchtower would let people see his exact location and wouldn't make his vision any better. The only reason David could imagine that he would need a torch was if they planned to use it for flaming arrows, but this too was strange since they were supposed to be the defending force, not attacking. The scene changed again to the troughs as the three men were making another trip with their liquid. A third time, the men went out and filled the troughs with the liquid from their buckets. Finally, one of the men climbed up to the watchtower and poured what remained of his liquid into the bucket at the guard's post.

They were building a trap! The troughs were filled with something flammable, probably oil, and there was enough to make a wall of fire when lit. Whether to stop an attack or ambush their retreat, it would be a devastating blow. This was precisely the kind of information David needed to inform Marcus about. His forward command center must be moved, and quickly. David turned to one of the guards with him.

"You there, I have a message for Marcus at the forward command center. Are you ready?"

"Of course, what is it?"

"There are troughs filled with oil laid across the field here, here, and here," David pointed to the crude drawing still on the makeshift table. The watchtower guard is ready to light them on fire on a moment's notice, and he will do it as soon as he sees anyone attacking. Our forces must NOT make a frontal assault across the field unless the threat from their planned fire wall is neutralized. Do you understand?"

"Yes sir!" The guard spun around, and was gone before the door even finished closing. David smiled. That speed sure must be nice!

David returned to the visions of the gem. He saw another group of their reinforcements reach the edge of the city. They would be to the barn in a few minutes. That was good news, because if he saw anything else, he would need to send his only other protector with the message. A minute later, he saw his first guard reach Marcus and begin conveying the information. Marcus dispatched others to reroute the forces into a new plan. David couldn't tell what the new plan was, but he knew Marcus had adapted and the new information would prove valuable. He went back to looking at the visions of his gem.

The scene changed back to the forward command center, and there was only one soldier there. Several soldiers came and left while David watched. He was probably serving as a clearinghouse for information to inform the others that the command center had moved. The scene changed again, and this time, he saw the northern watchtower. Marcus was standing on the tower behind the guard, then drove his sword straight through him. The guard fell to the ground without making a sound. Marcus immediately picked up his bow, lit an arrow and aimed for the troughs. From the festival side, they were a fairly easy target and the flaming arrow went sailing through the air, striking the left most trough with ease. Instantly, flames leapt ten feet in the air and moved all the way across the field. By the gradually disappearing stars, David knew that black smoke must be pouring out of the flames and filling the night sky.

The flames had their desired effect and the menacing black cloaked Sentries from across the festival moved from their hiding spots into the field to engage the enemy. The ruse had worked, and one by one, the King's soldiers moved in from behind the guards and took them out while they scanned the flames looking for their prey.

The scene changed and David saw Vic and his team. According to plan, they used the distraction to enter the festival path and quickly brought their cloaks around to cover themselves and re-sheathed their swords. They were now part of the crowd and moved as quickly as possible through the throngs of people.

The face masks gave the whole scene an eerie feeling. Virtually everyone had a mask, and most were mounted on a stick and held up to the face. They came in all different shapes and sizes. Vic almost ran into a short man with a dog mask, then he was bumped by a fat cat. Before he had gone twenty feet he had also seen monsters, birds, rabbits and goats. Some were flat with drawings on them, and others were more elaborate with protruding beaks or long ears. David couldn't really control the angle of what he saw and the faces and masks changed so rapidly it was hard to understand what he was looking at.

The scene changed again, and this time, David saw a face he recognized. It was Lord Dramon, in the same tent where he had seen him before, only this time he was there with a woman. He continued to watch until he realized with horror what he was seeing. The woman placed her hand over a pendant she wore around her neck and closed her eyes. A few moments later, she opened her eyes and said something to Lord Dramon. When she moved her hands away, there was a stone, just like his. Lord Dramon had a Watcher!

"Soldier, you need to deliver another message, this time to Vic on the strike force. Can you make it into the festival alone?"

"Yes, but what is it?"

"Dramon has a Watcher. I don't know how he found someone to do it, but she is using the stone against us. She is in his planning tent near the main meeting tent and must be stopped. We will never be able to attack Dramon undetected while she is helping him."

"Understood, but I cannot leave you until my replacement returns."

"Don't worry, I've seen another team on their way here. They will be here in a few minutes. Now GO!"

"Yes sir," and he was gone.

As the door bounced closed in the quiet and cold night, David realized what he had just done. He was again defenseless, just like last night.

"I'm not leaving this room," he said to himself. "And I have every possible defense."

He went back to the gem. The battle on the outskirts of the tent city was raging. The initial surprise had worn off and the next wave of Sentries had arrived. Both sides were taking casualties, but overall, things were going fairly well. He had to flash through several battle scenes until he saw what he really wanted to see. The team of reinforcements was now on Main Street and heading toward Clover Avenue. It looked like there were three of them, one older and two younger. A father with two sons? That would be just perfect. One to inform the forward command center of the latest news, one to inform Marcus, and one to stay with him. He wanted to continue to watch them, but the scene kept changing back to the battle and he felt obliged to watch. When it seemed like they had been a long time in coming, he figured they must have arrived at the barn but not known where to go. Finally, he tore himself away from the gem and decided to go out to meet them. He grabbed a small dagger that was hanging on the wall and carefully crept out of the out-building and headed toward the barn.

Considering all the violence going on less than a mile away, the night was strangely silent. Here in this small valley, little sound got through from the festival, so even the noise of partying did not make it to his ears. David rounded the side of the barn and saw them. Sure enough, there were two relatively young men and one older standing right in front of the barn wondering where to go next. He tried to whisper to them, but they were too far away, so against his better judgment, David ran out to meet them and then led them back into the out-building in the back. They introduced themselves as father, son and a friend. He explained to them where the battle was taking place and used the crude map to show the father and friend where to go. The son would stay with him. Once instructed, the two were off.

David went straight back to the gem. This time he saw one lone soldier coming into town on horseback, probably another soldier to join in the battle but he couldn't be sure. The scene was very brief and next, instead of a battle scene, he saw himself. At first he couldn't tell where, and then it became clear. It was when he greeted the new reinforcements in the street, and from this angle, he could clearly see that their movements had been followed from above. A scouthawk had watched the nighttime rendezvous and was heading back to report their location. This was bad news for them for sure. He took his hand off the gem and looked at the young man who was there to protect him.

This was going to be rough. After looking at him more closely, he realized his protector was really only a boy. He couldn't be older than fifteen, and was fidgeting with his sword like it was something new to him.

"So, what's your name?" David asked.

"John."

"John, do you know how to use one of those?"

"Well, not really. I mean, Dad taught me what to do and I sort of know, but I haven't actually had to use one before."

David looked down, and then back up at John. "John, I am almost certain that any minute now, there will be at least two of the biggest, evilest warriors you have ever seen walking through that door. They are here to get me, and if they do, you and your dad and your brother will likely be dead before tomorrow morning. You are going to have to use that thing, and use it well. Do you know how to move in the power of the stone?"

They boy's eyes lit up, "Oh yes, that I know how to do well. I used to run messages for my father when I was a boy. I was one of the youngest to master it."

David smiled, there was hope yet, "Good, then we have something in common. I know how to do what I do, and you know how to do what you do. The problem is, neither one of us is very good at killing Sentries and there are some very bad ones on their way to kill us right now." David paused to check the gem and see how much time they had. He instantly saw three Sentries on the side path beside the barn. They were probably thirty seconds away.

"John, you hide behind that hay over there." David grabbed a sickle off the wall and started climbing into the rafters. I'll get up here. When I strike, I'll take out the first guard and then climb back up high again. You need to take out the second one at exactly the same time I strike, before they have time to react. That will leave a one-on-one battle with the last one. Keep dodging him as best you can and try for a strike if the opportunity arises. But whatever you do, don't stop moving. If you do, you're a dead man for sure."

John nodded. David could see the fear in his eyes, but there was also determination. David could count on his will, even if he couldn't count on his steel. Unfortunately, this plan would only buy David a few more minutes before the Sentry scaled the rafters or burned down the building. Either way, he would have to get rid of that third Sentry.

David held his breath as the door creaked open. He had seen Sentries before through the gem, but never in person. For the first time, he saw the red glow of their eyes and the scaly arms protruding from their cloaks. They looked even bigger when he looked down on them from above. They were huge, and they let off an awful stench. He wasn't sure he could kill one even if he hit him straight on with the sickle striking with all his might. In any case, he didn't have much other choice.

The Sentries started going through the room examining possible hiding places. Once the second Sentry was in the best possible position with his back to John, and David had a clear shot at the first one, he swung the sickle down across the front of the Sentry with such force he almost fell right out of the rafter. The sickle hit its mark and sunk deep into the Sentry and a moment later, they heard a bloodcurdling scream and the Sentry vanished. Seconds later, while David was scaling higher and farther back into the rafters, he saw the tip of John's sword come plunging out the front side of the second Sentry and with another scream, the second set of clothes dropped to the floor. Now for the hard part.

John was out in the open and the third Sentry had a clear shot. He swung at him and John dodged the shot, but the second swing he couldn't dodge. It made full contact with his sword and a blue flash of light lit up the room. John jumped in the other direction and dove behind some nearby hay. It only took the Sentry a second to realize where he had gone, and with two strides, he was across the room and engaging John again. This time the Sentry got in two shots. With John's speed, he was able to block both shots, but David could tell that John would not last long under that kind of force. Each time their swords met, it took more strength for John simply to hang on to his sword. He was using both hands now, and the Sentry was backing him into the corner.

David had been so mesmerized by the fight, he forgot to touch his gem. He did and instantly, he saw the soldier he had seen earlier running full speed toward the barn. Help was coming, now if John could just hold on. "Go for the door!" David shouted from on top. The Sentry looked up just long enough to let John sneak out from under his grasp.

"I'm not leaving you!" John shouted back, and he attacked the Sentry in a feeble effort to strike. The blow was blocked with such ease it was almost a joke.

"Go for the door NOW!" David shouted, and this time, John realized the urgency with which David spoke. He dove out the door, pushing it open as he fell through it. The Sentry stormed straight for John to finish him off when he met with the last thing he ever expected. Another blade sliced through the air with such force David could hear the wind whistle. The Sentry was cut clean in two and the blade kept right on going, splitting the door and sending wood shards flying in all directions. The scream echoed through the quiet night sky. There, with John crumpled up in a ball at his feet, was Derek.

"Sorry I'm a little late. I had some other business to attend to."

David made his way down from the rafters and Derek helped John off the ground.

"As far as I'm concerned, you were right on time!" said John with relief. Derek and John pulled the remainder of door closed, and then Derek turned to David.

"You must be the Watcher. How is the battle going?"

"I've been a little distracted. Just a minute, let me check."

David grabbed the stone and looked at the battlefield again. There were battles raging at the north tower and at the south side, but the field which had been burning was all but abandoned. The fire had burnt out and the first strike had killed the Sentries assigned to that area.

"There is no fighting in the center of the loop anymore," David reported, "but I'm sorry to say, John, that your father is down. He is alive, but injured. He's being cared for by unknowing visitors of the festival. He should be fine. The other person who came with you is dead. That means the message didn't get through."

"What message?" Derek asked.

"Dramon has a Watcher."

"What??? How can that be?"

"I don't know how, I just know he does. She's a woman, and she's using the stone to tell him things. I saw it myself."

Derek grabbed David's arm and tried to keep from raising his voice, "What does she look like?" Derek asked with an intensity that scared David.

"She was very pretty, had long blonde hair and the gem was on a broach around her neck.

As he described her, Derek's face changed.

"Oh no. It's Catherine. She is the reason I was late and the one I was supposed to speak with, but she wasn't at her parents' house as planned. She wasn't at her aunt's house either. She needs to become one of us, but has not been introduced to the King yet. She probably has no idea what she is doing. She has the potential to be a truly great Watcher with some training."

"Well at this rate, she will never have that chance, if someone doesn't get to Vic quickly."

"Vic? Is he leading the team that is going to get Dramon?" Derek smiled. "Well that's great. Renatus must have had a hand in this. Good for Vic. He'll never kill Catherine, he's in love with her. She couldn't possibly be safer."

"Unfortunately, he's not alone, and the rest of his team won't hesitate for a second."

26. Strike Force

Vic had been making his way through the crowd and trying to scan every mask he saw. There were so many, it was hard to take them in so quickly. One passed by his left that was grey, but was not a fox. Another passed by right in front of him. Could that have been a fox? No, some kind of dog. It was maddening. He looked back, was the team still with him? He couldn't see. They had gotten separated in the flow of people. Maybe they would make it to the center tent, maybe they wouldn't. Either way, he had to make it there and get Lord Dramon. That was his sole mission and he wasn't going to fail. He would kill the grey fox once and for all.

The crowds began to thin. Good, he must be nearing the center of the loop. Since the middle was dedicated more to meetings than games and food, there were less people entering and exiting the area.

There it was: the main meeting tent. All the sides were pulled down, masking the large meeting table that took up almost the entire tent. Just to the north a smaller tent, probably Dramon's operations center. Out in front of the operations tent were two large wooden high backed chairs. Someone was sitting in one of them, with their back turned to Vic. That *had* to be Dramon. Vic maneuvered through the crowd to get a better look and just as he did, the person turned to look around. It was a grey fox.

His target had been sighted, now all he had to do was take him out. In his younger days, he would have presented himself and then taken on the challenge of beating his adversary in a fair sword battle, but no more. He had seen how these Sentries operated and if Dramon was even half as dangerous as those who served him, Vic was in for a very tough battle. He had no desire to lose when he was this close to winning, so he decided to simply strike. His task was to kill, and that is what he would do. Vic continued to work through the crowd until he was actually right in front of the chairs. Because the two high backed chairs were facing each other, Vic could use the one opposite the grey fox to block his approach, and then at the last second, leap out from around the chair and take him by surprise. A strike against an unsuspecting victim with that kind of force would surely be fatal, even if Dramon ended up having the strength of a Sentry.

Vic lined himself up with the second chair and started making his move. He began running as fast as he could while squatting so as to keep his profile within the cover of the chair. Two guards saw him run past, but before they had a chance to react it was too late. Vic leapt right over the chair and came down hard directly on top of the grey fox with all his might; but things did not go as planned.

Instead of striking his victim as he expected, Vic's sword met steel with a flash of blue light that almost blinded him. The sword that crossed his was as solid as a rock and took the full force of his blow, and then threw Vic's sword arm back into the air along the same path it had come down. Vic went tumbling onto the chair and the person in it, and together they both ended up on the ground. The grey fox mask was thrown to the ground and they both turned to look at each other.

"Catherine?"

270

"Vic?"

"What are you doing here?"

"What are YOU doing here, and why are you trying to kill me?"

"I didn't..." Whatever Vic was about to say, Derek was sure it wouldn't make any sense at all so he interrupted. "Sorry guys, no time for a lovebird reunion. Vic, get her out of here."

Vic looked at Catherine, "OK?"

"It's about time!" She was relieved to see Vic, confused at what had just happened, but glad to be leaving Dramon. The whole thing started to feel like one of their adventures back home, and this was the spot when Vic stepped in and got her out of trouble. She had been watching for Dramon throughout the night, and had seen much more of his brutality than his kindness. She knew that if there was a war to be fought, he was on the wrong side. She was still confused by what James had said, but she knew that of all the people in the world, the one she could trust without question was Vic.

As the two scrambled to get up off the ground Catherine heard the voice she had come to know all too well.

"Leaving so soon?" It was Dramon's voice, and it was as cold and heartless as ever. With a matching grey fox mask in hand, Dramon emerged from the tent where he had been planning his troop movements. "Guards!"

Sentries came from out of nowhere toward them. Vic knew he could outrun them himself, but Catherine wouldn't have a chance running on her own.

"Get her out of here," Derek shouted, "Head south toward the main entrance." Derek spun around and dove back toward the Sentries surrounding Dramon.

Vic didn't argue. He immediately engaged the first Sentry he saw and as he did, felt the speed of the gem assisting him. He dodged the first blow and ran behind him, taking out his knees as he passed. The second Sentry he dispatched almost as easily. Then he stopped and felt time catch back up. He must stay with Catherine. She was running toward him and he returned to her just in time to stop a Sentry that was barreling down on top of her. Their swords clashed in a flash of blue light and this time, they engaged four, five, six times in a row before either gained the upper hand. Vic locked swords with him again and this time, pushed himself back with all his might and did a backwards flip off the two swords. The movement was just what he needed to gain speed from the gem again, and he flanked the Sentry for just long enough to throw him off balance. With a smack he kicked the Sentry and sent him to the ground. Vic was right on top of him and a second later, the familiar scream filled the air.

Vic spun around. Where was Catherine? There she was, hiding in a vendor tent nearby. She came out to meet him.

"Catherine, I need to know if the meeting has started yet. Do you know?"

"I don't think so. They were all assembling in the meeting tent and Dramon was about to go over there, but he never got there. He has a guard posted at the door on the inside, so none of them can leave."

"Catherine, we have to let them out, or everything we tried to accomplish tonight could be wasted. Exactly where was the guard standing?"

"Come on, I'll show you."

Vic followed Catherine around the back side of several vendors who were near the apex of the loop until they had a vantage point of the back side of the meeting tent. "You see the third tassel? About there."

By now, the rest of his team had arrived and were engaged in full battle with the Sentries protecting Dramon. Any festival visitors still in the area had run screaming from the scene, leaving only the combatants, but no one had emerged from the meeting tent. Thanks to Catherine, Vic knew his mark, but he would have to pass through some of the hottest part of the battle to get there.

The barons inside knew that there was a war going on outside, but they had been shown a Sentry for the first time. Dramon made it very clear that the only way they would live was to stay in their seats until the fighting subsided and that his Sentry would kill anyone who tried to leave. Though some of the barons complained about being held against their will, the sounds of the battle outside convinced them that it was safer to obey Dramon's instructions.

As Vic began his run through the battle, he felt the power of the gem aiding his steps. Everything around him began to slow, but he still couldn't walk through steel or bodies. Several times, he had to block a blow or climb over someone or something to make it through. An arrow flew through the air and just barely missed his forehead as he jumped through the air. Fortunately, Catherine was correct about the Sentry's location and when Vic landed the jump, he put his sword right through the canvas wall of the tent and right into the Sentry on the other side. He followed his sword through the canvas wall and ended up landing right on top of the large wooden conference table they had all been sitting around. He picked himself back up and stood on the table.

"Gentlemen, this party's over. I suggest you go back to your realms and do not come back here again!"

Vic didn't have to say it twice! All the nobles jumped to their feet, found their respective servants, aides and guards and scattered in different directions. They left through the smaller side slits in the canvas rather than through the front where the most intense fighting was. Just as he was turning to leave, Vic paused to notice the crest on the seat in front of him. It was the same family seal he had seen at Catherine's farm. Catherine had followed him into the tent and was standing just inside. Vic pointed to the symbol and looked quizzically at Catherine, "Your chair?"

"Nope, mine was outside. I think this one was empty all evening, but it certainly is our family seal."

"Hmm. I suppose I should take the lady to nicer places, now that it seems she is nobility."

"It's about time you showed me a little respect!" she smirked back at him.

"We'll have to investigate this further with your dad when we get home."

When the barons had all left, Vic thought it was time to see what was going on outside. He threw open the wide canvas entrance and there, standing in front of him, was none other than Lord Dramon himself.

"You think you have won this battle, but beware for this war is far from over."

Catherine knew that Dramon had not seen her yet, and she wanted desperately to disappear. She could not bear to see what he would do if he saw that she had betrayed him. She quickly slipped out the back of the tent so that she could peak through and watch the scene, but found herself running straight into Eunice.

"In a hurry, my Lady?"

Catherine froze. Would he turn her in? They had spent so much time together training. She learned that he had done some very evil things, but that it still hurt him to do them. There was so much she wanted to say, but no words came out, until she finally said one.

"Please…" Tears welled up in her eyes. There was nothing more she could say.

The stone face of Dramon's closest advisor began to soften. He looked down, then back to Catherine. He knew they both had a choice to make, and she was making the right one. For a brief moment he thought about going with her, but it was impossible. Where could he possibly go? Dramon was his life, and he would have to live with it, but she didn't have to. He too could find only one word.

"Go," and he let go of her arm. A moment later it was business as usual and he spun around and headed back around the corner of the meeting tent. She peaked back through the slit in the tent that she had retreated through earlier. Nothing could have prepared her for what she saw next.

Vic and Dramon were still facing each other at the far end of the tent, and Dramon was growing more and more agitated as he talked.

"You fools. I am the one you should be serving, not that elusive prince of yours. What does he have to offer? Sacrifice and pain? I give you power, because I have power to give. This land is mine, and neither you nor he will take it from me. You have not even begun to taste my power!"

For a few brief seconds, Dramon's entire appearance changed. Gone was the commanding presence of a rich and powerful baron with his debonair fox mask, and in its place, the fangs of a cobra beneath red cat eyes glaring at him fearlessly. The being said nothing but exhaled a hideous hiss that emitted not poison, but fire from its mouth headed directly toward Vic.

There was nowhere to run, and no time to escape. He wished he was holding a shield, but all he had was his wrist guard. He pulled it up to his face as if it were attached to the shield he wished he had.

To his surprise, instead of scorching fire he felt only mild heat and saw a blast of light from the gem so bright it was all he could see. It was brighter than the brightest part of the cave. It was gone in an instant, and so was the fire, leaving only the lingering smell of the cave's incense in his nostrils. To his amazement, he was unharmed.

Dramon stood as if nothing had happened, back in his usual form. He looked mildly perturbed, but not surprised. "Guards!" He pointed to Vic and from behind him four Sentries began advancing. Lord Dramon turned and walked away into the melee.

He had survived Dramon's attack, but taking on four Sentries at once didn't sound like much fun. Instead of engaging, he spotted the support ropes that kept the canvas curtains around the side of the tent in place. When the Sentries were just under the canvas sides of the meeting tent, he cut the rope with one swift strike and the canvas fell onto the Sentries, tangling them up only long enough for Vic to escape in the other direction. Catherine was still behind the tent and greeted his retreat.

"Going my way?" she said as she opened a canvas panel.

"Absolutely!" He grabbed her hand as she helped him through the opening, and then they both headed into the chaos of the crowd. Two steps later, he stopped so quickly Catherine almost fell over. "Not again. Are you going to get us into more trouble? I thought that was my job!"

"We need to send the signal. Someone has to light the tent on fire to let the rest of the teams know they can retreat." Vic jumped up onto a vacant vendor's booth and pulled himself up onto one of the supporting poles. From this vantage point, he could see over the crowd and all the way across the tent city. There in the Northern Watchtower was a single face lit by the light of a flaming arrow in hand. It was Marcus, waiting for the signal.

Vic caught his eye and then motioned to him, pointing at the meeting tent. That was all the instruction Marcus needed. In one swift movement, he launched a flaming arrow at the main meeting tent. It sailed through the air and met its target. Vic waited only long enough to see the flames catch. He knew the job was done, and now they could leave. Catherine and Vic disappeared into the chaos of the departing crowd and it wasn't until they reached the outskirts of the town that they breathed a sigh of relief and slowed their pace.

Vic wanted to rejoin the team at the barn, but with all the people streaming out of the festival to get away from the chaos, there was no way they could swim upstream until the crowds had diminished. In the meantime, they climbed up a nearby hill and sat down under a large sycamore tree where they could watch the flow of people leaving. With so many travelers carrying torches, the road was lit up like daytime.

Vic kept his sword on his lap and both kept a close eye out for anyone climbing up the hill to join them.

27. Starting Again

When the mass exodus diminished, Vic and Catherine went back down the road and made their way to their original meeting place behind the barn. The team had taken serious casualties and was ragged and tired, but Vic was glad to find many of the men he had met earlier. They were reassembling and telling tales of their adventures. As he entered the out-building, he was about to join in the frivolity when he realized how awkward Catherine must feel. He raised his hand to address the crowd and they quickly became silent.

"Gentlemen, I would like to introduce Catherine. Thanks to your efforts tonight, she has been saved from the clutches of Lord Dramon. I'm sure in time, you will all come to know and love her." Catherine gave a slight curtsy and a heckler from the back yelled out "I'm sure we will!" The place burst into laughter.

As everyone went back to their talking, Vic heard a voice right behind him that was like old times, "And it's a good thing you didn't kill her, too." It was Derek.

Vic spun around, "How in the world did you…."

Derek smiled and then nodded at David across the room. Vic turned to David, who smiled back, and it was all clear. David was a better Watcher than Vic had ever expected, and it was a good thing too. "In any case, thanks. It's great to see you again. I'm glad you made it."

Derek gave him a good slap on the back, "wouldn't miss it!"

Vic knew the answer, but asked anyway, "Did you get Lord Dramon?"

"Unfortunately, no. His escape was well planned. He disappeared into the crowd. There were too many innocent civilians that would have been hurt if we had given chase. We will have to finish this assignment another day."

As Vic and Catherine worked their way around the room, they greeted the men who had fought that night. Catherine leaned over to Vic and whispered in his ear, "They all have gems like mine, and you do too. Where did you get them?"

"The same place you should have gotten yours. I'll show you when this is all finished. I have someone you need to meet."

When they arrived at David, Vic gave him a big bear hug. "I'm glad you made it," David said to him as they finished.

"Me too," Vic smiled back.

David turned to Catherine, "And now I see why you almost got us both killed wandering around Rochester looking for her." He bowed and kissed her hand gently, "A pleasure to meet you Miss Catherine."

She shot Vic a quizzical look, then turned back to David, "The pleasure is all mine," Catherine replied gracefully. She didn't know exactly what to think of this band of soldiers reveling in their accomplishments, but she certainly enjoyed being treated like a lady.

She turned back to Vic, "You were looking for me?"

"Let's just say my unplanned stop in Rochester was not such a good idea." David and Vic chuckled together.

They stayed a little while longer but soon, the stress and struggle of the day began to wear on everyone and they dispersed to find lodging for the night. Most of the general public had left the festival when the fighting escalated, so no one had trouble finding rooms at the inn. Catherine's room wasn't near as grand or polished as her plush room in the castle the night before, but somehow she felt much warmer and safer even without a fire, knowing that Vic was in the room next door. Her thirst for adventure was satisfied, for the moment. Now it was time to rest.

The next morning, they all met in the tavern at the front of the inn together with the rest of the soldiers who had served in yesterday's battle. Marcus addressed the group.

"My fellow soldiers, you have done extremely well. Last night was Dramon's hour of glory, and not only did we deprive him of his victory, but we took away his prized possession." He gave Catherine a smile and a slight bow. "This victory was not without cost, and we will remember those we lost. Service of the King is not easy, but the rewards are beyond imagination. Today is a new day, and you should all be pleased to know how proud he is of each of you. I have served the purpose he gave me and led you into battle. Now I return you to his care. Seek your next assignment for yourselves. You have my unending gratitude. King's favor for your journeys."

After a cheer, everyone began to make their way out when Marcus found his way to Catherine. Vic was by her side.

"The rest of these soldiers can take care of themselves but you, my lady, require special attention. You know that Dramon will not stop until he finds you and there is nothing more important right now then bringing you to meet Renatus. Vic, this is your most important task. See to it that she gets safely to the cave."

"Yes sir."

"King's favor on your journey." Marcus turned and walked away.

"A cave?" Catherine asked, "are we going spelunking? Sounds like fun!" She had that twinkle back in her eye that usually spelled trouble for Vic. It was nice to see it again.

"Like nothing you've ever experienced before!" Vic knew that this time, he was right!

They stepped out into the morning light to find the town outside a mess. Workers were cleaning up the town everywhere they looked. It was again becoming the small town it usually was rather than the party atmosphere it became once a year. Vendors had begun the tedious process of packing up their goods and breaking camp, and the streets were now filled with pack animals instead of travelers.

As they surveyed the site, David came out and greeted them. "Vic, I found another group that will be passing through Clavis and I think I'll head home with them, if that's OK with you. I expect you and Catherine have some catching up to do."

"Are you sure? Last time we got separated it wasn't a good thing."

Bradley came up behind Vic and patted him on the back. "I think we can take care of one particularly good Watcher, don't you think, boys?" Vic heard some laughter from behind and realized that Bradley's whole team would be with them.

"You're in good hands, David. Safe journey."

"Vic, I would be pleased to work with you again anytime the King wishes," David replied.

"The honor would be all mine." Vic felt like he and David had been through their worst defeat and their best victory together, and was eager to work with such an excellent Watcher again.

When the group had departed, Catherine asked Vic the question that had been burning in her mind all morning, "What is all this talk about a King? Who is Renatus?"

"That's who I'm taking you to meet in the cave. Will you go there with me?"

"Vic, I don't care where you're going, I'll go with you. If you liked the cave, I'll like the cave, only this time let's stick together."

"Absolutely!" It felt so right to finally be going on an adventure with Catherine again, and to know she was safe.

"Vic, when we're done, can we go back to Mayport? I have lots of questions to talk with my father about, and I think you have some unfinished business with him too."

With all the excitement about the mission, the festival and the battle, Vic he had completely forgotten about the seeds. He grabbed his sack and rummaged through the contents until he was able to remove the bag of seeds from the bottom. He carefully opened the bag's mouth and let some of the fine golden seeds fall through his fingers.

"Think your father might want these?"

Catherine smiled as they both watched them shimmer in the sun.

"Actually, we should make a stop on the way to the cave. The other half of your father's seeds is in Clavis with a friend I met along the way. He's recovering there, and he's also the one who showed me the cave. I'm sure he would love to meet you, and it might be nice to have him around when I try to find that place again!"

"You did have quite an adventure, didn't you?"

Vic smiled, "Nothing like the ones we're going to have!"

Dramon's carriage careened around the corner at breakneck speed and then ground to a halt to meet three of his couriers. He reached out of the carriage and grabbed the first one by the shirt and yanked him inside the carriage.

"Find her. Find her right now. I want every outpost of mine notified immediately. They may have ruined my festival, but they have only postponed the inevitable. I will control the barons and she will help me. Either she will use her talents for me, or she will not use them at all! I'll make sure of that. Now go!" and he threw him out of the carriage and onto the ground outside.

"GO!" he yelled up to the driver, and they were off again. The carriage made a sharp turn into the driveway of Widow's Castle and then ground to a halt on the gravel of the great round driveway. The driver's brake stopped the carriage much faster than the horses appreciated and they panted in their harnesses as sweat poured off their bodies and foam dripped from their mouths. Dramon leapt from the carriage and up the steps to the castle. He waved his arm and the massive wood doors blew off their hinges. Never slowing for a moment, he went straight into the main hall. He paused only for a moment to locate the Widowmaker, then marched straight up to her.

"I need more Sentries, and I need them now."

She seemed unmoved by his demand. "Then you will have to bring me more willing victims."

"What have you been doing here? Your hall is always full and the wine always flowing. There are men everywhere, so give them to me."

"They must be willing. You know that. It has been more difficult to find them willing. Ask Grithos, maybe he can deliver them faster."

"All Grithos cares about is the money…"

"Of course he does, that is his trade."

"And even at the prices he is charging he still can't deliver."

"Then you must be patient."

Dramon slammed his hand down on a nearby table. "I will NOT be patient. We need more of us here to complete my plan, and I will not be denied. Maybe if you didn't consume so many maintaining that pretty face of yours we would be done by now."

The Widowmaker's eyes narrowed for a moment and ever so faintly turned into the red cat eyes of a Sentry as she hissed back at him, "Do you think that would make me better at my trade?"

Dramon turned his head away. "You know what I want."

Her countenance resumed its usual glow, "Yes my liege, and I will send them when they are ready."

Epilogue

Vic survived his first battle as a soldier of the King, but has much to learn. He is relieved to be reunited with Catherine, but she desperately needs to meet Renatus. Homeward bound together, Vic hopes to learn the story of whether Catherine's family comes from nobility, and to hear more from Derek and Jason about the Great War and the new kingdom the King will usher in when he finally arrives.

Unfortunately, their time of celebration could be painfully short lived as Lord Dramon seizes every opportunity he can to take revenge on Vic and capture Catherine, the Watcher who betrayed him. His operation to bring more of his kind into physical form obsesses him and he enlists many other powerful beings to wage a war for the hearts and minds of the people. Never before have there been so many blatant demonstrations of raw power as he tries to bend the barons into submission.

New friends and new enemies clash all along the way as Vic must protect his love from Dramon's relentless attacks, learn the secret of the Sentries, and find the key to defeating Dramon and his growing army.

About the Author

Robert Ming is an elected City Council Member and Mayor of Laguna Niguel, California, and a practicing lawyer. Robert has grown up living, working and going to school in Southern California. Presently, Robert is a Managing Director and Associate General Counsel at Jefferies & Company, Inc., an international brokerage and investment banking firm.

Robert is a founding Co-Chair of the Laguna Niguel Military Support Committee and founding president of the Laguna Niguel Military Support Foundation. He was the founding president of the Association of California Cities - Orange County, and helped launch the Bonner Institute for the Advancement of Choral Music and sits on its Board. Robert is also Chairman of the Board of Stoneybrooke Christian Schools.

Robert and his wife Susie have been married for 20 years and have four children, Jonathan (17), Katie (14), Wesley (3) and Grant (2). Robert's complete bio is available at www.robertming.com.

10933257R00180

Made in the USA
San Bernardino, CA
02 December 2018